I0843120

Also by K Jwancio

ROMANCING THE PAGES SERIES:
Romancing the Pages
Behind the Pages

THISTLE FIELD ESTATE SERIES:
Bed...& Breakfast
Breakfast in Bed
Thistle Field Estate

SPELLBOUND IN THISTLETON SERIES:
Spellbound in the Stacks
Spells and Wedding Bells
Spells and Belly Swells

HOLIDAY NOVELLAS:
The Gift Across the Street
Long Lost Valentine

Enjoy the

Nailed at Home Plate

playlist!

ISBN: 979-8-9888132-9-3

Cover design, formatting, and interior art by Iwancio Inspired Design.
Cover character art by agingerpanda.
Interior character art by michillart.

Nailed at Home Plate

A Philly Sillys Romance

K. Iwancio

This is for my dad, the biggest Philadelphia sports fan I know. I spent my childhood listening to Harry Kalas so much that I can hear his voice in my head. I'm sorry it took me so long to fully understand your love for our hometown. I miss sharing this fun with you. Know that you're in my heart and by my side at every game I watch.

P.S. But Dad, for the love of God and baby Jesus, please skip all the dirty chapters while reading this in heaven.

P.P.S. For those of you wondering, the chapters are 12, 14, 15, 17, 18, 19, 21, and 22.

This book was written for everyone who has ever fallen hard for the one on the field, the movie/TV screen, or within the pages of the book. Here's your chance to feel what it's like for him to call you **"mine"**.

TRIGGER WARNING:
This book contains two consenting adults exploring various minor kinks which include (in no particular order): toy play, sexual exploits outside of the bedroom, dirty talk, squirting, surprise facials, anal play, jizz in gray sweatpants, numerous sexual baseball innuendos, and condoms in sugar bowls.

FUN FACTS:
"Cum" is mentioned 9 times.
"Fuck" is mentioned 95 times.
"Cock" is mentioned 45 times.
"Ass" is mentioned 88 times.
"Dick" is mentioned 10 times.
"Fucking" is mentioned 119 times.

CHAPTER PLAYLIST

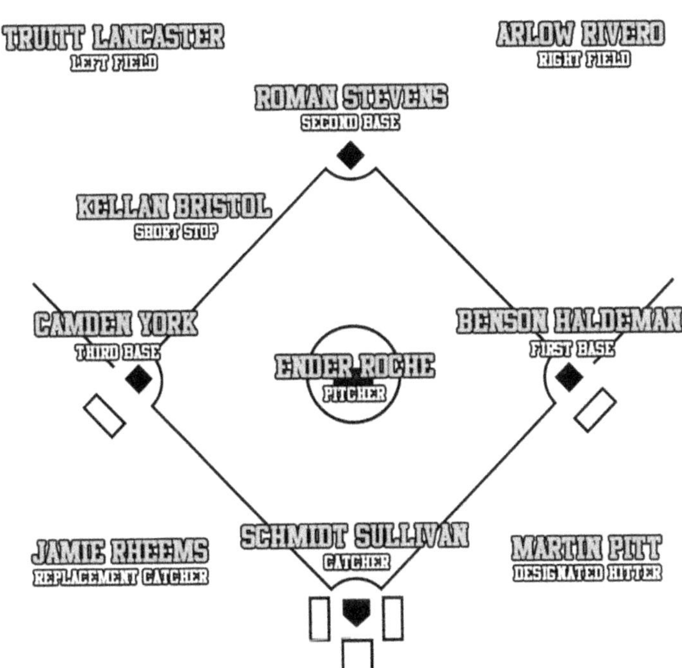

The Philly Sillys Starting Line Up

WORKIN' ON IT

MEGHAN TRAINOR

"Alright, put your damn shirts back on!" I shouted to the team, in between my breaths of laughter. "We don't want to blind the poor people in the stands with your god-awful farmer tans." Another day, another choreography practice of utter chaos.

I wouldn't have it any other way.

I'd been with the Philly Sillys teams since their very humble beginnings. The Philadelphia Phillies finally decided to start their own Entertainment League Baseball, or ELB, team. Which was decidedly overdue.

All of this nonsense started with the quick rise to fame of the Savannah Bananas and Party Animals. Both teams played a new twist on baseball. It was more about entertaining the crowd than scores and stats. From there, numerous other teams across the country quickly joined the league, with more being added every season. The Bananas had been kicking ass and taking names, showing the industry that you could have fun and play baseball. Well, their version of baseball. And damn, was it ever fun.

The Sillys had their small stadium south of the city by the train tracks and industrial docks near the

Delaware River. It was a bit out of the way from the big sports complex area, but I didn't mind. There was less city traffic here and I enjoyed the view of the river from the stadium.

When I heard Philadelphia was adding its own ELB team, I jumped at the chance to find a job in the organization. I'd been a huge fan of Philly sports since the day I was born. All thanks to my dad who was also a product of the City of Brotherly Love. I was born and raised in the northeast Philly suburbs, on the other side of Roosevelt Boulevard from the Northeast Philadelphia Airport. My blood was made of wooder, soft pretzels, and cheesesteaks "wit wiz". Where the polite greeting to strangers during the appropriate seasons was "Go Birds!" and "Go Phils!". My roots were deep in the area from generations of Andrews' living here since the pre-Revolutionary War era.

I was athletic in my own sense. My background was in dance and gymnastics. I just happened to be well-versed with the Bananas' method of baseball, after watching any game I could that was aired on ESPN. So, when I saw the job listing, I jumped at the opportunity. I submitted a resume and audition video for the position of Team Choreographer.

To prepare for my interview, I rewatched every Bananas game I had access to so I could understand the format of the game-to-entertainment ratio. I made sure to wear every Philly sports jersey throughout the audition video. They were always hanging in my closet, waiting for their season. Between my talents and knowing the ins and outs of the new sport, I got the job.

It also helped that baseball recently moved up the hierarchy of my sporting loves. Eagles football had been my first for the longest time. But when a particular dreamboat was traded to the baseball team, that brought my attention *fully* to baseball for the past few years.

Football and hockey players wore helmets, so it was difficult to discern the hotness of the players during the games. With basketball players you only got a fleeting look as they ran past. But baseball? Most of the time was spent with the players in stationary positions so you were able to get an eyeful of each one every so often. So, when I locked the icy blue eyes of the new Phillies catcher, Jamie Rheems, it was all over. Goodbye football. Baseball was now my life.

The infatuation initially started when the team unexpectedly ended up with a Wild Card spot in the postseason. Seeing that they had a chance to get to the World Series for the first time in almost two decades, I was glued to my television as the team managed to inch closer and closer to the Commissioner's Trophy. Being a Philadelphia sports fan, we were used to our continued disappointments and holding our breath for an entire season. When the Eagles nabbed their first Super Bowl win, it started a wave of varied success throughout the city with the sports teams.

I started watching just to see my home team, hopefully, get to the World Series. Instead, I ended up with a brand-new crush and yet another disappointment in my history of watching Philadelphia sports. The team ended up losing in game seven. But damn, what a ride.

Even with the demanding schedule of the Sillys, I watched baseball games live when I could. If not, I caught up with them later on the recorded replay. On the rare occasion I had a day off while the Phillies were in town, I usually tried to scoot down to the stadium and take in a game. Even if it was standing room only. The vibes at the ballpark were absolutely unmatched.

"Hey Cadence, next time go easy on us." First baseman, Benson Haldeman, huffed at me as he gathered his water bottle and shirt he'd shed during practice. Why he and Truitt chose to have a beard while playing a summer sport was beyond me. The only part of baseball season I didn't like was the insufferable temperatures of summer we had to contend with.

"My secret is I always go easy on you guys." There was a chorus of groaning from the team, and I could only laugh. For the most part, they were cooperative with what I threw their way. But it didn't mean that I didn't get sass for it. It was a playful love/hate relationship with the guys.

One would think that spending the better part of my spring and summer with a bunch of hunky guys would be a single woman's dream. For some, sure. As for me, the novelty wore off pretty damn quick.

I just *couldn't*. First of all, they were coworkers. Secondly, I saw them all more as dorky, goofy little brothers. Little brothers who had very nice bodies. Not that I ogled them anymore. The stink of sweaty man bodies and locker rooms had a permanent place in my nostrils. Knowing what they smelled like at their worst deterred any sexy factor for the lot of them.

The guys saw me as just another guy on the coaching staff. Which also meant that none of them scattered when I had to walk through the locker room while they were changing. Most managed to somewhat hide their junk to avoid any embarrassment, but I did my best to avoid walking through in the first place.

Philly Sillys' coach, Bert Topper, made me feel like an equal on his staff. With a few decades of minor and major league ball under his belt, the organization had to drag him out of a cozy retirement. *Had* being a strong word. Turned out he was rather bored anyway and was willing to give the new sport a chance. Despite his usual monotone demeanor, he was a great fit for the team. All business and no-nonsense. A stark contrast to the rest of the team

He'd call me into his office, which was only accessible through the locker room, from time to time, not caring what sort of minefield I'd have to walk through to do so. Between the team and coach, I was thankful that they saw me as one of their own. Just because I had breasts and a vagina didn't mean that I should be treated any differently in the workplace.

The guys were more of a walking HR sexual harassment complaint to *each other* than they were to me. What was it with guys in sports and spanking each other? Kinky. They wouldn't dare touch me like that. I was just someone who they got goofy or smart-assy with from time to time.

Skinny jeans and team T-shirts were my usual go-to for the ELB season. For practices, it was typical workout or dance gear. Tank tops or sports bras and Soffe booty shorts for the hot days. Ball caps and ponytails were the only suitable hairstyle. I typically cut it into a shortish sort of bob before the start of the season after letting my hair grow over the winter.

"Aww come on guys, you know you liked it." Catcher Schmidt Sullivan chimed in, which only brought on more groaning. Schmidt was my sidekick, giving the guys a much-needed morale boost during practice and games. Party guy extraordinaire, he usually gave the mascot and my best friend, Tiffiny Roberts, a run for her money in getting the crowds hyped up, right along with the team. I'd never seen the man have a grumpy face in the entire time I'd known him.

"Schmidt you're such a kiss ass." The left fielder, Truitt Lancaster, chided as he stroked his beard. I felt like I was roasting if my hair even brushed against the back of my neck. No wonder he kept it wet all the time. It made more sense to cut it all off instead of dousing it with water every chance he got. But, to each their own. Guys are weird.

"You still love me though." Schmidt grinned as the last of the guys joined us to head back to the locker room. "I'm irresistible."

There was a more avid chorus of groans. Schmidt was one to milk his audience, whether they liked it or not. The fans were keener on his nonsense. The guys were to a point, even though they didn't openly admit it.

"Now boys, be nice to each other. Or else practice tomorrow will involve *quiet* yoga." That earned a proper grumble and a few swear words from the team.

"Yeah, y'all remember what happened last time." Right fielder, Arlow Rivera, reminded the guys with a smirk. The man was dark and hunky, with wavy black hair that came over his eyes. Women were constantly trying to woo him, but he was cautious. He was a single dad and wanted to be a good role model for his adorable daughter, Lily. Sometimes Arlow would bring her to practice to hang out with us, but most of the time she was a permanent staple in the front row at games. She was more of a hardcore Sillys fan than I was.

"You mean the last *few* times," Roman Stevens, the second baseman, added with a snort laugh.

"Tru here and his melodic ass." It was Camden York, third basemen, and Truitt's partner in most of the chaotic crimes around here. His cropped, blonde curls bounced as he chuckled. Truitt answered back with a punch to Camden's bicep.

"Hey, the ladies love my ass. Its musical talents are just a bonus."

That got me to laugh. It was never a dull moment with this squad and their seemingly unending antics. They knew not to mess with me, but they did go out of their way to try to humor me. Laughter seemed to be the energy they needed to keep up with their nonsense on the field to entertain the crowds. Laughter and cheers.

With the crowd sizes not being where ownership wanted yet, the boys had a rough go from the established date of the team. Except for me, I was always entertained by them. They thought I was always a worthy audience. Considering my good nature and love for humor, I was probably a prime person for their audience.

Some days the boys got on my nerves. But most of the time they were adorable gigantic knuckleheads. The more absurd they were to me, the more obscene the dance moves and training I made them do. They hadn't caught on yet. Or perhaps they were just indulging me. I couldn't tell.

All the guys were charming in their own right. At that moment no one was seriously dating anyone. Designated hitter, Martin Pitt and Schmidt were happily married. Sure, I heard about the occasional conquest from the single guys. Mostly while on the road. Philly girls weren't as keen on their antics.

The guys were *intense*. With an equally intense work schedule, it was difficult for any of us to have a lasting relationship. Martin and Schmidt lucked out with getting married before they became serious ball players. Once the season kicked into full swing it was baseball all day, every day. The ELB had more off time than the majors, but the schedule was still hectic. If you didn't have an understanding partner, it was a tough life to support.

Not that I overly minded it. Dating wasn't a huge focus in my life. It added unnecessary complications. I loved my job. My job was my life. Not many men could understand that. Especially due to the fact that I was around attractive baseball players for six months out of the year.

Maybe I would have more of a chance to have a lasting relationship if I found someone in the offseason. But even then, it took a few months to mentally and physically recuperate from such a vigorous season. I needed to focus on myself before trying to split my attention with anyone else. It wouldn't be fair to them, and it wouldn't be fair to me.

Sometimes the quiet overwhelmed me and I found myself wishing to have someone to hang out with. To have a body to snuggle up to. Someone to chat with about everything and also nothing at all.

I've had people tell me, "Why don't you just date a baseball player?". Okay sure, it kind of made sense. We'd have similar schedules and training demands so we could be supportive of each other, right? Well, that would only work if we were part of the same organization. And it would only work if said organization was cool with a player dating a member of the admin team. Which was pretty much the equivalent of a CEO dating their secretary. Not a smart idea.

But I did what any sensible person would have done when an attractive baseball player asked them out. I said "Yes". Just once though. Roman was the only one that I sort of had a crush on at first, even after working with them all for a few months. Neither of us were stupid about it. We made sure we didn't do or say anything suspicious around the guys. Our dates were always outside of the city, so we had less of a chance of being caught by anyone who even had an inkling of who we were.

While it was a lot of fun we ended it as friends. Or well, I ended it as friends. Things got too real for me. Roman wanted to make it into something more serious and I…I just didn't feel that way about him. He was a nice guy and I had fun, but that's all it was. Not something that I could see being forever. It just wasn't fair to either of us to keep it going when we had to do so much to hide it.

"Cadence?"

"Huh?" I blinked and suddenly center fielder Tomas Lopez's face came into focus. His Dominican lilt made my name sound like music as it left his lips. I thought he looked like a charming lawn gnome with his always joyful and expectant expression.

"Yo, earth to Cadence." Truitt had to add in his two cents with a dramatic wave of his hand in front of my face.

"Yeah, yeah. I'm here." I batted Truitt's hand away and sidestepped the crowd of guys who looked on in some mix of concern and humor. "I was…just going over my grocery list. To pick up. On the way home." The cadence of my voice was choppy. I could tell from the looks on the guys' faces that only half of them believed it.

"Shit, I don't even remember what's in my fridge," Kellan Bristol added, looking rather worried as he massaged the leather of his glove while deep in thought. The guys cracked up in laughter. Thank god for the lanky, blonde-haired shortstop. He broke the tension and turned the attention of the guys off of me.

Hurrying down the hall, I made a beeline to my office to leave the guys to shower and head out for the day. It wasn't exactly a secret that I had "zone out" moments here and there. Mostly I was just deep in thought. For some reason today my brain wanted to hyper-focus on my dismal dating life instead of dreaming about the next dance routine.

Call me old fashioned, but I only wanted to date guys that I had a spark with. A connection. Someone who I could see myself with forever. Dating just for the "fun" aspect of it wasn't me. It was such a sappy and outdated notion, but why waste my or anyone else's time when the next one could be forever love?

It was probably my dad's fault for getting me hooked on Molly Ringwald movies from the 80s. *Sixteen Candles* was his cult classic favorite. He only ever admitted it to me, but his favorite part was when the heartthrob crush, Jake, showed up at the church in his fancy little red sports car. Sometimes I caught my dad in the middle of a dreamy sigh as he watched the scene unfold.

So yeah. I was looking for my Jake. A man who was a literal dream on two feet. Someone who smiled whenever he thought or spoke about me to anyone. The kind of man that would be happy to see me when I got home, even when we were in our eighties.

Someone like Jamie Rheems.

Well, at least that's what I imagined.

Jamie Rheems. The star catcher for Philadelphia. The man I rushed home to see just a glimpse of his face behind the wire cage of the catcher's mask on television. The man with corded biceps and forearms that flexed with every catch and throw. The man with an ass I could bounce a quarter off of.

The man that didn't even know I existed.

The man that I'd never had a face-to-face interaction with. The man that I'd never spoken to. A man that I didn't have to work into my hectic schedule. My imagination worked him in for me. In all the delicious ways possible.

It wasn't always a full-blown fantasy per se with a house and a future. It was just little glimpses of a shared space with the man. A smile that was just for me. A darting look into the crowd to see me in the sea of people. A lingering touch of those strong hands as we…

A knock on my office door made me jump almost three feet in the air. Unless I was showering or changing, I always kept the door open. So, it was safe to say that the new rookie pitcher for the Sillys, Ender Roche, saw my startle.

"Hey, Cadence?"

"Oh uh, hey Ender." I managed to get out, still breathless from his sudden appearance.

"You forgot your hat." With a bashful little smile, he stepped into my office and handed it over. His Venezuelan accent always made me swoon. With a baby face, he still looked like he was fresh out of high school, even though he was in his early 20s.

"Fuck, right." The guys were rather rambunctious today as practice concluded. I must have left my hat on the field when I was trying to show one of them how to do a proper cartwheel. "Thanks, Ender." Even with his promising potential, he was the sweetest guy on the team. Well, maybe he and Roman were tied for first.

"Don't let the guys get under your skin." He probably told me the same thing once a week so far this season. At this rate, all I could do was laugh and nod.

"I know, they're just a bunch of overgrown goofballs. Some more than others. I'm good though. I'm used to it." I dismissed him with a laugh and a wave. With a quick grin and a nod as he left, I found myself in silence once again. Well, as much silence as the closed double doors to the locker room could offer. Silence was not in the team's vocabulary or know-how.

Glancing at my watch, I swore under my breath. It was that time again. Grabbing my purse, I made a beeline for the parking lot. I had to get home to watch my imaginary perfect guy squat behind home plate.

2

MONEY & FAME
NEEDTOBREATHE

"**Y**ou have got to be fucking kidding me. The Philly Sillys?" I slapped my hands down on the wooden conference table. Standing abruptly, my legs shoved the chair hard enough to hit the wall. "They're a fucking joke. I'd rather go on IL permanently. Hell, I'll even take an early retirement."

Injured leave, or IL, was certifiably a death wish next to being benched in major league baseball. Especially when it was going to be long-term. It was an unsure storm of what-ifs as you recovered. Would you be as strong as before you were injured? Will the injury only get worse? Time would only tell, and it was torture. Absolute god-forsaken torture. Torture that, up until recently, I never was a part of.

"And do what, Jamie? Work as a Little League coach? Dammit, man, you'd make all the kids cry. You're too serious about baseball. Don't be a fucking idiot." I shot my agent, Tom Allen, a dirty look. His language didn't match his sportscoat and khaki business casual demeanor. But he wasn't wrong.

I didn't have the most approachable personality. Baseball was my job. I didn't do it for the fame or the fans, I did it because I loved it. And you didn't need to smile because you liked doing something. "If you want any chance of playing this season to get your strength back up to get back in the majors, you need to do this. You're lucky the Sillys had an opening instead of the team benching you. Thank fuck it's nowhere near the trade deadline."

"Yeah, but the Sillys? They're just a sad excuse for the franchise to do whatever the Savannah Bananas are doing." At this point I didn't care who I insulted. I was fucking pissed that ownership thought this was my only viable option. "They just want me for ticket sales and the views on the Tock Tick or whatever the fuck it's called. The Sillys don't even play *real* baseball!"

Technically it was baseball, but with a bunch of extra over-convoluted rules that were more akin to kids playing backyard ball. It was purely for the entertainment factor. There was no end game, no World Series sort of pomp and circumstance. Hence the league being *Entertainment* League Baseball. They solely existed to put on a show for the crowd. It looked closer to a damn circus. Why the franchise thought it was worth throwing money into a team of a bunch of goofballs was something I had yet to fathom.

"But they're quicker games, Jamie. Two hours tops. Look, if you manage to not fuck up your body any more, and recover while still playing ball, you'll have your contract intact to come back to the Phils. Hell, maybe even before the season is over. But I can't emphasize it enough. You. Can't. Fuck. It. Up."

Gritting my teeth, I growled out of sheer frustration. I felt as if I was stuck between a rock and a hard place. It wasn't my fault I was injured. Not exactly. It was the repetitive motions from crouching behind home plate as a catcher. At my age, I was a ticking time bomb to perhaps an inevitable career-ending injury in the baseball world.

With ownership out of the room, I felt I could speak frankly. Albeit a bit too loud for Tom's liking, judging by his expression. The frosted glass could only hide so many sins.

It wasn't like I'd already been frustrated enough with the bullshit that life had dealt me lately. Being in my mid-thirties and still on a major league baseball team as the starting catcher was rare. I was on borrowed time. The injury only reiterated that fact.

My backup catcher was decent. I did my best to teach him all my tricks during the game. But he wasn't ready to go full-time just yet. Probably in another season or two. Or three. Time that I still needed to convince myself to retire with grace. Today was not the time, even though I was frustrated by this roster move.

Being a catcher meant that one needed killer multitasking abilities. Not to mention staying cool in a stressful situation. While everyone was staring at the pitcher, it was the catcher who studied the batters in-depth as to their at-bat habits so we could call accurate pitches in the heat of the moment. Throw in keeping an eye on anyone stealing a base, and it was certifiable chaos.

Because of the weight and prestige I had in my position, I put off telling anyone I was having an issue with my knee. Swallowing a couple of over-the-counter pain pills before a game took the edge off for the beginning of the season. It wasn't until I stubbornly hobbled into the locker room one day before a game that the team's physical therapist threw a fit as they sent me through a gauntlet of tests. Which was only bad news after bad news.

Unfortunately, I was familiar with the issue as I had the same thing happen to my other knee a few years ago in the off-season. At least that side of my body had better timing. Probably the only body part to have good timing. Everything else on me had piss poor time management skills.

I went in for surgery the same week. The recovery was four weeks before they eased me back into practice. Everyone expected me to be rusty the first week or so back. What no one planned on was the fact that my stats weren't getting better. They were getting *worse*.

Due to my prestige as a Gold Glove award winner and a few stints at the All-Star Game, ownership had framed this fucking awful turn of events for me to be the saving grace of the Philly Sillys. To bring Philadelphia's ELB team into the spotlight. No matter how they sugar-coated it, it still felt like a demotion with a slap in the face to boot. The first thing out of my mouth was the suggestion of pulling someone up from the farming system from players in the Single-A, Double-A, and Triple-A leagues of the minors. That was immediately shot down with the fact that they were keeping the guys on task for major league ball, not the Entertainment League bullshit.

They thought that my move from the majors to the ELB would kill two birds with one stone so to speak. Having a star major league player starting for the less popular team would draw crowds in and hopefully give a reason for ownership to stop worrying about the fact that investing in the auxiliary team might have been a bad idea. That way I could still play some semblance of baseball with my slow as fuck recovery in something less strenuous.

I really fucking hated it.

I hated the idea so much.

"Look, think of it as something short-term. Give the Sillys a few weeks of your time and then you'll be back before the postseason."

As much as Tom was maybe right, I didn't want to entertain the other outcome. I didn't want to admit to myself that this could be my last season as a major league ball player. Especially if my stats remained in the toilet.

From a sensible aspect, it wouldn't be the end of the world. My yearly salary was in the very healthy eight digits. Not that I did much with it aside from putting it into savings and investments.

I kept a somewhat modest penthouse that I bought outright near some wetlands on an offshoot of the river over the bridge in New Jersey. The commute was a bit longer, but I liked the quiet time to zone out. The views reminded me a bit of my hometown in North Carolina. The only thing that I did manage to sink some decent money into was a top-of-the-line pickup truck with all the bells and whistles. It was safe to say that I wouldn't have to worry about work after baseball was over.

But I didn't want baseball to be over. I never wanted it to be over.

If I knew what was holding my body back from its condition pre-surgery, I would have already done everything in my power to rectify it. As soon as I was cleared by the doctor and trainers, I was back in the weight room. Everything pointed to me healing perfectly. So what fucking gives, body?

"If you want to stay in this organization, I highly suggest that you take their offer. I've had guys let go for less. *Much* less. They see something in you that they want to keep."

"Yeah, but they don't like me enough to throw me to Triple-A. Hell, Single-A even. Instead, I get drop-kicked to the bottom of the barrel."

"Only because of your prestige." I stop pacing and glance at Tom, who still looked hopeful. With a sigh, I collapsed back into the desk chair I'd gotten up from. "Heck, maybe you can do what they're asking and boost attendance in the first week. Then maybe you'll be back here in two weeks. Tops."

I shot Tom a look that said all he needed to know. I wasn't buying any of the kiss-ass shit he was offering. Even if I did boost attendance numbers, I still needed to get *my* stats back to, well at least near, where they used to be before my knee started giving me issues. That was the major hang-up here for me.

"Look, just give it a chance. Maybe it will be something you can do in your sleep. Fewer games, shorter games, more rest. Think of it as a mid-season vacation where you still get to play ball." Tom stood slowly with a nod. "Just make sure you give the team their answer before the end of the day." With that, he left the room. I was all alone with my thoughts.

If only it was as easy as everyone kept telling me it was going to be. It was almost as if they were spoon-feeding me shit and calling it chocolate. A change of scenery was not going to be the answer. Being thrown onto the Sillys was going to be more like a total shock to the system. Maybe, just maybe, it could turn into something good.

Or maybe it was really going to be like a shit show.

As much as I hated their offer, I wanted to keep my position and stay in Philadelphia. If that meant jumping through hoops like a trained circus monkey, then so be it. Philadelphia was the first place that felt like home since I started my professional baseball career. Even if coming back to the East Coast wasn't under the best of circumstances.

I jumped from college ball to the San Diego Padres minors' farming system, to the majors for a few seasons, only to be ultimately traded to Philadelphia. I dated on and off in that time, but it wasn't until I found a home in San Diego that I saw myself maybe settling down. My last girlfriend, Vanessa, and I had been together since right before I was called up to play in the majors. We made a home out in California and life was, well, content.

Unfortunately, professional ball was an unforgiving bitch. A player was there for ownership to do what they could for a team to get a win. If the franchise said you're being traded, you can't bitch about it. You can only say "Where to?" and "How soon do I need to pack?" You can be pissed or disappointed by it, but you had to follow where the money and contracts led to.

While I was excited to be back on the same side of the country as my folks, Vanessa, unfortunately, was not. My career and I weren't worth the cross-country move. I did have to give her some amount of respect for breaking things off instead of leading me on through the whole sham of a marriage. So many guys in this industry have been chased down by gold diggers and spotlight hounds. Shallow women with even shallower personalities.

I didn't want a pretty woman with no soul. I wanted a real relationship. Something tangible. Something that would last forever. Something like what my parents have.

Sure, Dad razzed Mom every chance he could get, and Mom bossed him around to no end. But it was all in love. They were well into their early 60s, and I still caught them kissing at random intervals when I was home for a visit. Hell, they still went on dates, even as empty nesters.

Baseball wasn't a money grab for me like it was for some guys. It was what I loved. I wanted a life partner who respected and appreciated that. But a woman who was supportive of this life was like finding that one home run ball that had soared clear out of the park into the parking lot beyond.

The schedule wasn't for the faint of heart. I had no idea how some of my teammates played professional ball and juggled raising a family. It was a lot to even think about, but I was a bit envious of them. I always wanted a family. One day.

Now here I was, at the fucking terrifying crossroads of my life and career. Despite this shitty hand my career decided to deal me, I wanted to play ball. And I wanted to play ball in Philadelphia. Which only left one option.

Donning a new uniform and playing for the Philly Sillys.

3

SKIN

SABRINA CARPENTER

"I honestly have no fucking idea how you deal with these guys on a daily basis," Tiffiny mumbled to me from our current view of the field. For most of the games, I liked to wander around the stadium so I could see the dance routines from every angle. Making dance moves visible from most of the ballpark at any given time wasn't an easy feat. Sometimes they needed to be tweaked or modified in some way or another until perfection hit.

"Why?" I snorted as I glanced at her. As much as I loved my best friend, sometimes her unhinged outbursts even took me by surprise. "If you ignore their antics, they aren't that bad." Most of the time it was difficult to have any sort of serious conversation with my fellow petite counterpart when she was still neck-deep in her mascot costume.

We were far enough away from prying eyes that no one would catch a glimpse of her as the headless mascot. My favorite vantage point in the park was the hidden mascot entrance because it constantly blasted cold air in the direction of the field to give Tiffiny a reprieve when she came for her usual breaks. Wearing a fuzzy padded suit, in the shape of the Liberty Bell, for a summer sport was no cakewalk.

"I feel like we have this conversation every season since I've been here. You must have invisible balls of steel to put those assholes in their place." That sharp retort got me to laugh.

"Call it 'tough love'." Turning to her, I caught the glassy stare of her character's hinged eyeballs, as the head of the mascot was tucked up under her arm. The cartoon-like slipper sneakers were always a hoot on her small feet. But the pièce de résistance was the fact that the damn Philly Sillys Liberty Bell mascot was named Ding Dong. I told the marketing team that they were geniuses when they showed us the concept.

Despite the rather goofy and delightful grin on Ding Dong's face, the person inside was anything but. Tiffiny was charming in her special way. That is if you liked sarcastic abominable snowmen with razor-sharp teeth. But she sure as fuck knew how to charm the fans and get tons of laughs when she was in uniform. I joked a lot that she made Ding Dong into something like the Philadelphia Flyers' infamous orange fur-covered mascot, Gritty's, toxic and insane ex. She had a gift.

To the normal person, it seemed like a weird schtick. But to Sillys fans, she was an utter hit. The marketing team even set up a social media account for Ding Dong. Most of Tiffiny's free time was spent coming up with more and more unhinged content. Even in the off-season. While most of us had a few months off, she had to do her best to keep the mascot, and the Sillys, relevant throughout the entire year.

Her personality grew on me during the season last year, when she was hired. In the off-season, we commiserated in our mutual misery and became forever friends. I mean, who else could understand the utter insanity that I had to go through on a daily basis?

For the games, Tiffiny did her own thing. Sometimes she joined the guys on the field for a routine. But there was just something there that made her reluctant to do so regularly. I mean, I get it. Being on the field in front of a crowd was rather intimidating. That's why I never tried it myself. I was more than happy sitting in the outfield and looking on with pride. Or well *cringing*.

Sometimes the guys took their own *creative* liberties. Usually, it worked out in their favor. How were the fans to know that the routine wasn't supposed to go that way? Then again it could also turn out to be an epic fail that ended up on social media. Which then fell on my shoulders. How the fuck was I supposed to keep them in line during a game? Remote-controlled shock collars?

Believe me, I suggested that already.

Squirting them with the field's watering hoses was a very close second. Also vetoed.

"More like herding cats." Tiffiny's gaze hardened the longer she stared out at the field. "Smelly, off-beat, howling, hairless cats."

I snorted. "Geez let me get the bullhorn out and immediately tell the guys what you think of them."

"Oh, they know."

Even with her attitude, I knew Tiffiny loved this team almost as much as me. Although if she had to deal with the players regularly, like I do, her *charming* description of them might skew a bit differently. But only a bit.

"They aren't that off-beat today," I added after taking a long, hard look at them mid-routine.

"Yeah, *today*."

I cocked my brow at her. "Well, you're in a rather chipper mood. Throwing out compliments left and right here."

"It's the heat." She dismissed quickly as she squirted some water from her Sillys water bottle into her mouth. Her brown hair was plastered to her forehead in misshapen ringlets. The suit did have a fan/air conditioning contraption, but it only offered a tiny bit of relief in the insufferable summer humidity.

"You know…wearing a fur suit isn't exactly the most conducive for people who despise the heat–"

"And what the hell am I going to do with my Masters in Theater Studies? Teach a bunch of stuck-up kids how to do shitty Shakespeare in a private school in center city? Hell no. At least here I can work solo." She hooked a fuzzy thumb in the direction of the team. Subtlety was definitely not her middle name.

"Hey 'Shitty Shakespeare' does have a nice ring to it… You might want to trademark that as a backup plan. Or at the very least that would make a fantastic band name."

That at least got some semblance of a smile out of her.

"Sure, let me pull together all that money I have lying around while I pay off my student loans for the rest of my natural life." Tiffiny let out a huff, almost as if she tried to hold back laughing at her own joke. "Speaking of money, how's that *boyfriend* of yours?"

I felt the heat rise to my cheeks. With it being baseball season, it was a given that neither Tiffiny nor I had any semblance of a significant other. Which could only mean that it was one very unattainable person she was referring to.

"Oh…uh, Jamie's, um…fine." The incredibly hunky catcher had graced my apartment almost nightly since late February. Although "graced" was a stretch. The man showed up on my television, not nearly enough, thanks to there being other players on a baseball team. Sometimes I wished I could bribe someone to keep a camera solely on Jamie for the entire game.

"Any homers lately?"

Only in my fantasies in the ballpark of my bed.

"Not since before his surgery." I sighed. The franchise nearly broke my heart when they announced all of a sudden that Jamie was going on the IL due to knee surgery. That was the longest few weeks of my life. Tiffiny got me through most of it with movie nights and gorging ourselves on appetizers at our favorite local haunts. Although not without some rather heated teasing about my "boyfriend", as she calls him.

"That's too bad. It's probably because you didn't send him any flowers." I rolled my eyes. "Or topless pics." That comment earned an elbow to her upholstered bell curve.

"You're such a brat."

"But you love me."

"Only sometimes."

"That's fine. I can only tolerate you sometimes." We both cracked up with laughter. It was always a loving but insulting back and forth. A love language for both of us.

"But really," I sighed as the fantasy I had of Jamie hovered in the back of my mind. "Who would want to date one of these guys anyway?"

"I don't know. Some parts of them are appealing. Money. Fame." Tiffiny offered with a shrug. "Hot bodies."

I snorted. Baseball was the one sport where you didn't necessarily have to be physically fit to play. I'd seen some pitchers and basemen who had pot bellies that Santa would be envious of.

"Well, like you, I like being a quiet swamp witch in my apartment, thank you very much."

"Yeah, that doesn't seem like Jamie's vibe at all." I rolled my eyes.

"You don't know that. Maybe he's a witch-loving homebody." When Jamie wasn't on the field, I was usually combing through interviews and articles about him. There was never much. It was like he was allergic to the spotlight. When he did manage to interview somewhere it was typically to talk about his position and what the team was doing. Outside of baseball, he was seemingly an enigma.

Some of the other Philadelphia players didn't shy from the spotlight. They were found out on the town, taking photos with fans or in the arms of some pretty model or influencer. Not that I knew who any of the women were. Nor did I care.

I liked to think that Jamie was a guy who was more comfortable at home. Maybe he had a dog or even a cat. Or maybe he was close to his parents and siblings, and he spent his free time hanging out with them.

"Come on, the man is too pretty. He can't sit and waste away at home."

"You do." I quipped back at her. The unexpected compliment spawned a quick quirk of a smirk at the corner of her mouth. "Aren't you the one who is supposed to be encouraging this infatuation instead of giving me shit for it?"

"Oh, right. I need something to razz you about daily. Well, until one of us finds a real guy and not one from a book or on TV." We glanced at each other for a moment before erupting into a fit of uproarious laughter. A real man? Who were we kidding?

BLINDING LIGHTS

POP GOES AMBIENT & VANCOUVER SLEEP CLINIC

I t wasn't a game night, nor was it the night before an away series. So, pulling up to the Sillys' stadium left me with a sense of worry. I'd been utterly perplexed by the emergency call from Coach Topper himself. The man only made gruff and to-the-point phone calls. Good or bad, his voice never wavered. So, it was always a crapshoot on what to expect.

But this call was different. Part of me was worried that something bad had come down from ownership. If there was even a hint of something off in any aspect of my life, my body went into immediate. "doomsday protocol", complete with stress sweat and body-aching anxiety. Sometimes I was even treated to a "high heart rate" alert on my smartwatch. I had two alerts just on the drive over to the stadium.

It was no secret that trying to get this whole Entertainment League Baseball thing off the ground had been pretty rough. We still hadn't managed a sell-out night since the stadium opened its doors. You'd think with all the amazing comedians from the Philly area that this place would be ripe to accept a baseball team like the Sillys. It seemed that Philly sports fans were keener on the *serious* sort of sports. Hell, the professional soccer team was still trying to get its footing with the fans. And they'd been around longer than we had.

To quell the stench of my pure unfiltered anxiety, I kept my car window down in the hope that the fresh air would give me the smell of Philly pollution instead of BO. Not that I would have much to worry about in the basement-smelling Sillys locker room.

Whatever it was, I hoped the news was good. The guys needed a little boost of something. It wasn't even close to mid-season and I could tell they were losing a bit of steam. The dance routines of late were a bit half-assed and without the usual spunk. It was also deep into the fiery and unpredictable hell that was Pennsylvania weather. The hot and humid temperatures always made things unpleasant.

As I made my way down the steps, there was a murmur coming from the locker room. It was an odd sight to see the guys in their street clothes and not their usual workout gear or uniform. They invited me out from time to time, but that was outside of the ballpark.

"Yo, Cadence, do you know why Topper called us?" Arlow looked up from his seat on the bench, straddling it as he leaned his elbows on his thighs. All eyes turned to me, even the ones from the other coaching staff members.

"What makes you think I know anything? I was just about to ask if any of you guys knew." There were some murmurs of "no" and a whole lot of shaking heads. That made this meeting even more unsettling. What the hell was so important to call us all in on our day off but not tell anyone anything?

"Do you think it's something bad?" Schmidt stood as he rubbed the back of his neck nervously. The guys all exchanged looks as if they all had the same feeling.

"I sure as fuck hope not." I gave them a half-assed awkward smile to reassure them in some capacity. "I mean, if it was something serious, I'm sure Topper wouldn't have been so casual about the meeting place for *whatever* it is he needs to tell us. If it really was bad news, he would've invited us all someplace that had readily available alcohol."

That at least got me some enthusiastic nods. Not that I had anything to compare this event to. In all my years with the Sillys, I couldn't remember a time that we were all called in to meet under such mysterious circumstances. I tried to put on a brave face for the team.

Muffled voices grew louder beyond the main door to the locker room. The strain to hear made the room so quiet that one could hear a pin drop. It was the first time I'd ever experienced any measure of time where all of the guys were this silent before.

From what I could tell, there were at least two voices beyond the door, so it was a surprise to us all to see only Topper make his way into the room. He was in his usual team-branded gear. I once joked to his wife that I wouldn't be surprised to know that he had Sillys-branded pajamas that he wore to bed. For Topper being such a grump of a guy, he sure loved this team. Maybe to an unhealthy level.

As soon as the door clicked shut it was as if the shaken bottle was suddenly uncorked. All the guys went off at once, standing to confront Topper with their barrage of questions. It was times like these that I wished I wore my whistle around my neck at all times. Not that the guys would have shut up. We were all a mess with anxiety.

"Alright, alright, settle down gents." Topper shot me a look with a quick nod. "And ladies." He never needed to personally address me, apart from the men, but he always went out of his way to do so. There was some charm to his rough exterior.

I was always the one who was the first to shut up and listen when the typically quiet manager spoke up, unlike the guys. It was like corralling a room of sugar-high preschoolers most days. "We have a…new player joining the team tonight."

There was a murmur throughout the room as I cocked my brow. Since I was a part of the coaching staff, typically I was briefed when we had a new player join the Sillys. I reviewed their audition tape and talent background so I could figure out where in the entertainment lineup they would fit. But that was always at the beginning of the season. To have someone join at such a weird time was suspicious indeed. From the looks around the room, it seemed that Topper was the only one akin to this information.

"This came down from ownership today and y'all need to be on your best behavior and show him how it's done around here. Just because he has more of a *status*, doesn't mean that we will treat him any differently. Especially since he will be with us for the foreseeable future while he recovers here."

Now I was completely perplexed. Ownership? This shit had to be serious. Did they find someone in the farm that they wanted to bring up to the big city?

Players had to work their way through the minors' farming system as ownership cultivated them for the big leagues. Was this some hotshot player that they found out of the blue?

"Please give a Sillys welcome to our new starting catcher," The curious murmurs reverberated throughout the locker room. What player could make ownership pull Schmidt as our starting catcher? The man was the team's single cheerleader. I mean– "Philly's own…Jamie Rheems!"

My heart and eyes collided with the brick wall that was the absolute vision of Jamie Rheems as he slipped through the locker room door.

Oh my god.

He was *here*.

In the flesh, standing easily a head and shoulder taller than Topper. The man of all my fantasies of late was standing in the locker room of *my* workplace.

As the newest member of my team.

As in, someone I will have to train.

As in, someone I'm going to have to face, on a daily basis, for maybe the rest of the season.

The only time I'd ever been close to Jamie Rheems was from at least two dozen rows back at the ballpark behind fencing and security. Not six or so odd feet away from the man that I had *literally* orgasmed to thoughts of last night.

Oh, dear god, I was so fucked.

And not in the good way.

Something of a scowl curled at his bold bow of a mouth. He didn't look happy to be here. Which, granted, made sense given the situation he found himself in.

The Phillies currently had the best record in baseball. They needed to keep the momentum going. A half-assed catcher wasn't going to get them to the postseason. Aside from the designated hitter, each team member had to pull their weight. They both played their position and had a chance at bat. When the star catcher, in the number two batting spot at the beginning of the season, dropped down to the number eight, something was drastically wrong. Maybe that's why he was here?

None of it made sense. The Sillys didn't need the help. Our roster was solid. Maybe Topper knew something we didn't.

My eyes couldn't leave the man as Topper slowly introduced Jamie to the players. I couldn't believe it. My heart was racing so fast I thought it was going to make a break for it, up through my throat and out of my mouth.

Jamie was in his mid-30s and quickly coming up to the "out to pasture" years for a major league ball player. Especially as a catcher. Squatting for long lengths of time and throwing from a crouched position was hard on the human body. Despite all that, he was still giving the younger guys in his position a run for their money. At least before his injury.

Goddamn, he was so fucking *fine*.

Well-built in all the right ways and with a jawline that made your gaze want to linger, he turned heads with fans. Even with his head in a ball cap, his rich dark chocolate hair was always tousled so perfectly when he took his hat off. His hair color paired so well with his stunning blue eyes. The color was so intense you could easily see his irises through a television screen.

Which was why it was so difficult for me to believe that he was currently only a few feet from me and headed in my direction. I tried to remain calm and desperately wished that my face didn't give away the distress that I was feeling inside. Topper was making sure that Jamie met with everyone. Since dancing was a healthy dose of the Sillys' training, meant that he was headed directly for me at the end of the line.

I resonated with a deer in the headlights as Jamie inched his way closer to me. There was a subtle five o'clock shadow along his jaw, his skin softly tanned from the hours on the ballfield. Throughout the baseball season he went from being clean-shaven to a rough stubble but never let it get long enough to be considered anything but. Either look for him sent my female hormones into *"fuck me hard"* overdrive.

His scowl only deepened as Topper turned to me. My heart came to a complete and shuddering stop being this close to Jamie Rheems, the man of my dreams in my fantasies. I couldn't help but feel my usually warm, glowing fantasy shatter into a zillion pieces as I faced this grumpy front of his. Those blue eyes were as cold as their icy color.

Great. We were already off to a rough start and neither of us had said anything yet. Those enchanting eyes of his drifted down and back up my body as if he was trying to figure me out. I had to suppress what would have been a delicious shiver. He was sizing me up. Given my five-foot height, it didn't take long. The thirsty bitch inside me hoped it was for a thorough devouring, but unfortunately, I wasn't one of God's chosen ones.

"Cadence Andrews here is the boss on the field when the ball isn't in play. You listen to her and her alone in between plays for the routines. Half of practice days are for field and batting work. The rest is for choreography." Jamie's eyes went dark as his brow furrowed. There was a tightening of his jaw which made me want to slap his sour mood right off his face. This wasn't at all his normal demeanor.

I wasn't even blessed with a voiced agreement. All I got was a curt nod. But hell, his gaze was intense. It was akin to his usual look on the ballfield with his game face on, calling pitches to the pitcher. The man was all business. Oddly enough, the longer we were in each other's personal space, the more intense his look got.

Oxygen slowly vacated my lungs in one long, shaky breath as the duo slowly turned away from me to speak with the other coaches. Holy fucking seven circles of hell. I honestly didn't know if I should be weirdly turned on, ready to pull out my mace spray or cry.

Jamie Rheems was going to be a tough nut to crack.

That is if I could survive being around him every day first.

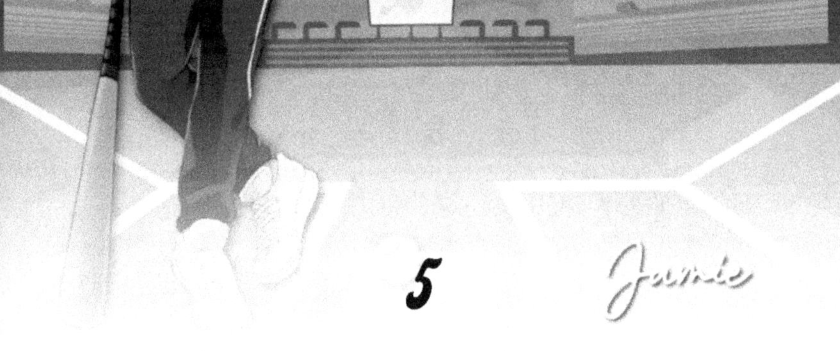

5 *Jamie*

I KNEW YOU WERE TROUBLE

TAYLOR SWIFT

"I walked into a fucking Disney movie," I muttered under my breath as I saw what looked like chaos set to music. My new teammates were all spread out in the outfield, working on what looked like some oddly complicated dance number. An overplayed pop radio hit blared over a rather large wireless speaker by a woman's feet as they all attempted to follow her lead in the outfield near second base.

The one woman who sucked the oxygen from my lungs the second I met her.

The one woman I couldn't find words to utter a simple greeting to.

The one woman who I couldn't stop thinking about.

The feeling had been peculiar, and it still had me in a tizzy this morning. Or maybe it was from the piss poor night of sleep, stressing about walking into this bizarro circus that ownership tried to convince me was baseball. The only semblance that this field had *anything* to do with baseball was the fact that there thankfully were three bases and a home plate. But that was it.

37

Dancing had never been my strong suit. Hell, it was never even on my radar. Between high school and college, all I focused on was baseball. I didn't even go to my senior prom. I had a ball game to be at the next day. God bless my supportive parents for dragging my sorry ass to ball games near and far. But they knew that I loved it. And all that hard work paid off.

Well, it *had* paid off. Up until a few days ago.

Now here I was, standing with a bag full of my practice gear, and feeling like I was facing a midlife crisis. A washed-up baseball player with nowhere to go but down.

This fucking can't be my life right now.

"Hey! Jamie!" The crew of chaos stopped for a drink break when I was spotted. The shortest man in the bunch with dark wavy hair and a trimmed beard was excitedly waving me over. From what I could remember from yesterday's introductions, he was the man whose job I'd be replacing. At least for the time being.

Might as well get this stupid thing over with.

As I reluctantly shuffled my way over to the group, the woman from yesterday caught my eye. It was difficult to miss her. She was wearing a rather sinful pair of bright pink workout leggings. Sinful in the sense that none of her feminine curves could hide from the skin-tight fabric. Her wavy coppery blonde hair was up in a pony, revealing the sad excuse for a t-shirt that seemed more holy than a Catholic Sunday. Which only led to rather *unholy* thoughts as I caught sight of the matching sports bra through the artistically placed holes in the cotton.

In the off-season I'd seen countless women workout alongside me in the gym. Some much more scantily clad. None of them gave me this sudden and rather visceral response as my new *coach* did. Which only made me feel even more frustrated about this entire absurd situation.

Women were rare in the majors. Most were part of the medical or therapy teams. The others were involved with promotions and social media, so we didn't interact with them much unless they needed some sort of nonsense filmed. None of them would have dared to wear such *clothing* to the ballpark.

None of them had to teach us guys how to fucking dance either. That sort of entertainment was singularly the mascot's job and the furry green dude at the ballpark did a rather bang-up job of it. But that was the mascot's *job*. Not the team's job.

With a grumble, I tossed my bag down with the rest of the random piles of gear from my new teammates. The woman was seemingly startled by the commotion. What was her name again?

That's right.

Cadence.

I caught her glance over her shoulder at me, only for her to look away as quickly as she had initially turned. As if she had been burned by even the thought of looking at me. There was an excited murmur among the guys as I surveyed the sad situation in front of me.

"You're late." Her icy cold tone cut through the chatter and was a harsh contrast to the already humid summer air. I didn't care that she was right, it was how the words came across. On the other hand, the guys on the team looked stoked that I had actually shown up. But my new coach looked nonplussed. *Great, way to go, Jamie.*

"I'm just here to play baseball," I muttered back as I shifted uncomfortably with all the eyes on me.

"It's choreography practice first." The reminder was bristly. I couldn't recall ever meeting anyone this tart. The fact that she wouldn't even look at me didn't bode well either. What the hell was up her ass?

None of the other guys seemed phased by her attitude. There were even a few snickers with her comment. Maybe that's how she was.

Ignoring her, a few of my new teammates sauntered over to reintroduce themselves or extend friendly pleasantries to welcome me in. At least they were nice. But they were more thrilled about this situation than I was. I could only kind of pay attention to the greetings as I kept my eyes on her.

How she didn't have this misfit group of ball players salivating at the mouth was beyond my comprehension. She probably had put them all in their place at one time or another. Perhaps she even dated one or two, or all, of them. Or maybe we were barking up the wrong tree.

With the distraction of the team on me, Cadence busied herself with whatever was on her phone. There was just something about her that was...*odd*. Whatever it was I didn't exactly want to piss off any members of the coaching staff by interrogating people about the only female member of staff.

Perhaps I had offhandedly offended her at our initial meeting? Or maybe she was a real stickler for being punctual. Normally I was one of the first guys to the locker room on game and practice days. But here? I wasn't feeling the same excitement to come to work.

"Alright boys, the break is over." Cadence's sharp voice broke up the chatter. "Let's tighten up the seventh inning stretch routine we've been working on." She found whatever she was looking for as music started to pulse from the speaker in the grass. I watched as the guys listened without a second word. I almost jumped myself as she suddenly appeared next to me. Hell, she was short. I could see straight over her head. Her harsh tone dropped to a volume that was solely for me. "Fall in line with the other guys and follow along. You missed warmups."

There were a few rumbles of low whistles from the guys as I found an empty spot towards the back of the group. Warm welcome my ass. But I'm sure I probably deserved it for not being my usual prompt self. They probably all thought I was the pretentious major league asshole that could show up whenever he wanted. Of which was the complete opposite of the usual me.

"Alright Sillys… Five, six, seven, eight!" The guys quieted down as all eyes went on Cadence. I kind of just stood there and took it all in as her vibrant outfit broke through all the drab tank tops, t-shirts, and shorts. For the most part, the guys followed her move by move. A few went the wrong direction or were off tempo just a smudge.

All I could manage to do was stare, completely perplexed by the entire situation before me. Cadence didn't call out any moves or offer verbal instruction. The guys just magically fell into line in front of her as they copied her moves.

How the hell was I supposed to follow this? Was I supposed to do what she was doing? Was I supposed to go the opposite way because she was facing us? There didn't seem to be any rhyme or reason for the nonsense. Maybe I could kind of half-ass it until it was time for fieldwork. Exactly how much time did the team waste on such pointless exercises?

I could only stand there, metaphorically scratching my head. Nerves were starting to churn in my gut. It had been quite some time since I did training in which I had no idea what the fuck was going on. It was almost as if it was like the first day of school.

The group did a little spin and then a single clap. All I could do was offer up a panic clap a few moments after theirs in a vain attempt to sort of follow along. Which only brought all of their attention back to me. The music cut off sharply.

"Mr. Rheems if you weren't aware, you are *required* to participate." Her words sliced through the sudden quiet. She did tell me to follow along, but how could I when I had no idea what the dance moves were? I had no clue how this all worked.

"Dude, just move. Even if you fake it." The man to my right whispered under his breath. His dirty blonde beard was neatly trimmed. Which made it easy to hide the fact that he was talking to me.

"Don't fuck it up or else she will make us do quiet yoga again." I cocked my brow as the younger guy in front of me turned around to share that interesting little tidbit. What kind of fresh hell was this place?

"Kellan is right." Cadence interrupted, loud enough for everyone to hear. Fucking hell *and* she had super hearing? For a woman who had so much authority she sure couldn't look me in the eye as she scolded me. Her face was pointed in my direction, but her eyes were off to the left. There was a telltale bit of mirth to her smirk. "Personally, I like quiet yoga days."

I almost jumped from the resounding groan that echoed through the guys. Like Cadence, I didn't mind yoga. It sure as fuck was better than dance practice. But the yoga she threatened them with had to be some wicked sort of hell for this ice queen to procure such a response from the team. Maybe it was safer just to attempt to dance. I didn't want a reason for my teammates to be pissed at me from the get-go.

The music started again after a drawn-out, steely, indirect stare from Cadence. A shiver went down my spine, almost as if her eyes were glacier-like.

Despite her clunky demeanor, she moved with effortless grace. Her body was toned like a dancer. She was a brightness in the crowd of heather gray and navy blue. A goddess on the ball field.

Why the fuck was I haphazardly swaying to music and musing about my new coach's body? But she was much more appealing to look at than a bunch of sweaty men shaking their asses. Much more appealing…

My foot tangled with my other and I tipped forward before catching myself. If I wasn't careful, I'd end up with another injury. An injury that would be more embarrassing than just being an old-as-dirt baseball catcher. This dancing stuff was more dangerous than having 90-mile-per-hour fastballs chucked at my head.

What was it about this woman that had me all tangled up in my thoughts? And limbs for that matter. She was like a perplexing enigma that moved with such effortless grace. With a sway to her hips that would even make a blind man take a second look.

I glanced at each of the guys, trying to gauge how they felt about her. From what I could tell, no one was ogling her with wagging tongues, waiting for her to bend forward so they could get a better view. Despite her chilly output, she held the guys' attention. She had to be a hell of a woman to keep this bunch of guys in line.

My trail of thoughts had turned aggravating again. Why was she so stuck in my brain? It had to be from her piss-poor attitude and *not* about how good her wider-set curves looked in spandex.

After the less-than-ideal breakup with Vanessa, I promised myself no more relationships. Not even a tryst. It wasn't fair to bring a woman into this life on the road, no matter how willing she was. Because it was the overly willing ones who were the gold diggers or who wanted to share the spotlight.

I hated the spotlight. I wanted to be as far away as possible from it. I wanted someone who didn't want it either, someone who was understanding and genuine. The women I encountered previously were the farthest things from it.

Sure, there were decent ones in the bunch. My colleagues in the majors somehow managed to find incredible partners and some of them…not so much. Some of the younger guys were there to party and enjoy all the other various nonsense that came with it.

It wasn't like I hadn't tried. Between my teammates trying to set me up on dates to managing a few on my own, it never ended well. The demands of my career were the biggest contention. Even if I needed to blow off some steam, I wasn't going to sleep with a woman for fun.

Call me old-fashioned, or my southern North Carolina charm, but I needed to have a connection with someone if I was going to take them to bed. Sex wasn't just a physical thing for me. It was mental. Emotional. Just like baseball. Whatever that switch was that most men had that focused on getting off with the next hot thing, I didn't have it.

Although it didn't mean I wouldn't *look*.

I would admire an attractive woman as much as the next guy. Especially ones with soft pink curves…

That mental distraction somehow put me in the way of the guy in front of me with messy black hair and deeply tanned skin. He spun around with his arms out. Ducking away from the man tornado, my face avoided the brunt of his helicopter as he backhanded my shoulder. Which only sent me stumbling forward into the next row of players doing the same motion.

There were a few shouts of surprise and grumbles before the music came, once again, to a sudden stop.

"Mr. Rheems! Seriously. Is there a problem?" The hips that distracted me in the first place were cocked to one side, with her hand perched on the tasty jut of her hip bone. *Move your fucking eyes elsewhere, Jamie.*

"Uh…no." My gaze shot up to hers, completely called out on multiple fronts. All eyes turned to me along with some chuckles as the guys took the interruption to grab water or wipe the sweat off their faces.

"Good, because I'd hate to bring you front and center." There was a playful chorus of "oohs" from the peanut gallery. "Alright, guys, from the top!"

On second thought, maybe retiring wouldn't be such a bad idea after all.

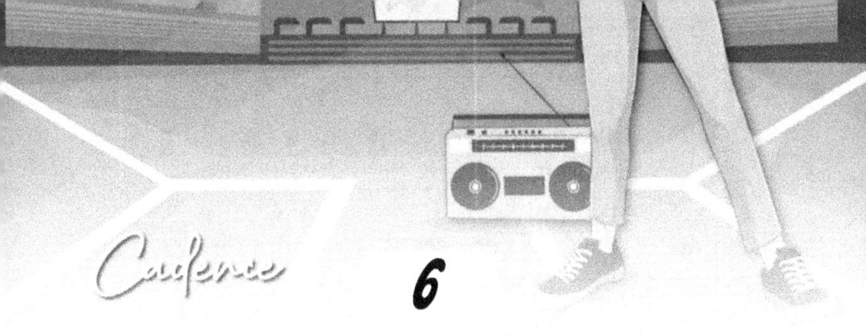

6

DON'T BLAME ME

TAYLOR SWIFT

"**S**o, how's your *boyfriend* fitting in?" Tiffiny clinked her beer bottle against mine to get my attention. She texted me earlier about needing to get out of the house for a change of scenery. As much as I needed the same thing, my thoughts were an overflowing jumbled mess of all sorts of things. Alcohol wasn't exactly going to help, but having a friend nearby to distract me from said thoughts might.

"That man is the furthest thing from boyfriend material," I grumbled as I tipped my bottle back for a hearty swig. "Be lucky you can't meet your fantasy book men. You'll only end up disappointed. Because Jamie is the biggest, most stubborn grump on planet Earth."

"Jamie?" Tiffiny huffed, trying to find some common ground for my bitch fest. "What kind of fucking redneck 'Backstreet Boys' member dropout bullshit is that name anyway? What were his parents thinking?"

I rolled my eyes as my fingers danced over the condensation drips along the neck of my beer. This whole situation was shitty on so many levels.

Especially the part where Jamie wasn't anything like I imagined him to be in my late-night fantasies.

"I happen to like it."

Tiffiny rolled her eyes. "Guys like him are the reason why I read to find men. No chance of running into a *fictional* man on the street." A sad but dreamy sigh escaped my friend. "Unfortunately."

"I'll drink to that." I sighed as our bottles clinked together before we sagged into our bar stools. Why was it so difficult to find a decent man in real life? Or at least a tolerable one. Was it too much to find a man who was *lovingly* obsessed with their woman? Not in a creepy sort of stalker kind of way. Someone who was selfless and passionate in bed. Someone who thought about you even when you weren't together, then came home to *show* you how much they missed you.

Tiffiny was right. Those sorts of men only existed in books. Existed in books written by women. Some men wrote romance and some of those said romances focused a hell of a lot on boobs bouncing boobily. Cheers to women who wrote the kind of men we needed.

Not that I was actively looking for anyone. I was more into the whole theory that the one who was meant for you would just fall into your lap one day. I wasn't going to go out of my way to stalk dating sites or pick up random guys in bars. Nothing about wanting a man made me *that* desperate. Okay, so maybe *one* thing. But they had vibrating silicone stand-ins for that. Of which I had an entire drawer full of at home.

For the most part, I was content being by myself. I could watch what I wanted when I wanted. My free time was spent doing things that made me happy or being in utter silence without a soul to bother me. Sure, it would maybe be fun to have someone over to do something a little different from time to time.

"We really picked the wrong career path for dating," Tiffiny mumbled as she dove back into the loaded nachos we were sharing. It wasn't the best choice for a dinner option, but it did carry all of the food groups. Plus, we needed to bury our stress and sorrows in some greasy food.

"Yeah, but who needs men when you're surrounded by loud and obnoxious ones all day long? A daily reminder of just what we're missing."

"True. We get our fill during the season and then spend all winter recovering." Tiffiny did a rather loud snort-laugh as she crunched down on an overloaded chip.

There was silence between the two of us as we ate. Something was bugging me about this sudden about-face in my personality with having the man of my dreams as part of my squad. I felt like all I did was yell at him.

He was trying my patience, whether it was on purpose or not. Maybe it was my protective instinct kicked into overdrive. I was uncomfortable around men I found attractive. I could only do the most awkward mating dance on the planet which included not being able to control the volume of my voice and overthought movements.

"You don't think I'm being too hard on him, do you?"

"Pfft. No. Those majors boys are used to it."

"It's just that…it's fucking torture to have him staring back at me every day. I haven't been able to look the man in the face, let alone have any semblance of a conversation with him. I feel like all I do is come across as pissed off."

Tiffiny burst out laughing with a mouthful of chips. At least she had the decency to cover her open mouth. But it did nothing to muffle her outright guffaw.

"Why? Are you constantly undressing him with your eyes?"

"You know, I'm not even going to dignify that with an answer." The joke was on her. Jamie *had* undressed in front of me, by accident, only yesterday. But that was because Topper had called me into his office for another Jamie update. Due to that visual, I had no cognitive function to give said report. "But no." *Technically.* "It's like I'm under hottie overload if he comes within ten feet of me. It's like I forget how to be a civilized human being."

"So…that's a yes then?"

"Shut up." I took a large swig of my beer in a vain attempt to ignore the flashback of the rather up-close and personal vision of a shirtless Jamie. It was an accident I swear. But there was no fucking way I was ever going to tell Tiffiny that little secret. I'd never hear the end of it.

"Come on, admit it." I reluctantly glanced at her, growing more afraid by the second just what she wanted me to admit to. "You still want to jump Jamie's hard…*bat.*"

The chip went down awkwardly in my swallow. Working with a man you've admired and fantasized over from afar wasn't something I'd wish on my worst enemy. This first week with Jamie as part of the team had been the most stressful week of my entire career with the Sillys. Hell, my entire adult life.

"He's making it easier and easier for me *not* to think about it." Which was technically true.

But also, a complete and utter lie.

I had to simultaneously be professional and also not lose my fangirl shit. Which, if I was being honest, my inner fangirl was still hanging on by a damn thread any time I managed to catch him without a scowl on his handsome face. But unfortunately, those times were few and far between.

The man was freaking gorgeous. Just being in his orbit was both heaven and hell on earth. The heavenly part was being able to see him daily and at such a close range that I could almost count each eyelash hair. The hell part was a tie between his icy attitude and the fact that I couldn't talk to the man in a civilized manner. It's as if he made my brain short-circuit to the point that *major staff sergeant bitch Cadence* came through.

Jamie made my heart race and bile come to my throat. A normal person should be used to having a baseball god in their presence by now. But for some reason, my body still had this immediate flight or fight response to him.

Maybe it was some sort of protective mechanism to stop myself from doing something stupid. Because if Jamie and I were ever alone, my body would definitely want to do something stupid. Especially with Tiffiny egging me on.

I wasn't the kind of person to fling myself at a man who made my panties wet. My reaction was to give the man a *wide* berth because something utterly absurd was sure to come out of my mouth. Or nothing at all. It was safer to stay back and maybe, just maybe, they'd approach me. Not that they ever did.

"Oh, come on, he can't be that bad. From what you told me before he seemed…*charming*. Is charming the word I'm looking for? I don't understand baseball." Tiffiny looked a bit confused as she raised her beer bottle to her lips. She was the furthest thing away from a sports fan. Her days were spent hiding in bed and reading. Being a mascot, all she had to do was get the crowd hyped and entertain them. Nothing about that needed her to completely understand the rules of the game.

"Considering how long you've been with the Sillys, I'm still surprised you haven't picked up one thing about baseball."

"I mean…there's the catcher guy." Her brown eyes looked off thoughtfully as she mused. "A baseball. Some gloves…and a ref?"

I was mid-sip when I snorted so hard the beer burned my nasal cavity. "Jeezus, Tiffiny. I mean…you're off to a good start." I desperately tried to keep my laughter under wraps, but it was a lost cause.

"Oh, it's not a ref, is it?" Tiffiny furrowed her brow as she thought about the matter. "Wait, refs wear those Hamburglar shirts."

It took me a moment to understand what she was talking about but when I did, I lost it. I couldn't help the deluge of laughter that spilled forth. I had to put my beer back down on the table lest I drop it in my unbridled mirth.

"I mean…you're technically not wrong." I choked out with tears in my eyes. All I got was a tongue out from her in response. Those vivid black and white striped referee shirts weren't easy to forget. Except on a referee they were vertical. "It's an umpire for baseball. The guys in all black behind home plate. And at first and third base."

"Oh." She nodded, rather noncommittal. "Yeah. Those guys." The tone of her voice led me to believe that she still had no idea what I was talking about.

"During all those games, you haven't watched a second of baseball, have you?"

"Nope."

"What the hell do you do when you aren't on the field?"

"Read."

I already expected that answer. For the most part, the mascot came out on the field during specific, previously scheduled intervals. Sometimes they had to go out to hype up the crowd during a tense part of the game. But usually, it was the same innings each game. Aside from how long each inning took, it was an easy-to-follow schedule.

"Lucky…" I muttered and nibbled on another nacho. Some days I wished I was the one sweating my ass off in a fur suit. It was a tough gig working with the team and with a man that I'd been salivating over for years.

I was essentially living every fangirl's fantasy. I went from watching my sports crush on TV to working with the man day in and day out. Too bad he was the equivalent of a male ice queen. But maybe, just maybe, I could chip away enough at that rough foundation surrounding his usually stoic nature to have him let loose and be the perfect addition to the Sillys. And me with a front-row seat to watch his *very* fine ass as he did it.

Unfortunately, the man had been reluctant every damn step of the way. The few times I dared to gently nudge his body to adjust his stance mid-dance might have inspired quite a few solo sessions between the sheets for me. The man was *hard*. No baseball player needed to have that kind of muscle definition to stand around, or in Jamie's instance, squat. That thought made my mind wander on just what kind of power that man had in certain body parts from straddling home plate day in and day out.

It was enough to make my mouth water.

I needed to be professional. The man was a major league player, and in injury recovery no less. All I had was a few weeks, months if I was lucky, to stare at him and boss him around before he left, and I went back to watching him on TV. I needed to enjoy every damn moment while I still could. Even if his attitude was a complete turn-off.

His piss-poor attitude did dull the perfect fantasy I had of him. The saying was true, "Don't meet your heroes, you'll only end up disappointed". While Jamie hadn't disappointed me yet, he sure had diminished the once-tasty fantasy I had outlined in my head.

Lately, my fantasies were inspired by his gruff demeanor. In my head, the man turned that attitude into full, unbridled passion towards me. It did nothing to help the in-person situation awkwardness for me.

If only it could be real life. The man all but recoiled every time I touched him to readjust his positions during a routine. He was a certifiable robot when it came to dancing. Which, in some dance styles, he would have done well with. But fuck if I'd ever explain the popping dance style accurately enough for him to *actually* want to try it. That would surely throw him through a loop.

I only had until the end of the month to get him ready enough to be out on the field with the rest of the guys. Topper was breathing down my neck to get him to Sillys' entertainment level. The Sillys social media team was already having a field day hyping up the fans to get them to come out to see Jamie's debut. Games were starting to sell out because of him. Maybe having him here would give the Sillys the morale boost they needed to get through the season with a strong finish. For once.

"Yo, earth to Cadence." I jumped in surprise as Tiffiny waved her hand in front of my face. "They're talking about your *boyfriend* on TV." Narrowing my eyes at her, I moved them to the television she pointed to.

"Vince, can you believe Philly sent Gold Glove catcher Jamie Rheems to their Entertainment League Baseball team?"

"You know, Adam, I can. Aside from hoping that Rheems' appearance in the league would get them some ticket sales, he was literally, maybe a game away from being benched for the season. Heck, maybe the rest of his career. His stats have been abysmal since he came back from the IL. I think it was high time for them to bring in some fresh blood from the minors…"

My jaw dropped.

I knew that Jamie hadn't had the easiest time since he came back from his surgery recovery. But I had no idea it was *that* bad. Topper never explained the sudden roster change for the Sillys but with the television commentary, it all made sense.

I knew the team didn't have the best ticket sales. They were literally in the MLB team's shadow. I had no idea that there was something else motivating this unprecedented roster move. The Sillys were Jamie's last stop before, maybe, being dumped by the organization that he'd given the biggest chunk of his professional career to. If he didn't get his shit together then he'd be out on his ass for good. Either forced into retirement or traded to another team for maybe a year or two before he'd find himself, yet again, in the same position.

"I…I need to go."

I didn't give Tiffiny a chance to protest. Tossing more than enough money on the table for my half of the meal and drinks, I made a mad rush for the door. If Jamie was going to be a part of Philadelphia, and my favorite team, for the foreseeable future, I needed to come up with a better game plan for him to get his head out of his ass and back in the game.

7

BEEN LIKE THIS

MEGHAN TRAINOR & T-PAIN

I never thought that baseball could be utter torture. And then I saw the Sillys play.

I mean sure, the games were over in a blink of an eye, but it was absolute unbridled chaos that happened in between the first and last pitch. It turned my stomach. How was this even considered a sport? And ownership thought this was a good idea? They had to be off their multi-million-dollar rockers.

Two straight weeks of watching this nonsense and I could barely keep track of the rules. A time limit on a baseball game? Insane. And the fact that you scored "points" instead of runs every inning? Complete lunacy.

Aside from the dancing, the games were mostly like normal baseball games. There was a batter and a pitcher along with a full field of players. But instead of doing everything normally, the guys went out of their way to try a trick catch or throw. During the last home game, left fielder Arlow caught the ball down the front of his uniform. Kellan at shortstop did a front flip as he threw the ball to home plate. The catcher, Schmidt, didn't blink an eye as he caught the ball and did a little spin on the ball of his foot before easily tagging the guy out.

57

While the game was chaotic, I had to admit, they looked like they had a lot of fun. Most of the time they were doing two things at once, playing baseball and dancing. It took a lot of skill to manage both. This game suited their personalities to a T. Whoever did the Sillys recruiting had done a stand-up job.

Coach Topper kept me benched for the games as he knew that I still was green around the gills with this whole endeavor. Even with this dumbass excuse for baseball, I was itching to get back into the game.

Maybe the change of scenery would knock me out of my batting funk. Or maybe I'd be the worst I've ever been due to the fact I was stressed out of my gourd about dancing in front of people. But the longer I sat in hesitation about officially joining the Sillys ranks, the longer it was going to take to get back to my rightful place in the majors' roster.

The Sillys guys were cool though. They were perhaps the only saving grace of my sanity. Even though they were rather insane themselves. I was pretty sure that you had to have some degree of insanity to play Entertainment League ball.

A few of my teammates from my old team checked on me from time to time. One even had a case of beer delivered to me to help "drown my sorrows". I think he also was hoping for an invite to tackle said case of beer. Because of that unexpected drink delivery, I did overindulge a bit more than I usually do during the season.

Playing ball while hungover sucked, but being hungover and then doing dance choreography? That was a brand-new circle of hell for me. Since then, the rest of the case of beer remained untouched. I figured I could save it for the end of the season. Whether it be next week or sometime in September or October. Whichever end of my life came first.

My new coach was relentless. A real pain in the ass drill sergeant. For some reason, it seemed that she had it out for me. I knew I was the new guy. I'll admit that I sucked at dancing, but she had a real kink for public shaming. Public shaming *me* specifically. I was legit terrified of my first game as the Sillys' starting catcher.

As much as I wanted to blow this popsicle stand, I was stuck here.

My knee was back to how it felt before it started giving me issues. So, it wasn't the pain that was holding me back from my job. Being behind home plate was my domain. I felt at home there. Literally and figuratively. Straddling the plate was no longer a chore thanks to the surgeon who put me back together. My reaction time was still a little sluggish, but I chalked that up to the downtime I had in recovery. One week of rest and recovery was like losing four weeks of conditioning. It was a huge hill to climb after being down and out like that.

It was my batting average that tanked the most in my off time. I was second or third in the batting rotation in March and April. Early batting rotation placement meant you were reliable enough of a hitter for the coach to give you more chances at batting.

As soon as I got the all-clear from the doctor, every spare moment I had was spent in the gym. I used to push myself, but now I stop while I'm ahead. Being my age, in a rigorous physical sport where you're bent in all sorts of positions, was just asking for trouble if I went beyond my limits. It sucked that I had to be more careful now.

My practice at-bats have improved since I arrived here. I still wasn't getting the power behind my swing, but I was finally hitting the ball more consistently with my timing. Having a change in coaching staff helped me more than I thought. It gave me some new insight into what I was missing.

Field and batting practice was only the half of this recovery nonsense. The other half was dealing with the coach-from-hell day in and day out, Cadence Andrews. I've had some real doozies for coaches but for some reason the short, strawberry-blonde, dancer with freckles across the bridge of her nose, took the cake.

First, it was her attitude that got me. But being stuck on her radar every day made it difficult not to admire her whenever I could. As for that, I couldn't *stop staring* at said freckles. Or her ass. Or the fact that I secretly looked forward to seeing a different matching sports bra and yoga pants outfit every practice.

Even though I couldn't seem to get her out of my head, she certainly couldn't be bothered to give me the time of day. It was as if she went out of her way to punish my ass for being a shit dancer. It wasn't my fault I had no rhythm.

Day in and day out it left me in this frustrating push-and-pull conundrum of daydreaming about the sway of Cadence's hips while simultaneously being pissed off at her. She was like a mental puzzle that I kept coming back to, unable to solve it. Everyone else had her figured out. Why couldn't I?

"You're making that face again." The first baseman, Benson, chuckled as he toed off his cleats while seated on the bench next to me in the locker room. He was tall but built with solid reflexes. An ideal man to have at the first stop around the baseball diamond.

"What face?" My head shot up as I attempted to nonchalantly rearrange my expression. With our fieldwork practice, I'd gotten to know the guys. They liked to razz me like a rookie, but they were a good group. A talented bunch of players.

"The one you always make when coach is around." Truitt leaned down to my eye level with a wicked, knowing grin that flashed white through his scruffy beard. My brow furrowed. Did I make a face around the head coach? Was it a bad face? A weird one?

"What? I don't make faces." I tried to make my face as impassive as possible before I bent down to unlace my cleats. "Topper's a good coach." And he was. He was a tough old bird with only one expression, but damn he was good at his job.

"I wasn't talking about *coach* coach." Truitt was egging me on at this point. From the corner of my eye, I caught his brows wiggling playfully at me as I fingered the tight knot in my shoe. "Coach Andrews. *Cadence.*"

There was a resounding mix of laughter and random chatter as I glanced over my shoulder at the rest of the guys. My heart traffic-jammed into my throat. There was no way that I'd been that fucking obvious. While I wasn't fond of the dancing portion of the daily schedule, I didn't make a face over it. At least I was sure that I hadn't. But now these guys were making me think otherwise.

"I *don't* make a face," I grumbled as I fumbled with my other shoelace. But my brain couldn't function normally. I was too fixated on the fact that the guys were giving me shit. Giving me shit over the one person that already had my brain all out of sorts lately.

"Dude, every day it's the same face." Benson laughed as he waved his accusing finger in my direction. "Even now you're making it."

"This is my normal face." I shrugged them off as I managed to get my feet free from my cleats. I wanted to bolt clear out of there. But that would make me look even more guilty of what they accused me of already.

"Dude you just have to give it right back to her." Arlow shrugged as he kicked off his grass-caked cleats, sending the thin blades into a chaotic flutter onto the concrete floor.

Fuck if my brain didn't go immediately to the gutter.

Once my thoughts got over their unexpected X-rated scene that starred Cadence and me with her bent over the bench I was sitting on, I let out a mental sigh of relief. They weren't giving me shit about staring at her. They were giving me shit for the permanent scowl that had been on my face from day one.

"Yeah, give her that attitude right back. She's all bark and no bite. Stand your ground. Even though she is pretty scary sometimes…" Designated hitter, Martin Pitt, thoughtfully scratched at his facial hair along his chin. He and Schmidt were the only two of the guys who were married. They probably had better suggestions on how to navigate uncertain waters with a woman. There was a resounding murmur of agreement from the guys within earshot. "Although she has been in a different sort of mood lately."

"Shit." Kellan's blonde head shot up from the process of peeling off his socks. "Maybe she's in the Danger Zone again?"

"For this long?!" Tomas' Dominican accent was almost sing-song in his exasperation.

"I said *again*, Tommy boy. You know, from that monthly thing?"

My eyes were certifiable ping-pong balls as they bounced from one end of the locker room to the other with all the guys chipping in on the conversation. Meanwhile, my brows could have knitted a sweater from their furrowed position of utter confusion. I didn't want to admit the fact that I was pretty sure her attitude was due to dealing with my untalented ass.

"Truitt, did you remember to bring Cadence her Twix bars during that last cycle?"

There was a moment of utter silence as the men waited with bated breath. Cycle? As in a baseball cycle, where a player hits a single, double, triple, and a home run? A resounding swear slipped from under Truitt's breath. All the guys groaned.

"Dude, it's all your fault. You fucked poor Jamie over!" Camden exclaimed to his teammate as he waved his hand in my direction.

"Uh…" I was lost. What the fuck was all this? Was this some sort of code? A weird superstition?

"Yo, guys, I didn't mean to!" Truitt wailed as he plopped his forehead into his hands, his elbows propped up on his bare knees. This entire conversation had gotten entirely out of hand in seconds flat.

"You'd better bring her some tomorrow," Martin warned as he whipped off his shirt. "Just in case."

"Appease the goddess." Benson chimed in as he flipped off his headband, sending his dirty brown untamed locks in all directions. The guys laughed. I didn't.

"Look, we're just joking." Schmidt laughed and slapped a hand on my back. "We love Cadence, we really do. But during certain times of the month…the goddess needs a sacrifice to appease her."

"Sacrifice ooh-ha-ha!" The chorus echoed around the room.

That's it.

They were all lunatics.

"Honestly, it's to save all of our asses." Schmidt slung an arm around my shoulders as he plopped down on the bench next to me. "I'm kidding. We know baseball is a guys' world. We're lucky to have such a kick-ass coach like Cadence. It's amazing she can deal with us assholes daily. So…when she needs it, we all bring her in a little something when she's feeling…*crummy*."

"Usually it's chocolate." Truitt offered since his forgetfulness of said sacrifice was now fresh in his brain.

"Or flowers," Schmidt suggested.

"Or candles!" The guys each took a turn offering suggestions for Cadence and appropriate "sacrifices". Even though they were a bunch of insane asylum escapees, they all had a heart of gold. A misshapen heart of gold, but a gold one, nonetheless.

"You know, for that time of the month." Rising, Schmidt moved back to his locker cubby. "Or whenever she needs a pick-me-up."

"Or breakups!" Ender added while the guys nodded in agreement.

"I take it that she dates a lot…?" I prodded carefully since the guys seemed overly willing to divulge information at this rate. Any glimpse into Cadence's world might help me figure out the enigma with curves to a more manageable point.

"Oh hell no." Benson laughed as he slid off his sweat wristbands and flung them into his locker. "At least not since Roman. And that was like two years ago."

"Wait…" I whipped around to glance at Roman, the team's second baseman. He bashfully shrugged in noncommittal agreement. My voice dropped as I leaned in towards Benson. "You mean…*that* Roman…?"

"Duh. Who the hell else names their kid Roman?" Benson snorted in amusement before getting beamed in the head with a balled-up sock by the same person he insulted. The irony was not lost on me as Truitt had told me Benson's mom watched too much *Law & Order: SVU* when she was pregnant.

"So…Cadence dated Roman?" The words came out in a sharper tone than I meant. The guys on the team treated her as if she was completely unattainable. Untouchable. Not that I was fishing for tips on how to ask her out or anything. Because that would be daft.

"Heh, yeah. He said they had fun on their handful of dates, but she bunted him right back into the friend zone." Benson shrugged.

"Oh, shut up, Benson," Roman muttered. There was a hint of disappointment there, but the man didn't look all that upset about the whole ordeal.

"Yeah," Benson snorted as he glanced back at me. "Cadence deserves someone better than the sorry likes of us."

"Talking shit about me again, Benson?" Cadence's sudden appearance had us all aligning our spines ramrod straight in surprise. Her playful quirk of a smile had molten lava pooling low in my belly.

That was until she spotted that it was me who Benson was talking to. Her vibrant gaze tore apart from mine as she moved to look anywhere but at me. The brightness of her smile melted into a muddy puddle. What the hell was it about me that she couldn't stand?

"Gotta get the rookie caught up on all the hot gossip while we do our nails." Benson laid it on rather thick with his pantomime. It got a snort out of Cadence. I let out an annoyed huff myself at the mention of "rookie". I hadn't been called that in years. But the guys seemed determined to overuse it. Even though I was the furthest thing from a rookie, with this team and their antics, I sure as fuck felt like one again.

"Yeah, your cuticles could go for some conditioning, Benson." Cadence jested right back after avoiding my entire presence in the room. Maybe if she ignored the fact that I was here she wouldn't be so grumpy. I decided to keep my eyes on the floor and my mouth shut to see if my assumption was correct.

"Maybe we need to go back to that nail salon you took us to last year." Schmidt chimed in as my brow went sky-high. Wait, Cadence hung out with this lot outside of work? On a semi-regular basis? At a nail salon of all places?

"Ooh yeah. The place with those massaging chairs!" Truitt butted in as I tried to make myself blend in with the locker room bench even more. As unhinged as this conversation was with a woman and a bunch of grown men, it was kind of nice to hear a taste of why the guys respected this woman so much. She didn't treat them like baseball gods, she treated them like they were her siblings.

"Not for me. Mine got stuck." Tomas grumbled and it sent the locker room into laughter.

"Aww, poor Tomas." Camden mock-pouted as he slung an arm around the shorter outfielder's neck. "I'm sure they fixed the possessed chair by now."

"You know you don't have to use the massage option on the chair, bud." It was Cadence's tender tone that cut through the lighthearted jesting in the room. "Although if it really is still possessed, I'll bring some Holy Water and be sure to unplug the chair for you. Or I'll just end up stabbing it with a nail file. Either way, I'll protect you." That sent the guys into uproarious laughter while Tomas grinned with relief.

She didn't bat an eye at the guys with their antics. In fact, she fed into it. Encouraged it. Maybe she was even a little unhinged herself.

During practice, she was one tough cookie. In the locker room, she was someone I could hang out with. Obviously, the guys saw her as such. This whole interlude had me rethinking that maybe she wasn't so bad after all.

"Yo, we should bring Jamie with us next time. He could do with some pampering." Arlow clapped me on the back. I froze. Had Cadence forgotten I was there? This was the true test to see if her issues really were just with me. Was she going to revert to her sour self at the mention of my name?

"Yeah, he needs to dissolve the rod up his ass." I rolled my eyes at Truitt's jab. He'd act the same way if he were in my demoted cleats.

There was an audible feminine squeak that shot my gaze in Cadence's direction. I only managed to catch her wide eyes for half a second before she took an immediate about-face with her entire body. That wasn't exactly the most appropriate reaction to hearing about a metal object existing in one's anal cavity. I guess she and I both weren't fond of the idea.

"Yeah, yeah. Maybe you guys are just too deranged for this ancient major leaguer." If they could dish it, I could send it right back to them. I wasn't a stuck-up asshole. I knew how to have fun. Although I was a bit rusty.

The guys cracked up even more. At least they thought I had a sense of humor despite the rod between my ass cheeks. Small victories.

My eyes moved to Cadence, who still couldn't look me in the face. Instead of sticking around for more fun, she made a beeline towards Topper's office. Thank fuck she hadn't arrived ten minutes later when she did. She would have gotten an eyeful from quite a few of the guys. How the guys treated her appearance in the locker room led me to believe that this was a regular occurrence. Guess I'll have to keep that at the back of my mind.

Women were a huge no-no in the locker rooms in the majors. Not even wives. Although I wouldn't be surprised if one of the guys snuck *someone* in down there at one time or another.

Cadence was the first woman I'd met that baseball was seemingly just as important to her as it was to me. This was also her world. Why was I even thinking about this? I didn't come here to find someone. I came here to play ball and hopefully get my life back on track and back on the majors' roster.

However, there was one grumpy dancer who was making that chance *very* difficult at the moment.

"Hey Jamie?" I glanced up at the mention of my name from Arlow, pulled from the haze of my thoughts. "You're making that face again."

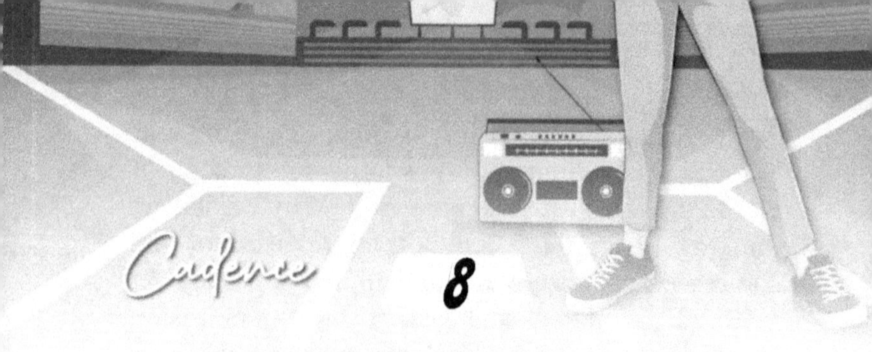

8

DANCING ON MY OWN

CALLUM SCOTT

The little chat in the locker room I stumbled onto the other day had me still in a tizzy. For a moment, I forgot that the hottest man on the planet was on the team. It was just another day of the guys chatting about their nonsensical nonsense. That was until I saw his stunning blue eyes from across the room. I ignored the fact that the sole reason I'd come into the locker room in the first place was because of him.

Topper wanted to chat with me about Jamie's status in his choreography training. The manager trusted me enough that he didn't feel the need to micromanage my practices. But that meant that I had to chance the walk through the minefield of the locker room to get to his office to give him regular updates. Which was sometimes when the guys were there either getting dressed or...*undressed.*

Despite Jamie's near-constant grumptastic mood, it still didn't change the fact that he was still visually the man of my dreams. There was this delicious tingle that raced up my spine anytime I was near him. Which was why I gave the man a wide as fuck berth anytime I had to be near him.

With the other guys on the team, I wasn't afraid to put my hands on them to adjust their positioning or to help them figure out the choreography moves. With Jamie I needed at least five feet of breathing space or else I was likely to keel over. Mostly I just gestured to which body part needed to move and where it was supposed to go. Maybe it was the man's ego that ate up the local atmosphere. Whatever it was, it was unsettling.

Unfortunately, the discussion with Topper wasn't all that great. Which only compounded my already testy mood of late. And it all had to do with the hunky catcher that was under my tutelage.

Ownership told Topper they wanted Jamie out on the field by the end of the month. That meant that I had little more than a week left to turn the grump into the goofy belle of the ball. To say that I was freaking out was the biggest understatement of the year.

This would all be so much easier if it wasn't for the one major pain in my ass. Jamie continued to be reluctant in my attempts to get him to cooperate. He did at least show up to practice, I'll give him that. But it was the fact that it was like pulling teeth getting him to do the dance moves in some semblance of a correct manner.

He was a grown-ass baseball professional, so I didn't feel like it was necessary for me to hold his hand throughout his initial integration into the team. He knew this sport inside and out. Instead of being a good sport, Jamie was a goddamn stick in the mud. He needed to be Philly Sillys star-worthy in four weeks from when ownership sent him to us.

Four, outrageously short, weeks.

And now there were only days left until Jamie needed to be field-ready.

No matter what sort of math you did, the equation didn't work out. Even though most, okay let's be honest, *all* of the issues were because of Jamie's negative attitude, it was still on me to snap him out of it and on with the program. He had no issues with catching and, from what I heard from the batting coach, he was making improvements. Except in my entertainment aspect of the game.

I had to make dancing tolerable for him. Make it into something he enjoyed. A rewards system maybe? I kept hearing Tiffiny's voice in my head making filthy comments about the *other ways* I could turn his frown upside down.

If only it was that easy and not frowned upon in the workplace. In the book or movie world that would totally fly. But I was in the shitty real world where women didn't end up with their gorgeous celebrity professional ball player crushes. I was in a world where all I could do was admire him from afar while simultaneously attempting to pull his head out of his pert ass. Or else I might end up losing my job.

Then the guys had to go and make a reference to Jamie's ass. Which drew an uninhibited questionable noise that came from the deepest confines of my body. I'd been doing so well with pushing my sultry thoughts of the man aside and saving them for when I was home. If Topper hadn't been expecting me, I would have gone and drowned myself in the toilets from the utter embarrassment.

Topper insisted I needed to get Jamie on the same page as the team *before* his debut. What the hell could I do that I hadn't done already? Did I need to spoon-feed him dance moves? Did I need to *physically* move his body myself for him to get it? Because don't tempt me. I would have done that already if it wasn't for the fact that I'd probably vomit all over his cleats just from being so close.

Teaching someone how to dance wasn't new to me. In college I taught kids dance at the local studio with whatever free time I could spare between my classes as my part-time job. But those were kids, and they were much easier to teach. Jamie was an adult who should have better listening skills than a child. If I hadn't seen the job posting for the Sillys I probably would have opened up my own dance studio in downtown Philadelphia for underprivileged youth.

Dance was not only my career, but I also used it as a way to express myself. It gave me a healthy outlet to do so. Sometimes when I was frustrated or angry I'd push the furniture against the walls in my apartment and let loose. Usually, it was slow and mournful music, and other times there were a hell of a lot of F-bombs and harsh beats. It just depended on my mood.

Working for the Sillys gave me more space instead of dancing around my apartment neighbors' schedules. Sometimes I'd get to the stadium first thing in the morning to enjoy the privacy and quiet when the dew on the grass was still fresh. I'd go out onto the field and just dance. Nothing beat the cooler air in the early morning or at twilight as I danced with my bare feet on the spongy grass.

I was good friends with the head groundskeeper, Joe. He was a kindly older gentleman with a heart of gold and was the biggest Philadelphia sports fan I knew, my dad excluded. While he was rather protective of his grassy outfield, he didn't mind if I came early to dance or warm up. He told me I was considerate of his hard work with the maintenance of the field, not to mention much lighter on my feet. He was always the charmer.

Joe was one of the first ones here in the morning to check the water levels and growth of the field before the heat of the summer day. The grass needed to be a certain height for optimum play. The mowing team was always ready to go during the baseball season. Before I came here, I had no idea that so much effort and science went into field maintenance. Whatever he did, it made the park look beautiful.

Since he was here so early, I knew Joe would be more than happy to let me in as long as I stayed out of his way. The mowing team never showed up until mid-morning when the guys took their lunch break. I liked to think that Joe held them off just long enough for me to get my dance work in.

After the meeting with Topper, I needed a good dance therapy session. I could always work on new choreography for the team or have a little fun freestyling my frustrations out. Today was certainly a *frustration* kind of morning. Namely one, big, Jamie-shaped, pain in my ass frustration.

I walked onto the field and spotted Joe headed towards his field office. Giving him a warm wave, I made my way over to the outfield behind first base. With the orientation of the stadium, the right field avoided most of the bright morning sun. Which was always helpful during the hotter days of the summer.

Today started with a soft breeze, which helped keep my testy mood to a low boil instead of blowing my top off the pot. The team was slated to arrive in another hour for their morning choreography practice before the landscaping squad arrived. Plenty of time for me to get a sweat worked up and to push some of the more aggravating feelings out of my system. Then maybe by the time Jamie arrived I could at least be more civil.

Tossing my bag onto the grass, I began my usual stretching routine to warm up my muscles. The chilly dew against my skin made it prickle. I knew that later I'd be wishing the weather was still like this when the summer sun was directly overhead. There was a heaviness to the air, it was, unfortunately, going to be humid today. At least it would provide a more physical distraction from my thoughts.

Popping in my earbuds, I swiped through my favorite music mix. I settled on a song that was more mellow than I typically picked for a mood such as the one I was in. But I needed a bit of chill empowerment before I got into the hard shit. An ideal choice for me to get through the more boring but necessary stretches.

Once I was thoroughly limbered up, I went for it. Cranking up the volume, I selected the carefully curated playlist that had thumping beats. Songs where I could feel the bass straight down to my toes. It was almost as if my heart pumped in time with the beat.

When I needed to mentally work out shit, I danced with my eyes closed. It was almost as if it was a sensory deprivation chamber within my own body. With my earbuds in and my eyes closed, I could focus solely on the music and how it flowed through my extremities. To let my mind and body go into a thought process where there was no routine to follow.

To feel free and move to what the music made my body do. It was passionate. Powerful. I danced with raw emotion as a way to process whatever I was feeling.

I felt comfortable dancing in the expanse of the Sillys' field. Although I always did set an alarm for about fifteen minutes before the start of practice so the guys didn't interrupt something that was clearly "me time". If they asked me what I was doing, I just told them that I was working out some ideas for future routines.

Dancing like this was my therapy. My safe space. The kind of place where I truly felt like myself. It was my freedom of feelings and expression. I felt…free.

Today was more for getting my aggressions out before I was tempted to use Jamie's pretty face as a punching bag. But there was also the fact that I couldn't bring myself to be anywhere near him. It was as if my feet were trained to have this strict distance between us.

The odd part about it was, aside from my feet, everything else on my body was screaming to be close to him. He had this aura about him that made me want to be near him. He probably gave the best hugs. But most of all, I wanted a front-row seat to one of his very rare, but genuine smiles.

Some days had been better than others. Some days he gave me a reason to hope. And then there were the days that I wanted to high-kick his face. Lately, most of the days were the latter.

The guys liked him. Of course, they'd also like a raccoon they found in the trash who was eating one of their old socks. They all had big, fat, goofy hearts.

Taking Jamie under their wing was just another day at the office. Maybe he didn't act that way around them, only I was blessed with that aspect of him. Or maybe they just ignored his grating behavior.

It wasn't just Jamie's poor attitude that had me dancing this morning. It was the fact that his success, his future, rode on *my* shoulders. Topper had it easy with the baseball stuff. All Jamie had to do was the same old stuff. Er, well, improve upon it. Maybe the baseball veteran could see something that the major league coaches didn't.

But me? I had to teach the major league heartthrob how to dance. He had to look like this demotion didn't affect him. Fans were going to come and see him. They didn't want to see a stick in the mud. And Jamie was a very muscular, firmly stuck stick in the mud of his attitude.

The odds were not stacked in my favor.

I wondered if I could get the guys to help. Jamie seemed more receptive to their feedback. Maybe I could coerce the guys into convincing Jamie to do something that could unlock his hidden dancing talent. But what? Maybe I could somehow ask them on the sly later. As for now, I needed to dance my frustrations out.

9

CATCHING FEELINGS

IÑIGO PASCUAL & MOOPHS

I arrived at practice earlier than normal. I couldn't sleep. Again. Most of the night was spent tossing and turning, the other long hours were spent thinking. I couldn't get my mind off my upcoming debut with the Sillys. It was looming like the breath of death along the back of my neck. And then there was also the endless deluge of thoughts of Cadence. For whatever reason.

Ever since the interaction in the locker room, Cadence had piqued my curiosity. Well, piqued it more than she already had. The guys had inadvertently alluded to the fact that she wasn't *always* this off-putting. I didn't mean to make the poor woman's life a living hell on purpose. But maybe I unknowingly had. As much as I didn't want to be here, it wasn't fair to take it all out on her. The guys noticed it. And if they noticed it, then Cadence for sure had. The thought made me feel like shit for letting my attitude be my personality of late. It was my fault that I was in this mess.

She was a woman with brains and two tons of attitude. Not to mention the humor to match. Cadence was nothing like anyone I'd ever met. She was a woman who loved baseball. Loved her team. Almost as if she was one of the guys out on the ballfield. The guys said that she didn't have to go to all the games, especially ones where they rehashed some of the older routines. Game after game, she was a constant presence at home games. As much as I hated to admit it, it was her dedication to the team that attracted me to her. Like, to an unnerving level.

Even with her keeping her distance around me, it only fueled my curiosity and the intrigue about her. What made her tick? What made her laugh? What inspired her to be part of the Sillys organization?

Maybe I was going about this all the wrong way.

As much as I hated the fact that I was demoted away from my beloved team, I had to be here. I *deserved* to be here. I wasn't playing the caliber of baseball that was needed in the majors. Maybe I needed to pull my head out of my ass and stop being in denial. To grit my teeth and focus on the here and now. This was a cold, hard, slap to the face to get my shit together. Would being stuck with the Sillys be such a bad thing? Probably not. Except for the teeny, little fact that I still couldn't dance.

After watching a few of the ball games, I knew I'd be the one who looked like an idiot on the ballfield if I was the *only* one not shaking his ass in some form or fashion. Either way, I didn't have much longer to get my shit together before my slated start. Topper let me have a bit more time to acclimate to the team, which I was grateful for. It was just a *lot* to acclimate to.

With the long hours of reflection during my restless night, I concluded that I needed to make a change. Today. Even if I had to hire a private dance tutor. I didn't want to lose my baseball career because

I couldn't get my head out of my ass long enough to learn how to dance. If I didn't do everything possible to keep my career afloat, I'd hate myself if I just gave up. That wasn't Jamie Rheems.

The overall Sillys experience was interesting. Maybe, just maybe, a bit…fun. Not just the dancing part, but the game part. It would be nice to play for fun again. To play for the love of the game instead of constantly worrying about stats and numbers and being nominated for awards or the All-Star team. It would be the first time in my life that I wouldn't be living every day just to strive for something greater.

With my sleepless night of clarity, I settled on resetting my attitude. Sometimes you just had to be a bigger man and admit that you were at fault. Even if it meant shaking your ass around like a jackass.

The southern gentleman part of me pulled at my good conscience to take the time to apologize to Cadence for my appalling behavior of late. Maybe that would thaw out her icy attitude towards me. Maybe just–

At the top of the stairs of the dugout, movement in the outfield stopped me in my tracks. She was an utter vision of grace and beauty floating in the outfield. The woman who'd been the bane of my existence, the subject matter of my thoughts at an alarming frequency, was dancing as if she was the last being on earth and had no fucks left to give.

Cadence was certifiably stunning. As awkward as it was to admit that about someone who was my coach. Stunning in a carefree sort of way. Here she was, in a ballpark, my favorite place on earth, dancing with effortless ease. She glided from foot to foot, twirling through the grass in the outfield as if she were one of those ballerinas in the old wind-up music box.

No music could be heard, which made the spectacle almost eerie. The vision of her took my breath away. It was wild, unbridled. Something I'd never seen before.

Her eyes were closed. Even with the size of the outfield, it was rather brave of her. What if someone saw her? What if the grounds crew was lurking about? The last thought made me ball my hand into a tight fist. No one should be staring at what was seemingly a private moment. Yet here I was, doing the one thing I was pissed about any other man doing.

Her fingers and toes came to delicate tips, extending the lines of her mesmerizing body as they expressed the emotion of whatever music she was listening to. Typically, she wore her hair up in a ponytail, but today it was loose and untamed in coppery gold waves. With each twirl, the strands surrounded her like a heavenly halo.

My brain was thinking anything but angelic things as I watched the talent my coach had. I had no idea that she was this *incredible*. The dance moves she taught us were usually comical or whatever was hot on social media. But this? This was something I could see on a big stage somewhere. She could be so much more than stuck in Philly dealing with my untalented ass. The strength and flexibility of her body had me imagining just what it would feel like to have her all tangled up in my arms. With legs like hers, she could wrap around me tight enough to go hands-free…

Fuck.

No.

Holy fuck I was literally an HR complaint waiting to happen.

I came here to *calm* the waters between Cadence and me. Not churn them up more with inappropriate thoughts. This kind of shit was completely out of character for me. If I did find someone worth pursuing, it was a slow and respectable sort of courtship. Not all these thoughts of falling into bed with someone each time my cock got hard looking at her.

This certainly wasn't the first time I was turned on by thoughts of my coworker.

I was ready to run back into the locker room and douse myself with cold water to get my damn cock to chill the fuck out before practice. Literally and figuratively. Cadence eased her dancing to a slow stop. Part of me wanted to duck away so she didn't see me and yet another part wanted to make a beeline at lightspeed for the woman just to get this all over with.

She slipped out her earbuds and grabbed her water bottle. I had to play it cool and not pretend that I'd been watching her for the better part of the last few songs. As Han Solo suggested, "I don't know. Fly casual." How the fuck do I maintain any sense of being casual after watching that performance? Shit, I didn't even have anything prepared to say to explain the past few weeks and I–

"Jamie?"

Fuck.

The more alarming notion was the fact that my body had moved of its own accord towards Cadence. Even though my brain had still been locked in a heated debate on even approaching her. Swallowing back my sudden fluster, I tried to remain cool.

"Uh…" *Off to a great fucking start, Jamie.* "Sorry, I'm here early." *Thank you, Captain Obvious.*

"That's okay." Dammit. Her voice sounded strained. I must have interrupted her quiet dance time before the insanity of team practice. Suddenly her eyes squinted shut and she shook her head. It caused the skin of her nose to ripple, bringing her freckles to the forefront. "Actually," She added suddenly. "Uh, there was um…something I wanted to talk to you about anyway. Privately."

My stomach bottomed out. *Shit.* Was she going to call me out? What about this woman made me so unnerved or pissed off? How did she have this kind of power over me? Even when she couldn't look at me square on.

"Oh?" I swallowed nervously with an equally unsteady laugh. "Hopefully it's not about me being a total lost cause."

"I mean…" *Fuck.* "Not…not technically." Giving her a cautious glance, she seemed to be just as tense as me. But that was only a passing thought as her sweat-covered dewy skin caught the sunlight. Suddenly I craved salt. "Look," The sharpness and urgency in her tone made me snap out of my salt lick daydream. "I understand that dance isn't easy for everyone. Sometimes you just need to find what teaching style works for you."

Wait, was this an underhanded way of kicking me off the team? "So…that means…?"

"Maybe we just have to think outside the box." I must have looked as lost and confused as I felt. Cadence bent down into her bag and procured her trusty hair elastic. Grabbing a fistful of her hair, she furiously wound the loop around her wild waves. I could feel the twitch of jealousy in my hand as I suddenly wanted to feel those silken strands knotted in my fist.

"I'm…almost afraid to ask what you're thinking."

"What, don't you have a sense of adventure, Jamie Rheems?" There she went with my full name again. The tone of it and how it slid off her lips sent a delicious shiver up my spine. "I know your coaches in the majors had you doing all sorts of interesting field work and wild things for batting practice. To name one, I seem to remember you chipping some golf balls from home plate."

I blinked at her. How did she know that? And for fucks sake, why was it a turn-on?

"I–yes."

"So maybe you'd be open to doing some country line dancing. Off the clock of course. The guys and I go a few times a season. You follow along, most of the time everyone fucks up in one way or another. I figured you'd fit right in." *Uh…thanks?* The words tumbled out of her all at once in a singular breath. Why did it seem that she was just as unsteady with us being this close as I was?

I bristled at her suggestion. Line dancing in a bar was slightly more terrifying than dancing in front of 20,000 fans at a baseball game. But this was exactly what I told myself needed to be done. I needed to change my attitude about this whole thing. I needed to learn how to dance if I wanted to keep playing baseball. I needed to do whatever was necessary to get back on the team I belonged to.

If this was something that Cadence said I should do, then…so be it.

"Well, I guess that's something I could try."

"Excellent!" The sense of relief in her body was noticeable. For fucks sake I've been a total asshole. "Thank you." I didn't exactly expect that enthusiastic response. She bounced on the balls of her heels for two beats and my eyes couldn't help but drift to her chest.

Fuck. Shit. Stop being a horny teenager. Do something else. Anything else.

"You're welcome, Cady." I rushed out in a single, charged exhale.

"Cady?" Her surprised tone hit me like a brick wall. Goddammit, we were doing so well. I had to go and fuck it all up because I couldn't help but stare at my coach's tits and say stupid shit. I needed to recover this word vomit if my life depended on it.

"Yeah…uh, like the chick from *Mean Girls*." Cadence blinked at me. I mean, fair. Most guys weren't into early 2000s teenage romcoms.

"Right." There was some skepticism in her voice. Her brow arched as her hands slipped to her waist. Shit, she needed to stop drawing attention to her body. Especially being this close to me.

"Yeah…I'm gonna call you Cady." All I could do was continue the lines from the movie. With a snort, she cocked her head to the side. How many men could quote lines from such an off-the-cuff cult classic teen movie?

"Are you a closet Lindsay Lohan fan or something?"

"What, you don't like *Mean Girls*?" Now it was my turn to be surprised.

"Oh no, I love *Mean Girls*. It's just…I don't know. It's weird you can reference it and then *accurately* quote it."

"Well, now I feel like you're judging me." The conversation became so easy all of a sudden. I felt dizzy from the sheer thrill of it. Maybe she didn't hate me after all? There'd been little to no animosity since we started talking. I was eager to continue this back and forth but then I heard the chatter of the guys coming onto the field for dance rehearsal.

"No. Just…impressed." She pulled my attention straight back to her so suddenly that I was afraid I had whiplash. As she turned away from me, I managed to catch her little smile. My heart knocked against my ribcage like a locked damsel in distress.

"Quoting movie lines is my superpower," I mumbled out. Anything to keep her from escaping so quickly. We had some good banter going on.

"I thought catching was." She quipped back with a snort. My ego surged at her response. Was…was that a flirt? There was a swirl of emotions inside of me. I didn't know what to do until words exploded out of me all at once.

"Depends on what I catch." I shot back, suave as fuck, with a wink to boot, as I caught her shocked gaze as she glanced at me from over her shoulder.

What in the actual fuck were you thinking, Jamie? Winking? Really? Next, you'll be asking the woman to dance with you.

In all honesty, I wasn't thinking. All thinking left my brain. It was only actions when I found myself alone around Cadence Andrews. Like I was a dumbass freshman swooning over the senior captain of the dance team.

No woman had ever left me this tongue-tied and completely unarmed. It was the first time she didn't look at me with hidden disdain. Or…whatever it was she looked at me with. I didn't know what to do with myself.

I was still inwardly cringing over how our interaction ended as choreography practice started. During practice, I channeled all of my utter confusion and frustration into doing whatever I could to follow along. I felt the guys' eyes on me, so either I was doing something right or flailing like a fish out of water. But there were no snickers or snide remarks. Hopefully, they were glances of approval or encouragement. Or, perhaps, it was pity.

I was still trying to gauge Cady's reaction. She hadn't said anything about the nickname, only smiled at it. It suited her.

The thought of her smiling made me smile. Or it could have been the fact that the routines were *finally* falling into a place in my brain where they made sense.

Holy shit, maybe I really could do this.

Cady made her way over to me as the guys did a run-through without her at the head of the pack. My spine immediately straightened as I found myself suddenly slipping back into her gravitational pull. This time her face wasn't some mix of horror and disgust as she looked at me. It resembled something of what looked like the lighthearted Cady from that day in the locker room.

"You…almost have it." She sheepishly interrupted. Timidly, she lifted her hands in offering. "Can I…show you?" Wait, did her voice just crack?

I couldn't dwell on that fact for very long. With a nod of my head, I agreed to something that I wasn't at all expecting. My eyes darted between her hands as they made their way to my arms.

I could feel the heat rise at the back of my neck as I stood incredibly still, waiting to see what she would do. Soft fingers gently adjusted the angle of my arms to something that more closely resembled how the rest of the Sillys moved in the routine. That was all I could think about at the moment. Because if I focused on how her touch felt, I'd have a hard-on in a hot second.

The touch was innocent, but my brain was thinking about anything but. Especially with her facing me while wearing one of her coordinating workout outfits. It was a front-row seat to her treacherous curves. Curves that needed a gigantic warning sign and flashing lights.

"Uh…see? There you go. Just…just some minor adjustments." Her breathless smile was inches from my face. The woman could have told me I was a second-time Gold Glove award winner but all I'd be able to focus on was the glorious way her skin felt against mine.

"Oh, right. T-Thanks, Cady." I breathed out. The continued use of the nickname brought a quirk to the corner of her mouth. She unexpectedly lingered, her hands still on my body. Oh, what delicious hell was this?

"Psst. You're doing it again, Jamie." Benson chipped in with a teasing voice. I shot him a look. Schmidt joined with a low whistle. If anyone else was going to put their snide two cents in, I was going to have some bloody knuckles before it was over.

"Alright boys, cool it." Cady snapped out of whatever spell that was between us and abruptly pulled her hands away from my body. "You're supposed to be encouraging Jamie. He's doing good work today..." My body inflated quickly and then deflated just as fast as I watched her wander back up to the front of the team.

What the fuck was going on with me? My skin was covered in goosebumps. Meanwhile, it was easily creeping into the usual Philadelphia summer heat and humidity. I was half tempted to fuck up even worse to tempt fate just to have her touch me again.

"Besides, I invited the rookie here out to line dancing with us tomorrow."

There was a rumble of laughter and murmurs before Martin playfully punched me on the shoulder.

"Oh really?" I bristled at the excited tone of his voice. "It's about fucking time! I never thought we'd see your tight-ass dance. And I mean *really* dance." Martin followed with a suave grin. My eyes looked up to Cady who'd gone back to avoiding looking at me square on.

"I…uh, yeah. I figured I should um, give it a shot." I gave the group of Sillys around me an uneasy smile. Well, there was no going back now.

"Alright alright, you all had better show Jamie how it's done." My cheeks went hot at her word choice. "Dancing can be…fun."

"Yo, Jamie should I get you some lube to get that rod out of your ass before we go?" Truitt could barely keep in his laughter. Once he got the jab at me, the other guys joined in. I rolled my eyes before they caught the same heated look on Cady's face that she had at the last mention of my ass. It made me wonder just what she thought of my hindquarters.

"I'm sure you'll do fine." Kellan offered his reassurance as the laughter tapered off. "Get a few beers into you and you'll follow along with any dance we put you through."

"Just…not before games, Kel. The whole point of this is to get Jamie to be, well…comfortable. Er…*more* comfortable." Cady added as she collected her things. "I'll see you boys tomorrow at the bar. And you'll need to be on your best behavior. We have a game in two days, Jamie's big debut. And you knuckleheads had better not fuck it up for him." There was an edge to her voice. All the guys took note, as her warning somehow scared them straight. Well, straight enough for the Sillys.

"Jamie?" Cady's voice softened as she stepped over to me. My heart went feral all over again, thudding against each curve of my rib. A rather vain attempt to throw itself at the woman.

"Yeah…?"

"Um…good job today."

"Uh, thanks." My ears went hot with her rare compliment. Maybe I didn't fuck up today after all.

Shit. I forgot to apologize. Perhaps it was best to attempt one thing at a time.

SHUT UP AND DANCE

WALK THE MOON

The noise of the bar was almost overwhelming. Anxiety had been eating away at my insides all day. I played World Series games and wasn't as nervous as I was today. But willingly walking into a line dancing bar, in a pathetic attempt to learn how to dance better, was infinitely more terrifying.

Ever since Cadence gave me that compliment yesterday, I was on cloud nine and more determined than ever to please her. She asked me to come here and give it a try. If a coach tells me to do something, I'm going to do it. Especially with my career on the line.

There was a ruckus off to the left, a group of line dancers in full swing on the dance floor. I noticed a few of the Sillys guys out in the mass of people side-stepping and swaying along to the music. The song wasn't country, it was something more in the pop genre. I was in over my head.

"Jamie?"

The voice sent a soothing warmth flowing through my overly tense body. It was an immediate response. I was rather taken aback by it. Especially since it was the same voice that had been the bane of my existence while with the Sillys.

"Hey, Cady."

"Oh, thank fuck, you came." The words were a breath of relief, but goddamn my body for thinking they were absolute filth. Because well, in any other context, it would be the dirty reason. I silently congratulated myself on deciding to wear jeans tonight. The denim had a much easier time hiding my half-hard-on.

Shoving my hands into my pockets to subtly give my cock a bit more breathing room, I shifted with a glance back over at the dancing masses. Cady must have sensed my apprehension as she reached out and caressed my bicep. The touch did absolutely nothing to help the situation in my pants. It only made it worse when her hand lingered longer than was technically acceptable between coworkers.

"I think you need a drink first." Her hand turned into a vice grip as she began leading me off in the direction of the bar and away from the dance floor. Nothing like getting right to business. She was much more comfortable around me than usual, which I found odd. Until I noticed the bottle in her hand. "Fuck," She suddenly stopped and turned back to me with an exasperated look. "I'm a total asshole. Do you drink or am I an ass for encouraging you to fall off the recovery train…?"

"No, you're fine. I drink." I laughed, still rather breathless from the last few minutes. "From time to time."

"Well, then that should make this a hell of a lot easier." Cady nodded and dragged me after her once again. "I've already been pregaming myself with

Tiffiny." She nodded to the brunette in the corner with her nose in a book. Squinting, I recognized her as the person behind the team mascot, Ding Dong. Tiffiny gave a half-assed little wave before diving back into her book. Cady snorted. "Don't mind her, apparently it's too peopley in here."

I held back my chuckle. While it wasn't overly obvious that Cady was tipsy, she was looser around the edges. Her having a much calmer demeanor helped me ease into this brand-new situation.

Placing my order with the bartender, the two of us lingered at the end of the bar. It was mostly vacant since the crowd was out on the dance floor making utter asses of themselves. At least I wouldn't be the only one in that aspect.

Cady helped herself to another round and the two of us made our way to a high top with barstools off to the side. There were a few bottles that lingered on some of the surrounding tables. They were soon reunited with their owners as the guys made their way back for a dance break.

"Jamie! You made it!" Truitt slapped me on the back as he took a large swig of his beer. A dribble made its way into his beard. A few other hearty greetings quickly followed. This was the kind of comradery a baseball team needed to have. Even if we were here for line dancing.

"Yeah yeah… Just let me get a beer or two in me first." I took a quick swig to emphasize the point. "Then maybe I'll attempt to make an ass of myself." That got a round of chuckles from the crew.

"Smart. Damn, I need another cold one after that dance." Schmidt shook his empty bottle and a few of the guys chimed in with their agreement. They wandered off to the bar which left me alone, once again, with Cady.

She'd been quiet during the little interlude with the guys, and for good reason. Half of her brand-new beer bottle was gone.

"Let's go." I cocked my brow at Cady. She swiftly downed the rest of her drink and abruptly stood up.

"Where?" I managed to choke out, still taken aback by how quickly she drank her beer.

"Dancing."

"But…they aren't line dancing now." I nervously glanced over to the dance floor which was no longer a pulsing crowd of dancers who were mostly going in the same direction.

"It's fine. I'll get you warmed up. I think you might like what I have in mind." There was a quick smirk that played at the corner of her mouth.

Jeezus fuck.

With words like that, compounded with my alcoholic buzz already going, it took every damn molecule within my body to not pull her petite body against mine. Instead of giving in, I concentrated with all my might on the familiar pop hit pulsing through the speakers next to the DJ. "I've got to get something through that thick skull of yours before both of us end up on the streets."

That pulled me out of my lust-filled haze. I bristled at the warning. Both? What did she mean by that? Because it wasn't like I would end up on the actual streets, just the metaphorical one. The one without a job doing what I loved. But what did she mean by *both* of us?

With new beers in hand, some of the guys on the team followed after us and found dance partners of their own. In some instances, numerous ones. But they actually liked dancing. Considering that about ninety percent of the people in the bar were drunk enough to be oblivious to my god-awful dance moves, it was now or never. Because she was right. If I didn't fall into step with the Sillys, I'd be out of the franchise. And no other team would want a washed-up catcher with a shit batting average.

"...Fine."

Cady leaned in and grabbed my hands. Being this close to her left me blessed with the heady aroma of something that was distinctly *her*. Something floral and outdoorsy. Fresh cut grass maybe? The woman was on the ballfield almost as much as we were. The scent was delicious and made me dizzy for a second. Or was it the alcohol? With a grin, she tugged me into the middle of the now-crowded dance floor.

"Since you can't seem to understand dance from a technical standpoint, you'll have to look at dancing as something else entirely." She spoke over the noise of the room as she pulled me to her. On the one hand, I was reluctant to give in but on the other, it gave me an innocent excuse to see just how well she fit against me. "Something more like…a workout." Her words were breathless with excitement as her hands guided me into position.

On second thought, this close proximity wasn't going to be good for another dancing lesson. Especially when my dick seemed to have a mind of its own with this woman.

"Yeah, an annoying workout," I grumbled, doing my best to suppress all the heated thoughts that were swimming in my brain with her this close. My one hand slipped into hers as she guided the other to her waist.

Her hands on my body were more of a hindrance instead of any measure of help. It was taking every ounce of mental capacity to ignore how close she was. There were parts of her body that were so close to being slotted right against the parts of mine that craved her the most.

"No." Her eyes shot up to mine as she grabbed ahold of my hesitant hips, smashing hers against them. That shut me the fuck up. If only my cock would do the same. Unfortunately, the move had the *opposite* effect on my dick. "*Another* kind of workout." The liquored seductive tone of her voice had my entire body paying rapt attention. "Considering you're rather popular among the ladies, I *know* you have the ability. You're just being stubborn about it."

Holy fuck she did not just say what I think she said. I couldn't decide if I was more annoyed with the fact that she insinuated that I slept around or the fact that she was adamant about reenacting the moves of fucking, but with our clothes on.

"But that…that's not…" I couldn't bring myself to admit it out loud. I was too flustered with the veiled remarks. Cady avoided my gaze as she busied herself making minor adjustments to my hands.

"If you really think about it, being intimate is just a dance. A *horizontal* one." She insisted, even though I had a difficult time understanding how she could compare dancing to sex. "When you rise to the balls of your feet…” She demonstrated with practiced ease, and it sent the curves of her body into the hard notches of mine like a finely weathered baseball glove around a baseball. “And press forward with a rock of your hips…”

The way her body met mine made my breath catch in my throat from surprise. I’d done some semblance of dancing before with women. Mostly just absentminded, off-beat swaying. But this? This was an unspoken invitation to join her body in something that I’d already been thinking about. As much as I didn’t want to admit it to myself.

The rocking of her hips was by far my favorite part. Despite us being fully clothed and standing upright in the middle of a noisy bar, her body was almost emulating the moves of sex.

“Cady…” I tried to swallow back the strain in my voice, but it was to no avail. The woman was all action, as always. There was no stopping her. But did I really want to?

“Shh…” She huffed out with her eyes closed. For a moment I could drink her in, from head to toe. Admire every smile line, every freckle. I watched in wonderment as she focused. “Shut up and dance with me.” She breathed out, continuing the motions without pause. Despite the volume of the world around us, I could only hear her. Between her hands and her hips gyrating in their hypnotic motions, I couldn’t help but arch my body towards hers in reply.

I was rewarded with a delicious hum and a soft little smile that played across her lips. She was difficult to say no to. Honestly, Cady didn’t seem to ever *let* me say no.

"Dance is an expression of your body. Don't think about it, listen to the music and let your body do the talking." She teased as one eye opened to gaze back at me. "Thinking about it like sex might motivate you on the field a bit."

I choked on my inhale. It was one thing to emulate the act of sex with her, but it was another thing to hear the word uttered from that mouth of hers. The little noise that absentmindedly escaped my throat brought on a cock of her brow. For fucks sake I needed a distraction. Maybe if I focused all my concentration on what she just said, before the sex part, I might be able to not only dance but forget it was my coach whose body I was molded against.

Pressing my lips into a fine line, I gave in to her demands. My hands settled on her hips and pulled her back in close. A puff of air left her all at once. Her delightful reactions spurred me on. Maybe it was time I took her by surprise. To show her, that despite my attitude, I'd been listening to every stupid little thing she taught me. Probably with more intensity than any of my other coaches ever got out of me.

"Let me lead, you follow. Do what I do. Or do whatever comes naturally. Go along with the music as best you can." The words left her mouth in a breathy huff. She pulled me off in a direction without a second glance back. It was as if she had eyes on the back of her head. Or maybe it was just her tipsy nature which lived dangerously and hoped for the best.

My hips echoed hers to the firm beat of the song. It had pep to it. Which made it easier to follow along and fall into step with. Not that I had anything anywhere near the correct beat, but I was close enough.

Spreading my fingers, I found myself sliding my hand from her waist, up the curve of her back, as I added a bit more oomph to the sway of my hips. I slid it up so high that the tips of my fingers brushed against the strap of her bra. I had to grit my teeth to ignore the sensation. Fuck, now I needed yet *another* distraction.

In an anxious panic, I grabbed both of her hands. I pulled her in and swept her up in my arms. I was blessed with a noise of surprise from her. It was all the encouragement I needed. With a subtle adjustment of our bodies, I spun her in place for a few rotations before managing to glide us both around the room and not step on anyone's toes. It wasn't quite a traditional dance style, but Cady didn't seem to have any complaints about it. In fact, she was *grinning*.

As much as I didn't want to admit it to her, she was right. Once I let down my stony walls, the music did something. Maybe it was the alcohol. Or maybe it was the warmth of Cady's body meeting mine curve for curve, move for move, that inspired me.

Being close to her was rare over these past few weeks, but now I could study the lovely curve of her face. Her golden copper hair shimmered, even in the dim lighting of the bar. Despite the overall sunny disposition of Cady, her eyes were an intriguing contradiction of gray and blue.

From afar they were blue but up close there was a stormy mix of gray, like the color of the seas in the middle of a hurricane. I couldn't help but find myself utterly intrigued by her. She didn't fawn all over me like other women. Nor did she put me on a pedestal because of my major league background. She treated me like any other Joe off the street. It was…*refreshing*.

Every day we were together made me want to get to know her more. There was something between us that I couldn't quite put my finger on. As much as we butted heads, I always found it to be a victory if I could manage to get some semblance of a smile out of her or even a lingering look. It might have been my imagination, but I was pretty sure I caught her mid-stare in my direction a few times. I wasn't the kind of man that looked for ways to fuel my ego but for some reason, Cady kept doing it without even trying lately.

I was high on the music. High on the fact that maybe I finally figured out this dancing shit. And I was sure as fuck high on everything that was Cadence Andrews. With my head still buzzing, an intrusive thought in the back of my mind kept bugging me.

Dip her.

I hesitated. I didn't want to drop the poor woman if I miscalculated all of this. But fuck, I wanted to see her continue to smile. It was now or never. Without further thought, I tipped her back. A squeal shot straight from her lips to my ears. It morphed into a surprised bubble of laughter. Her eyes fluttered open to find mine.

Her laughter caused my heart to race and my palms to sweat. When her eyes locked so firmly onto mine, it was almost as if there was an audible crackle of electricity between us. It drew me in closer as she was draped over my forearm and palm. Her body arched up towards mine in an open invitation as I held her there in the middle of the twirling dancers.

I felt as if I was locked in a trance. The only way to stop it was to lean in and ki…

Fuck.

My body jerked forward as a body part from someone on the dance floor bumped into my ass. I glanced back to see who the offender was. They ruined a moment that I was still in the middle of desperately trying to decipher. But by the time I looked back at Cady, whatever we had experienced was gone.

Rising of her own accord, she shot me a playful, breathless grin as her hands grasped onto both of mine. I felt about two degrees away from being a melted puddle at her feet. Why did she have such an unholy hold on me? She could crook her finger, and I'd follow without question. As if she had trained to do so.

I couldn't help but quirk some semblance of a smile back at her as her hands tightened their grip. She found her footing again but suddenly stumbled a bit in her steps. For someone so sure of her dance skills, it was unusual to see. Maybe it was just the alcohol hitting her all at once.

I dropped her hands and moved my firm grip back onto her hips to steady her. I took note of how her body moved with mine. A wordless call and echo to one another. Maybe this was…*fun.*

"See? You're not so bad, Slugger." Cady's breathed out as her eyes dipped away demurely. "Maybe we need to do more one-on-one practice."

Her suggestion took me by surprise. First of all, did she just lay a nickname on me? And secondly, my brain, *and dick,* went directly to the other sort of one-on-one practice with Cady's and my body rocking together. My breath caught at the thought.

And so did her foot under my shoe.

An awkward squawk of surprise twisted her face.

"Fuck! Sorry." I mumbled under my breath as I briskly pulled my body from hers. Despite the misstep, I was thankful for it. The last thing I needed was her feeling my hardening cock when the moment was already awkward enough.

"No, no it's fine! I'm just glad you're dancing." Her words were sweet. Excited even. Chancing a glance up at her, her smile hadn't faltered. There was a delightful pink tinge on her cheeks. It was probably from the dancing. "You aren't terrible. You need to give yourself more credit. I'd dance with you aga– OW!"

If I kept stepping on her toes every time the damn woman flustered me, she was going to take back her offer to dance. Or else she wouldn't have any toes left to dance on.

During games I could call pitches, keep an eye on runners at second base, and catch/return balls in a timely fashion. So why the hell couldn't I hold onto a woman *and* keep my feet from stepping on hers?

"You sure about that?"

Cady let out a snort before pressing her body in close again. It's not that I wanted to push her away, I stupidly wanted to mold her body against mine. Spread kisses down her neck…

Fuck. I really needed to stop.

Think unsexy thoughts. Think unsexy thoughts.

"Stepping on my feet isn't the worst thing a man has done to me." There was a quick roll of her eyes. "This is tame."

My skin prickled at the thought of anyone being mean to the little spitfire. How could she let anyone be mean to her? With how she spoke to me, it was almost impossible to get a word in edgewise when she went on one of her tirades.

"Dare I pry…?" I cautiously asked. This was the longest conversation I ever had with the woman that didn't revolve around work. As rude as it was to ask about past relationships, it was the only fodder I had to keep talking to her in my beer-hazed and semi-horny thoughts. And she did open the door to the conversation.

"Let's just say that it involved different boyfriends who all found greener pastures and didn't bother to let me know they moved on." Well, that was one way to put it. *Fucking assholes.* "Working around men all day long somehow diminishes the trust factor in a relationship. Once they get a look at my sorry lot, and the fact that I'm a female coach, they automatically think I'm fucking the whole team." Her lovely face curled into a sour expression. "What is it with men?"

I blinked at her. She spoke to me as if I knew. I mean, I kind of did. Not that I was anything like the past men she dated. I couldn't help but bristle every time I thought about Cady dating Roman. But now that I got to know the Sillys and Cady, these guys were like big brothers. Intimidating but harmless. They took special care of her, and she of them. Nothing sexual about it.

Even if I didn't mesh well with a woman or wanted to move on, I wasn't a dick about it. Unlike Cady's past knuckleheads, I at least gave my exes the courtesy of a breakup face-to-face. Even during my immature teenage days.

I was raised in a strict Catholic family. While I didn't believe in the whole "marriage before sex" thing, respect towards women, and others, was ingrained in me from the start. Even if a woman had treated me poorly, I never returned the favor.

Mom and Dad showed me what lasting love was supposed to be like. That love wasn't all black and white. It was messy. It was stressful. Above all, they had a partner who loved and respected them all while managing to find the fun in life together. That was all I wanted. A love like theirs. But playing major league ball didn't make it easy. And for once, there was a woman out there who understood that.

Cady had been given stupid excuses by stupid men. While I could understand the hesitation, especially with the notorious history of fellow ball players, Cady was faithful to a fault. In the short time I'd known her that was one of the first things I noticed about her. Her job and unwavering dedication to the team was her entire life. And all the men in her life had to be a fucking idiot to give up on such a passionate and beautiful woman.

Godfuckingdammit.

I'd be a lying Catholic in need of penance if I denied the fact that I wanted to be in Cadence's presence as much as possible. Despite her early animosity towards me, she was…oddly enchanting. Especially in quiet moments like this.

"Same for me," I added before I realized the words could be misconstrued. Cady's brow soared straight up her forehead to almost collide with her hairline. I realized that maybe she thought I was pitching for the other team. "I mean, uh, my ex, ex-*girlfriend,* she…uh, broke up with me when I was traded. Apparently, I wasn't worth moving across the country for. Which…fair. I suppose… It was a big move after all. And who knew if I'd be traded again and have to move once more." Despite my babbling, her face softened. "Baseball doesn't make a good bedfellow with those who don't get the industry."

That at least drew a laugh from her. A lovely, sparkling laugh. "Well…that's certainly one way to put it." Her words were still breathless from laughter as her mirth gently tapered off. Our dancing slowed as the song choice went a bit more mellow. We were talking with no animosity between us.

The words hurt to say them out loud. I hadn't thought of women or love since I arrived in Philadelphia. But now? I couldn't get a certain woman out of my thoughts. No matter how hard I tried, Cadence Andrews kept drawing me back to her. A very stubborn moth to an equally stubborn flame. A flame that could easily chew me up and spit me out if I crossed her in the wrong way.

The song drew to a close, but Cady and I kept dancing. It wasn't until the roaring cheers of the crowd jolted us from whatever kind of moment we were having.

"Looks like line dancing is gearing up for another round. Ready to give it a try?" Her hopeful smile did me in.

"Put me in coach."

Cady tossed her head back with a cascade of laughter before grabbing my hand and dragging me into the fray to attempt some line dancing.

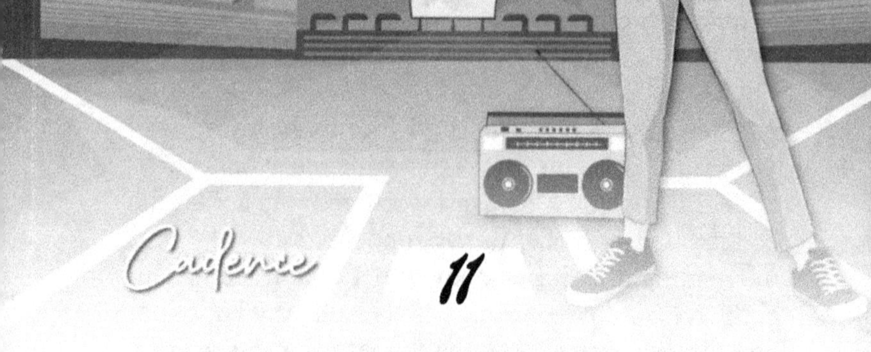

WHAT IS THIS FEELING?

ARIANA GRANDE & CYNTHIA ERIVO

"**W**as it my imagination or did Jamie and I dance last night?" The sunlight was entirely too bright as I made my way out of the tunnel and onto the field. I was fairly certain I went easy on the alcohol, on account of the routine work I had planned for today. That was until Jamie actually showed up at the bar last night. After that, things got a little fuzzy.

My strained question drew a snort out of Tiffiny as she walked beside me.

"Had I not known the history between you two I would have said you did everything *but* dance."

For fucks sake.

"Don't you fucking dare…"

"Girl, that was the hottest fucking thing I'd ever seen two people do with clothes *on*."

Groaning, I threw my hands up to my face. How much alcohol had I consumed? I thought everything that happened last night was all a dream. A glorious, steamy sort of dream. Or maybe I was stuck in an outright denial that we had come *this close* to kissing.

"That dancing was almost *Dancing with the Stars* worthy. Or a porno. Except that was a hell of a lot better acting than any porno I've ever seen." She outright deserved an elbow jab to the ribs for that side note.

I vaguely remembered doing some heavy grinding against Jamie last night. "Jamie was paying *rapt* attention to whatever you were saying to him." I rolled my eyes. "And look. Mr. Hunky Pants seems to be eagerly awaiting you today too."

My stomach did a funny topsy-turvy thing. Or maybe the alcohol was ready to make a reappearance? I glanced out towards the guys on the field and happened to catch Jamie *maybe* glancing in my direction.

"You mean Mr. *Grumpy* Pants. The man hates being here and hates what I make him do every damn day. It's like pulling teeth to even get him to smile." I ignored the fact that I got Jamie to smile no less than seven times last night. But who was counting?

"I don't know, he was doing some semblance of smiling last night with you." Heat hit my cheeks. It felt like my best friend could read my thoughts. Tiffiny's fingers danced along the brim of her ball cap as she adjusted it. "Maybe you just need to do some of that *mattress mambo* dance with him instead." I gave her another swift elbow in the ribs to which she responded with a backhand against my shoulder.

"There's no fucking way–"

"Cadence, for the last few years all I've heard from you is how hot Jamie's butt is and how luscious his biceps are. Among *other* things. Now's your chance to finally see what he's really like under the uniform."

"Oh right." I rolled my eyes. "I'm sure ownership would be thrilled if I went up to him and offered, 'Oh hey Jamie, wanna come back to my place for private dance lessons?'."

"See? Now we're on the same page."

"Absofuckinglutely not." Stopping mid-step, I turned to her. In the time that I've known her, I knew she was not going to drop this subject until she'd proven herself right. It was an admirable quality to her, but I didn't have enough of my brain cells working this morning to fight back. "Aside from the fact the man is a baseball god, ownership would have a field day. No man is worth me losing my job over. Not even the hottest man in baseball."

"Hey well if the man ever looks at you again like he did last night, you'll be on your knees. You'd be saying 'Tiffiny was right' but I have a feeling that your mouth will be full with–"

I was about 2.3 seconds away from slapping that smug ass look off her face. Just because she played the mascot and didn't speak during games, it didn't mean she didn't have two tons of attitude. Even with her being my friend, it wasn't below me to put her in a headlock. Her only saving grace was Ender who managed to step between us.

"Hey, Tiffiny."

"Get bent." She spat with such venom. Rather shocked at her visceral attitude change, I cocked my brow at her in silent question. My eyes flickered between the two. Typically, she was always a bit hostile to the players. But for some reason, Ender pulled a vicious kind of vitriol from her. Almost constantly. But today was especially wicked.

"Nice to see you too." From the tone of his voice, I could tell he was even taken by surprise. He looked a bit apprehensive to continue the conversation, lest he receive another verbal snap. Proverbially licking his wounds, he turned to me. "Um…hey Cadence. I have to grab my water bottle, but I'll be right out."

Once he was out of earshot I shot a look at Tiffiny. "The fuck was that about?"

"None of your fucking business." Muttering her response, she stormed out the last few feet of the tunnel and onto the field. The way she stomped off left me scratching my head. Was it a full moon or something? Practice was going to be really awkward if I was going to have to deal with Tiffiny, Ender, Jamie, and whatever the hell happened last night.

The guys were out on the field doing some warm-up stretches. Today was the last day before Jamie's big debut. With his performance last night, there was a flicker of hope within me that he wouldn't crash and burn as epically as I thought he would. I was easing him into it, and I'd be right in the dugout to encourage him.

As I walked towards the outfield, Truitt and Camden were mid-stretch, but I was fairly certain they were sneaking in a nap on the warm grass. Usually, when we all went out as a group, they were the ones that partied the hardest. Sliding my sunglasses down onto my nose, I pinched the bridge of my nose in a vain effort to quell the headache that was brewing.

I definitely had my hands full today.

If I could, I'd be on the grass right next to the guys, snoring away in the early sunlight. I wasn't really in the mood to attempt to nail down a new routine for tomorrow's game and play babysitter to everyone. So, we were going to go in, nice and easy with a few run-throughs of tomorrow's dancing interludes. The last thing I needed was for someone to get maimed at practice. And by everyone's apparent current attitude, I would be the one doing the maiming.

Thank fuck some semblance of the routine managed to nestle into the brains of the team. Even after a night out at the bar, they pulled out three mostly flawless run throughs from out of their asses. But it was a hell of a rocky start. For a while there I felt like I was trying to teach cats. Inbred cats. Inbred cats that had spent the night festering in tubs of beer.

After practice, I was in desperate need of painkillers and an entire jug of electrolytes. I escaped into my office to eat lunch and maybe a quick snooze on my couch while the guys did their fieldwork practice.

Instead of zonking out after picking at my lunch, all I could do was pace. The guys had enthusiastically suggested that since Jamie did such a great job last night, that maybe he needed one more session of pointers before his big day. Apparently, *everyone* had seen us dancing together the night before. And the guys thought it was a good idea for Jamie to have another round of solo dance lessons after practice today.

With me.

My heart had been in my throat, choking me out like a morally gray character in a dark romance ever since the guys brought it up in conversation. Me, alone with Jamie? Last night had been a tipsy fluke. All of our practices and dance outings had been with the entire team and me. Never Jamie and I *alone*. I hadn't even come close to mentally preparing myself for such an endeavor. Now I only had minutes left to pull my fucking shit together enough to get through an hour or two of just me and Jamie.

Even though I was losing my shit over it, one-on-one lessons were probably a smart idea. Jamie had only shown minor improvement in the group setting of choreography practice. He blossomed at the bar last night when it felt like we were the only two people in the entire building.

I hoped that without eyes around, Jamie would be more willing to comply with the private lesson. Maybe this would be a repeat of last night. And maybe, just maybe, if and when we did get close, we wouldn't be *interrupted*.

The look on his face as he sauntered back onto the field looked as if he wanted to be anywhere but here. *Great.* Tiffiny had been blowing smoke up my ass. She probably got our dancing chemistry confused with whatever she'd been reading in her cartoon cover romance book at the bar.

"Hey Jamie, I'm glad–"

"Let's just get this over with."

His unenthusiastic mumble made me bristle. I felt that little balloon of hope deflate with an exaggerated raspberry noise as it zoomed around my insides. Of course. Last night had just been an alcohol-induced hallucination.

Even though his attitude was back in the toilet, something about it felt…*wrong*. Almost as if it was forced, maybe? I eyed him suspiciously as he avoided my gaze with his arms crossed defiantly across his chest. There was a tenseness in his toned biceps. If it had been any other moment in time, I would have admired them for a moment longer as I fumbled with the speaker and music.

I made my way back over to him and slowly held out my hands. Maybe he was just in a bad mood. Maybe he was all choked up on his nerves about tomorrow. Whatever it was, I wasn't going to fight fire with fire this time. He'd been so open to my tutelage last night. Jamie stood there, looking at my hands, almost as if he didn't know what to do with them.

"I thought we could just keep this fun. Like last night." I reminded him as I managed to pull his hands out from the knot of his arms across his chest. My mouth went dry as sober me did my best to not go out of the way to feel up the star catcher.

There was a hard set to his jaw as he reluctantly unwound his arms and let me take his limp hands into mine. Tiffiny's mocking voice about getting on my knees to get him to cooperate somehow seeped its way into my brain. With a hard swallow, I dismissed the idea. This Jamie looked like a man who wouldn't be bothered by oral stimulation at the moment.

Tipsy Cadence was a little more willing to bring Jamie up against her. Nervous and irritated as fuck Cadence was a lot less enthusiastic to take that step. So instead, the both of us made this infinitely more awkward, like two middle schoolers at a dance kept an arm's length away from each other by an overly watchful teacher.

Even though he agreed to this, the man was anything but a willing participant. He was grumpier than ever. There was no heart to his dance moves. With my head clear, all I could focus on was the fact that Jamie Rheems was just inches away from me. I could feel the warmth and strength of his hands, yet they seemed reluctant to grab a hold of me like last night.

He knew I was a tough bird. I wasn't some wilting flower. I worked with a bunch of completely insane baseball players. I could survive a firm grip of a man as we danced together. Instead, Jamie's hands almost hovered over my body like an unnerving tease. Maybe he was pissed at me? Annoyed that I coerced him into this nonsense? His body language was keeping my thirsty bitch of a body at an imaginary arm's length.

"Come on, man. You can do this. Don't be afraid to grab onto me." My mouth went dry, but I was desperate at this point. "Anywhere you want." I caught the subtle pink tinge on his cheeks, even in the light of the early evening. His fingers did the tiniest little flex against me, almost as if he was battling something deep within.

What was he fighting against? What was he so unsure of? Did he want to touch me? Did he feel awkward?

"I'm good." He refused to meet my eyes and his reply back was soft. Why was he so adamantly against this? I thought we had a breakthrough. We were this close to greatness barely 24 hours ago.

I even played some of the songs we danced to. Nothing. Not even a budge. He was fighting this with every fiber of his being. Did he forget all that? Did he even realize that this was the last stop? That he had to get his shit together or else this was the end of him in Philadelphia?

By the end of the first hour, it was a wonder if I had any molars left. I was gritting my teeth so badly to stop me from saying anything that would get me into trouble. I had to gauge my words carefully.

"Where's the Jamie from last night?" I managed to eke out in a vain attempt at some humor to lighten the situation. My voice didn't sound as confident or as amusing as I hoped. "I'm pretty sure you shut some of the guys up with your moves at the bar."

They always said that you get more flies with honey. I was trying to land me a juicy one. But to my disappointment, he didn't look flattered or encouraged in the least bit.

"That Jamie and this one both don't dance." He said flatly. *Oh boy, hold me back. This Cadence is ready to go off.*

"Well, that's unfortunate because since you're on the Sillys you *have* to dance." I tried to hide my irritation with a laugh, but I don't think it came across. No paycheck was worth working with this kind of bullshit. Even if I had a crush on the man. But if he kept up with this nonsense any longer, he was going down a few notches on my crush list.

"Last I checked, only the mascots danced in baseball." He misstepped and landed on my foot. I grimaced. Whether his stepping on my foot was purposeful or not, it only added to the souring mood.

"Last I checked, you weren't in the majors anymore." I shot back icily and immediately regretted the words. That got a visible wince out of him. It was harsh but considering the only weapon I had were my words, and not a slap across his handsome face, it got me the same reaction.

"This is such bullshit." Jamie spat out as he violently pulled away from me. His attitude was going to ruin every decent thought I ever had of the man.

"Yeah well…" I shouted after him as he grabbed his stuff with haste. All I could hear were Topper's words in my head. That Jamie's success here fell on *my* shoulders. "Maybe you should stop being so…so *fucking selfish*!"

Jamie paused in his steps as he headed toward the dugout. He didn't seem like the kind of guy that would be so full of himself. Despite his gruff attitude about his situation, his fieldwork and batting practice participation was flawless. I bet those coaches didn't have to deal with such bullshit. And yet I was going to be the one who got shit for it. The one that ruined everything.

"Maybe there are some others who have our necks on the line too." I choked out. As distressed as I sounded, I wasn't worried about me, I was worried about my favorite baseball player crashing and burning into a horrific ball of flames all at once instead of retiring with the highest respect.

Lingering for just a moment, my heart shot up to my throat with hope that maybe I had struck a nerve. Instead, Jamie adjusted the strap of his bag on his shoulder before storming off towards the dugout. The fucking audacity. The longer I stood watching him retreat, the more I let the anger build into toxic fumes inside of me. Oh, that was it. The fuck with my crush. The man was just demoted. Big time.

I'd had it with Jamie Rheems.

12

MINE

BAZZI

Being sober and this close to Cadence Andrews, for an extended period of time, was going to end up with one, or both of us, being embarrassed on account of me. Ever since last night, my brain had been chanting Cady's name constantly. As if my heart was beating to the cadence of her literal name.

Something happened on that dance floor.

Something...*changed* between us.

Or maybe it didn't. Maybe I'd just become more aware of something that had been bugging me at the back of my mind ever since I arrived here. Now that we were face to face, with no one to distract us, I felt that whatever this was, could slide into dangerous territory real quick.

I was legitimately terrified.

Never before had I felt something like this with someone. Not with any of my past girlfriends, not even with Vanessa. She was the one I thought I was ready to spend the rest of my life with. With Cady before me, it sent my heart into overdrive. A coworker was the last person on the planet I thought I'd ever feel this way about. Hell, she wasn't just a coworker. She was a *coach.* My coach.

Part of me didn't want to be here. I wanted to be home, in my condo, trying to focus on not fucking up the game tomorrow. I didn't want to be at this one-on-one practice. All the guys just had to butt in with the suggestion after seeing Cady and I dance together.

Which only worried me even more.

I mean, I felt something, but I didn't think it was obvious to anyone else. I didn't know any of this chemistry stuff. Or what any of it meant. I was afraid to touch her. Because if I got that close again, I wouldn't be able to stop myself from completing that kiss we missed out on.

Instead, I put my walls up and was a total stiff dick to Cady. I couldn't very well go and ask her out on a date when I was pretty sure that she *barely* tolerated me as a person. But fuck, I really wanted to. This was all going on inside my head while she was just trying, with one last ditch effort, to help me dance.

Now she was fuming. I had no idea how to act around her now. So instead, I hid. Hid behind a stern face and a forced reluctance to touch her.

I ran from her after our blowout on the field. I didn't want her to be pissed. I wanted, with every fiber of my being, to dance with her like we had last night. But we already had one close call with a kiss while the woman was inebriated. Even if she claimed it was only a little, I didn't want to take advantage of her in a moment of weakness and have her regret it the next day. I didn't want to risk her career, or mine, with temptation.

My heart thudded in my throat as I ran down the steps from the dugout into the locker room. I needed to get out of here. The woman was out for blood, and

I was the sole person on her murderous rampage radar.

Aggressive steps followed me and echoed endlessly off the metal lockers.

Shit.

I was cornered.

"You know what? I'm really fucking sick of your shit. So is everyone else. You think you're all high and mighty because you play for the majors. Now that you're back from the IL and barely batting over .200! Your reflexes are rusty! Every guy on this team is better than you."

Cady's sharp words hit me like a brick wall. Here I thought she was all dance moves and attitude, but I underestimated her knowledge of baseball. I did my best to ignore her truths as I whipped off my ball cap and threw it into the depths of my locker station.

Electricity was palpable in the air. My brain was a blur of emotion. I was pissed I had to be here. I was annoyed that Cady wouldn't give me five seconds alone to collect my thoughts and figure out what happened last night and with practice today. I was crushed that she then had to go and admit to me all my faults this season in one breath.

Because she was right. She was *right*. I hated to admit that every single thing she said was true. It didn't make me any less pissed.

"You really need to get your head out of that *very fine* ass of yours and back in the game. A routine surgery shouldn't be holding you back like this. Especially since you had it before. Look, I get that you're used to major league ball but, playing for the Sillys is where you're at right now." I tried my best not to flinch. But goddammit those words stung.

"So why can't you just do your job? You're here. Now. At the Sillys' ballpark. All you have to do is listen to me and follow…*simple* directions. Why do you have to be such a fucking stick in the mud all the goddamn time?!"

The normally cold but docile Cady was suddenly unrelenting. I didn't know there was this much passion and fire in someone so petite. The words she spat in my direction were nothing but ice and fire. It wasn't just…

Wait.

Did she compliment my ass?

I'd been ready to charge right back at her but now I was thrown off course.

Godfuckingdammit.

Why the hell did my brain have to hyperfocus on that one line of her tirade? They were words that I never thought would leave her mouth but actually *did*. Cady might, just might, be attracted to me? It was the opening I'd been waiting for with bated breath, but I'd been too much of a coward to admit it.

I'd never been in this sort of situation before. What do I do? Do I fight back? Do I laugh it off? Do I ignore it completely? Why were women so goddamn confusing?

It wasn't until that very moment that I suddenly realized why all this animosity had been going on between us. Of why I bristled every time she got near to my body. Why I could barely string a few words together around her. Why almost every waking moment of my life over the past few weeks was spent thinking about Cady.

I really wanted to kiss her.

The need to kiss her was putting my tumultuous feelings *mildly*.

I chanced a glance at her off to my right. Had this been a cartoon, there would have been smoke coming from her ears. With her hands on her hips, she looked seconds away from charging me like a damn bull. There was something in her eyes. Something aside from her anger glittered there in the stormy depths. Was it…concern?

"You'd better be fucking listening to me Jamie Rheem—"

Before I could realize what I was doing, my body moved of its own accord. It was on autopilot and Cady's curves were the target. It only took two strides to confront her. The resolve in her squared shoulders melted as her hands fell from her hips in surprise. She wasn't fond of having a taste of her own confrontational medicine.

It was an out-of-body experience for a moment, as I found myself nose-to-nose with the woman. Well, I had to tilt my chin down to do so. I caught the whites of her eyes as my hands reached out to grip her hips and simultaneously closed the gap between us. It was almost as if the bowstring pulling us apart was suddenly loosed, sending, me the arrow, straight to the captivating target that was Cadence *fucking* Andrews.

My brain sat back in utter shock for a moment before it stood up and slow-clapped my body for *finally* doing what it wanted to do. I was a puppet and had some kinky motherfucker pulling the strings. I wasn't in control of my body anymore. Or…was I?

I pushed her ass firmly against the equipment lockers behind her. They clattered as our bodies made contact. In one smooth motion, I hefted my hands around her thighs and slid her petite body up the wall so that we were eye-to-eye. Not breaking our stare down, I reinforced her position by cradling my hands along the dangerous underside of her thighs.

A soft squeak left her mouth, curling her lips into an enticing O. Her hands shot out to grip my shoulders. From the look on her face, it seemed as if she couldn't decide whether to shove me off of her or embrace it. But the moment she made her choice; my *entire* body knew.

Her gaze met mine for only a single thudding heartbeat before there was a desperate mutual effort to bond our bodies together. This woman was a mouthful of petite sunshine and fire at any given time. Whatever she was lacking in height she made up for in attitude.

I couldn't get enough of her.

Even when she annoyed me to no end and made my blood boil by bossing me around in this weird excuse for baseball. Now that I finally had her right where my body wanted her, I couldn't help but think about all the ways she had made mine flush with awareness and need.

With our bodies pressed so intimately together, it only exacerbated the fact that I'd been in utter denial about how badly I wanted this woman. Between her devotion to baseball and love for her team, she was literally someone who could have walked straight out of my dreams and into my arms.

Every part of my body was screaming to kiss her. Fuck I wanted to. *Needed* to. Despite her astonished look, there was something there in the deepest depths of her stormy blue eyes that was *begging* for it.

My eyes drifted down to her parted lips. There was a subtle quiver there, enticing me. I could see the flicker of her quick pulse along the column of her throat and my mouth started to water. Was she excited? Nervous? Terrified? I was a little of all of the above myself. It felt as if time wandered on for a century as we stared at each other, wide-eyed and panting.

"Fuck it."

With one mutual inhale, our mouths collided, hard and hot. I wanted to moan from the sheer relief and utter satisfaction of it all. It was as if I'd been a starving man, in my last moments of life, and given the Holy Grail to drink from. I wasn't going to let a drop of Cadence Andrews go to waste.

As soon as our lips made contact, all of my hesitations and doubts dissipated in an instant. The humming chaos of the world was gone. All that was left was me and Cady. Something about that, about this, just felt so…so *right*.

My hips kept her body pinned to the wall, hands-free. I needed to touch her. To feel the heat of her body beneath my fingertips. To trace those treacherous curves that haunted my dreams and commit them to memory.

My breath caught as I felt her answer me in kind. Her fingers threaded through my hair, pulling me closer. *Oh, fuck yes.* The feelings, whatever feelings they were, were reciprocated. With that thought, our mouths slanted, mutually devouring one another as our bodies pressed together in a vain effort to be closer than was physically possible.

Her little breathy noises of want slipped into my hungry mouth. That alone had my dick ready to drill a hole straight through her and into the wall of lockers. *Fuck.* I'd been trying so hard to tell my cock to keep its cool, but now it was utterly impossible. My damn body betrayed me all thanks to the hobbit-like spitfire writhing with pleasure in my arms.

It especially betrayed me when she arched her body and rocked her mind-boggling hips into my aching cock. There was no doubt she felt it. With a moan, her hips thrust into my dick again. I could feel the heat of her cunt through her skinny jeans.

It's not like I could tuck that sucker away like a damn magic trick. It was trying to do its brainless best to poke a hole straight through my pants and find its way deep inside her.

If it wasn't her body that had me in a chokehold, it was her damn mouth. She tasted exactly how she acted, like honey on a spring day with a kick of spice. It was just the thing to melt through my icy demeanor. The Kryptonite to my steely resolve. The one thing about me that I was so sure would never find an antidote to. And yet it showed up in a five-foot-tall bundle of chaos at what I thought, was the lowest point of my life.

The desperate way her hips were grinding into mine wasn't going to end well for me. I couldn't recall a time that my cock had ever inflated as fast as it did when our lips met. My blood rushed south so hard and fast that I was feeling delightfully lightheaded.

Fuck. I was close. Embarrassingly close to blowing my entire load in my pants. Between her excited kisses and her hips emulating sex every damn second, there was no hope for me if I didn't put a stop to it.

My hands moved from their position of cradling her jaw down to her hips to stop them from her unknowingly getting me off. But I severely underestimated her core strength from years of dance. If anything, my hands on her hips spurred her on more to the point that she let out a needy little moan, picked up her pace, and it was all over for me.

I choked on my own moan as my hips bucked from the force of my ejaculation. My brain shorted out to nothingness as my balls unloaded the masses directly into my boxer briefs. With a final violent shutter, I broke our kiss and pressed my forehead against hers, trying to catch my breath. With every fiber of my being, I hoped that she had no clue what had just happened south of the border.

It took a bit, but my tunnel vision finally subsided. It was then that I realized where the hell we were. As much as I wanted to continue this hot interlude and consume every square inch of her, the stank of the locker room reminded me that this was the last place we should ever kiss.

Nor should it have been the place for me to jizz my damn pants.

"Holy fuck that did not just happen." Cady panted out as I caught her wide-eyed stare. My heart stopped that very second, utterly terrified that she knew that I messed my pants. With one sentence, she broke the spell that I was having a very difficult time waking up from. Or it could have been the fact that I was still trying to recover from a hell of an unexpected orgasm.

My eyes drifted back to her swollen lips as I licked her residual sweetness off mine. Which only drew her vibrant blue eyes back to my mouth and everything we'd been doing for the last few minutes.

"I'm…sorry…?" I still wasn't exactly sure if her exclamation was a good one or a bad one. She still looked dazed out of her mind and her breathing was rough. Maybe she got something out of that too?

"No, no. Don't be." She managed to blink as her taut body relaxed in my arms. Her pointer finger absentmindedly twirled around a lock of hair at the base of my neck. "I've only been dreaming of what it would be like to kiss you since-" Those beautiful blue eyes of hers went as wide as home plate as her entire body froze. She quickly avoided my gaze. I kept my disappointment at bay as her hands shot away from my body and flat against the lockers behind her. "Oh, my dear god I did not just say that. I did not just say that to Jamie *fucking* Rheems."

My brows went sky-high as my eyes darted across her face to decipher what underlying meaning her words had. This woman, who had been the bane of my existence since I met her, had fantasized about kissing me? I was so sure she hated my guts. I needed to get to the bottom of this while I still had her bottom in my hands.

"Since…?" I tried to channel as much of my nonexistent sexy swagger as I could muster. We were so close to greatness here and I didn't want to fuck it up.

"Pretend I didn't say anything." Cady continued to avoid looking me in the eye as she attempted to wriggle from my grasp. But there was no way I was going to let her loose until she admitted whatever she had haphazardly alluded to.

My hands flexed along the back of her thigh and the roundness of her ass to remind her exactly where she was. The breathy little noise of surprise only added an arch of my hips to the mix, effectively repining her to the wall.

"I believe that's a bit *hard* to do at the moment…" I gritted out. Because it was the inconvenient truth. How the hell was I *still* hard? Even after all that? The cum in my pants didn't exactly make this conversation easy. It was difficult for me to ignore what was going on between us when my hips were the only reason she was still mid-air.

"Please stop making this worse." Her brow furrowed with a grimace.

"Worse?! You're the one who complimented my ass."

"I–" Her eyes darted as her brain rewound the last few minutes of conversation. "I did not." She shot back.

"You said, and I quote: *'You really need to get your head out of your very fine ass and back in the game'.*" Sometimes my memory came in handy for things other than reciting movie lines.

Cady's mouth opened in retort, but nothing slipped from those kissable lips of hers. It pulsed in a gape, much like a fish out of water. That was until her brow furrowed violently. She knew I was right.

"Oh, fuck you."

"To be honest, I was hoping that's where we were headed." The words might have slipped from my mouth of their own accord, but they weren't a lie. I swallowed dryly, afraid that I overstepped. But the swiftness in which the rosy color hit her cheeks was the telltale sign I was onto something. "Shit. Sorry. That was too presumptuous of me."

Her body went rigid as her eyes finally met mine for only the briefest of moments. The pink in her cheeks went straight to red. Squinting her eyes shut, she shook her head.

"No. Nope. I'm dreaming."

I couldn't help but chuckle to myself at her dramatic response. Fuck, my heart was beating a thousand times a minute since she admitted there may be something mutual here. Even with our weeks of spicy animosity.

There was only one thing to do when a person insisted they were dreaming.

I pinched her ass.

Her back arched sharply as her eyes shot open, pressing her breasts into my chest. It was my turn to have my breath catch. But I did prove to her that she wasn't dreaming.

"Cadence…" I was sure to use her full name instead of the pet name I gave her. It was difficult to keep the tone of my voice level. "As much as you aggravate me to the utter end," Her eyes guardedly met mine as she looked at me through hooded lashes. "That kiss was…*fucking everything*. And I'd be lying if I said I haven't thought about what it would be like to experience some of those dance moves of yours. *Horizontally*."

Her jaw dropped once again and all it brought me was a mental picture of those open lips around my cock. *Dammit*. There was no hope for my body. But I couldn't take advantage of this woman. We were coworkers first and foremost. Although, I guess it was a little too late now.

"Jamie…" There was a tinge of warning in her breathless voice. At this rate, I was ready to carry her all the way to my penthouse. "You're just saying that."

I was taken aback. Sure, I was a major league ball player, but I wasn't a player in the other sense of the word. My parents raised me right. Hell, I hadn't even slept with or dated anyone since Vanessa.

That was because I hadn't met anyone like Cady before.

"What, I'm not allowed to be honest?"

"Well…yes. But…" She let out a rough sigh. "Maybe the reason is because there's only three, maybe four, layers of fabric between you and *permanently* attaching me to the wall." My cock outright twitched as the exact words I was thinking escaped her mouth. "A guy would say anything to make it *zero* layers."

I huffed at her.

While she wasn't wrong in general, she was wrong about thinking that way about me. Women weren't a conquest. They weren't just a place to empty your balls. They were beautiful, fun, deserved to be romanced, with golden copper waves…

"Well, I'm offended." I was sure to exaggerate my words and might have added a bit of a playful southern drawl to them. "Not all guys are assholes you know."

"Yeah, well most of the ones I know are. The team excluded." She grumbled with a huff as she continued to avoid my gaze. Her words brought me back to our conversation last night at the bar. There was no fucking way that I wasn't going to let Cady believe that she was anything less than deserving of anything and everything.

In just the short time I'd been with the team, I could see that she was the damn glue that kept everyone in line and together. The team looked up to her. Respected her. She deserved that in every aspect of her life, both on and off the field.

"Okay…fair. But I'm not one of them." Squinting my eyes shut, I shook my head to get back on the track of kissing Cady again. Having her in my arms like this just felt so…right. Dangerous. Exciting. "Because, unlike other guys…I have some *rules*. Decorum if you will."

"Rules…?" Her eyes went wide before she cocked her head to the side.

"Contrary to your popular belief, I don't take women home. I have a few stops…before *that*." Shit, I was babbling but I had to get these boundaries out. This woman made me nervous as fuck. Especially with her steely gaze staring me down from such close proximity.

That pulled one of her patented snorts from her and broke the uneasy tension between us. I wanted to show her that all I had were good intentions. Okay, *mostly* good intentions. I didn't want her to think that I was going to chew her up and spit her out like a mouthful of Big League Chew. Although she was making it fucking difficult to stick to my rules at the moment with her hips glued to mine with her ass in my hands.

"What, do I need to stop by your lawyer's office to sign an NDA?"

"What?" I recoiled a bit in surprise before my face twisted in confusion. Who the actual fuck had she dated? "What? No. *I* uh…have rules. For me. I don't like rushing into…well, anything."

"Ain't that the fucking truth." I rolled my eyes. "So what are these…*rules* you have?"

This single-handedly had to be the most awkward conversation I've ever had in my entire life. Especially with my briefs full of jizz and my cock still thinking we were at "go" time. No matter how flustered and ready I was, this conversation was a firm boundary. Not only for myself but in respect of whomever I wished to date.

"First rule: Connection." That earned me another cocked brow. "Second: Oral Communication." I watched as her brows turned to furrow together. This was not going well. "I think we have the first two well in hand."

"Well, now."

Damn, that sarcasm of hers.

This was my time-honored system. Even though the guys in my life razzed me about it, I always stuck to it. If I was going to sleep with a woman, it had to mean *something*.

"So that just means I can take you out. Courting is the next one." Was that the flicker of a smile on her lips? Even though it sounded so antiquated, it was better than the word "dating". I liked to think I was more distinguished than that. "Then…kissing."

"I think you went out of order there a bit, Slugger." A full-blown smirk blossomed on her lips.

I knew it was unusual, this list is what I did for me, for the women I brought into my life. It had never steered me wrong. Cady, on the other hand, didn't look completely convinced.

"So…your so-called rules are a load of COCK."

"I, no…*what?*" I sputtered. She really didn't say what I thought she just said.

"Connection, Oral Communication, Courting, and Kissing. C-O-C-K, cock. Your rules spell *COCK*." She gave me a curious once-over. "You really haven't thought this through, have you?"

If she said cock one more fucking time, I wasn't sure I'd be able to hold myself back from doing something I wasn't completely sure she was on board with yet. But of course, it was Cady who would be the one to upend my carefully crafted set of standards.

"I certainly have. And since we've already made it through C and O…" I paused as her eyes made their way back to lock with mine. "And well, K," My voice softened. "Courting is next. And…I'd like to take you out to dinner."

"Dinner...?" She hesitated.

"I want to show you that my intentions can remain strictly…respectable." Her face twisted and I sighed. I was fucking this up so bad. I had to turn a hot as fuck moment utterly cringy. "If I'm being honest, I'm a bit rusty in all of this. I had a long-term girlfriend back in San Diego, but we broke up because of the trade. It's…been a few years since I've done this stupid song and dance."

Cady's eyes flashed in surprise. As she took the time to consider my request and overload of information, I gently lowered her back down to the floor. Maybe I messed up my only shot

"Okay. Fine. Dinner. We'll see if we can tolerate…*whatever* this is."

Putting my hands up in surrender, I tucked them into my pockets to show her that this outing would be

as innocent as she wanted it to be. But it was also to
subtly adjust my dick to a position that I could more
easily hide my, finally softening, hard-on as I slowly
pulled away from her.

"Great." I let out a breath of relief. "There's
something I need to do before we go. Just…give me
a second."

"For what?"

"Because I need to shower and change my
fucking boxers," I grumbled out and avoided her
gaze. I didn't wait another moment to see her
reaction. Instead, I opened my locker behind her,
grabbed a fistful of clean clothes, and headed off to
the shower room.

13

CATCH

BRETT YOUNG

I wasn't going to be able to tolerate *not* jumping Jamie's bones. Especially when he left himself wide open at home plate. In the Sillys' locker room of all places. I was pretty damn sure that I actually made him cum in his pants. Just with our *first* kiss. That fact had my ego inflated as big as a balloon in the Macy's Thanksgiving Day Parade. And that smug bitch was in no mood to deflate in this lifetime.

It was as if every fantasy of mine came true in that one heated moment. Despite our attitudes towards each other, that kiss was flaming hot. It was going to take *days* to air out my downtown.

There was something in that kiss. A flicker of something deeper, something that was ready to consume my very soul. The feeling scared me to no end. I couldn't. We couldn't.

He's a major league *player*. Which meant he was completely out of my league. No matter what sort of COCK-filled rule system he had, he could have been blowing smoke up my ass. Because there was no way the man of my fantasies had kissed me senseless, ejaculated in his pants, then asked me out to dinner.

After all that heart-pounding excitement in the locker room, I found myself staring at him in utter disbelief across a restaurant table. Jamie seemed more at ease. Did that kiss change something? Did it mess everything up? I was so sure that the man loathed me. Especially after that disastrous one-on-one practice today.

"Something on your mind?" Jamie's voice pulled me from my tumble of thoughts as I mindlessly swirled my straw in my diet soda.

"I'm not sure which one to address first. You left me with a lot of shit to process."

"If it's about what happened in the locker room, I'm–" I cringed. Because of course he was sorry. Shit like that was always a mistake.

"Actually, if we could pretend that didn't happen and just get on with our lives, that would be super."

"But Cady–"

"Just…drop it, okay?" He looked defeated as he went quiet and put his beer bottle to his lips for a sip. The moment we talked about it meant that this blissful thing that happened between us in the locker room would be over. I didn't want to hear the words come out of my crush's mouth. That it had all been a big mistake.

I imagined this sort of scenario so many times but on much happier terms. What would it be like during the in-between times with one's crush? In between all the dirty, hot, delicious fantasy sex. What would the dinners out be like? The walks home? Just driving around in a car together? But now that I was kind of sort of experiencing it, I didn't know what to do with it. Especially when I felt so wishy-washy about what Jamie *really* thought of me. The man had been full of mixed signals since the moment I met him.

That kiss had me feeling things that maybe, just maybe there was *something* there. The way the heat slithered its way from his lips to mine and fed through the tributaries of my limbs was something I hadn't felt before. Maybe it was the surprise of the kiss or maybe I just needed to kiss him again to see if that sort of feeling was going to be an *every time* thing.

This was all a stark contrast to his usual self. He'd been stone-cold and stand-offish to me every moment on the field. The dance lessons and choreography only hardened his steely reserve. Except for last night at the bar. I mean, I get it. I wouldn't be happy if I got demoted from being in the majors to a team that danced every inning either.

So, what changed?

The server hesitantly stepped up to our table. Even she could sense the tension between us. And it wasn't the mouth-watering sexual tension from earlier. Maybe it was better that we hadn't gone further than kissing. I couldn't even imagine what the tension would be like now if we actually had sex.

All of this reality was hampering my fantasy.

"Cady, I really think we should talk about what happened." I felt my stomach flip and then promptly drop like a lead stone. I didn't want to talk. Because if we talked it was a risk of this delightful fantasy bubble being popped by the ugly bitch called reality.

"Maybe after we eat something?" Anything to stall. The last thing I needed right now was to hear that my crush just wanted to get that out of his system and move on. I prayed that the server put our order in with post haste.

"Fair enough." There was a blissful bit of quiet as I took in the ambiance. But Jamie's follow-up shattered the singular moment of peace. "But I do want to talk about it. Especially since I still have to get you home."

Shit.

Right. We came here together. I must have blacked out, lost in thought over our kiss still. He had to drive me back to the stadium to get my car. Great, let's just keep prolonging the awkwardness for all of eternity at this point. Because why not, universe?

"Fine. We can talk. Just…be gentle." I winced a bit, but Jamie's reaction wasn't at all I expected. There was a flash of surprise before it turned right back into that goddamn mouth-watering smolder.

"I'm always gentle."

Dinner was such a fucking bad idea.

Thankfully the bar was rather quiet, so the food arrived swiftly. I just wanted to eat as quickly as possible and get the fuck out of dodge. Not wanting another awkward thing to come out of my mouth, I dove into my wrap sandwich.

"I know I didn't exactly go about this the smart way." Jamie started sheepishly. "Do you think…we can restart?" Jamie's question came out of left field, but I was thankful for the abrupt change of subject.

The man sat there, watching me, as I stuffed a rather large bit of sandwich into my mouth. So much for not being awkward. I noted the subtle bob of his Adam's apple as I adjusted my jaw to a more ladylike bite.

"Uh…sure." Using my napkin, I mumbled around my full mouth. Jamie visibly relaxed and shot his hand out across the table.

"Hi, I'm Jamie." My eyes darted from his hand to his eyes. Oh, he was serious about starting over. Like, over over.

I took a moment to swallow my food before slipping my hand into his. That jolt of electricity was still there. Perhaps, it was even stronger than the last time. His touch lingered for a moment before he turned to address his plate of food.

"You work for the Philly Sillys baseball team, huh? How long have you been with the organization?"

"Since the beginning," It was then I began to relax too. He was right, we needed this. A fresh start. "I never thought I could combine my history of dance and my love of baseball, and well… Oddly enough it worked out."

"I'll say." Jamie chuckled as he took a large mouthful of his sandwich. My eyes stayed on him; my food forgotten. He was so pretty to look at in this casual state. But I sure did love the man when he was in his uniform in his natural habitat too. "You're good at what you do, Cady." I felt the heat rise to my cheeks. The conversation needed a redirect before I melted into a puddle in the wooden chair.

"So, a professional baseball player? Did you always want to play baseball?"

"Yes and no, I guess. I played both football and baseball in high school and college." He took a moment to wipe the side of his mouth, drawing my eyes back to it. "I was majoring in business, but then there were whispers of the possibility of me being drafted. I graduated with a third-round MLB draft pick. I figured if baseball didn't work out, I at least had a backup plan." Sitting back in his chair, he chuckled with that signature sinful grin of his that he let slip when he made a great play behind the plate. "And well, that was like ten years ago now. But…I can't play baseball forever."

"Yeah well, I don't exactly think you'll have to worry about getting a part-time job when you retire. Especially with your contract." *Shit.* That was too much. It was easily accessible public knowledge, but it still meant that I kind of maybe online stalked him. Just a little. Completely innocently of course.

Jamie's brows shot up his forehead. "So, you've heard about me?"

"Well, I…uh, kind of…have to research all the guys that join the team." *Smooth, Cadence. Real smooth.* "I need to have some sort of uh, understanding of their background. A few of the guys are retired MLB players. Most played college ball. Some play as a hobby with some wicked ass bat or ball tricks." I couldn't help but let out a crazed laugh. "Sometimes I feel like I'm some sort of elementary school teacher trying to get the dirt on new students. Ninety-eight percent of them have no dance experience."

"Including me."

"*Especially* you. Honestly, you're the worst of the bunch." My laugh was much more genuine that time. It wasn't fair. He had this air about him that made me relax. That is when I wasn't thinking about how hot he was.

"I didn't exactly expect to have to dance to play baseball," Jamie said flatly. I let out a hearty sigh and plopped my fry back on my plate.

"Look, I get it. But would you want to be on the bench, or worse, at home watching the games from afar? Or would you rather be on the ballfield seeing some action but at a level that's much more suitable for where you're at right now?"

Jamie froze, staring me down but said nothing more.

Oh no.

I broke him. He sat in stunned silence as he blinked at me.

"No, you're right." A heavy sigh escaped him as he sat back in his seat. "I've been in denial since I got here. Even ownership said the same thing as you. It wasn't really until a few days ago that I finally came to terms with the truth."

My heart did a flip flop to hear him admit what I knew I saw that night at the bar. Something had finally gotten through that thick skull of his. But he wasn't giving himself enough credit now. He made huge strides. I finally felt confident that he was going to do just fine tomorrow.

The conversation had turned serious again and I needed to lighten the mood. This lighthearted chemistry between us was addictive and I wanted to keep it up. To keep his mind in a positive mindset. I leaned forward and cupped my palm behind my ear just to sass him.

"I'm sorry, can you say that again? Because I'm pretty sure that you said, *'I was right'*."

It was only a tease. A smile quirked at the corner of his mouth. He tried to hide it by looking away from me. His arms crossed his chest as he shifted in his seat. I felt my body flush with awareness.

"You're lucky you heard it the first time, Cady. Just take the win." He shot me a look as he grabbed the beer bottle and tipped it back up to his mouth. It did nothing to distract me from his smile.

Shit, were we…*flirting*?

I couldn't help my own smile as we finished up the last few bites of our dinner. So, it wasn't entirely awful being alone with him. There was only a hint of his grumpy self, even then it dissipated quickly. And maybe, just maybe, he was fun to talk to. Outside of the pressures of work, that is.

"Do you want another drink?"

"No, I'm good. I think I'm ready to head home. I've had…*quite enough* excitement for one day." My pulse suddenly started racing as if I'd shot back three espressos at once.

Jamie offered a nod in agreement as he gestured to the server for the check. I reached for my purse and pulled out my wallet, but he tutted me.

"No, I've got this. I invited you out."

"Pfft, barely. But really, I–"

"Truly, Cady. Let me treat you." His stern tone was back as he took the bill. Out of the corner of my eyes I saw his gaze flit back over to me as a little smirk quirked at the corner of his mouth.

"Fine." I sighed with a roll of my eyes. Dammit, why did saying he wanted to "treat me" turn my insides into goo? "But I'm paying the tip." I didn't wait for any sort of acknowledgment as I pulled out enough cash to cover my half of the bill. If he wasn't going to take my perfectly good money, then the server could have it.

Jamie didn't offer any protest as he finished with the check and downed the last bit of his beer. He only had one that he nursed the entire time we were at the restaurant, along with a glass of water. But you could never be too safe. My playfulness was begging to be let off the leash again.

"You alright to drive, Slugger? Or do you need a designated driver?"

"Why, do you want to give me a sobriety test?" He rose from his seat with a smirk under his ball cap, turning it around on his head. *Oh fuck, not the backward hat move.* My heart began to palpitate.

Pocketing his wallet, he turned around to walk *backward* out of the restaurant, easily avoiding each and every table and chair that was potentially in his way. For good measure, he threw in alternating arms to tap the tip of his nose with the tip of his pointer finger. For fucks sake, why was this banter so damn easy?

"Alright, fine," I said with a staged huff of annoyance over the fact that he had to show me up. "Showoff."

"Do you want me to drop you off at your place or…?"

"Nah, the ballpark is fine," I answered quickly. My voice cracked and I cringed inwardly. "I'll just take my car home."

"Well, if you don't want to make the extra stop tonight, since it's late, I can pick you up and take you to work tomorrow. I don't mind."

This major player was being a *major* gentleman.

But that meant he'd be at my apartment and damn if I wasn't already tempted to invite him up. Between our dinner banter, and let's not forget about *that kiss*, it left me feeling all out of sorts about Jamie.

We both climbed into his pickup truck and closed the heavy doors. I hoped the comfortable quiet between us would continue as he drove me back to the stadium. Maybe with the distraction of dinner, he'd forgotten all about what sultry happenings had occurred in the locker room. That maybe, just maybe, I had managed to divert that line of questioning from ever happening.

"There's no ears or eyes around." Jamie glanced at me as he went to turn on the car. "Do you think we can finally talk about…you know?"

I guess he didn't forget.

Dammit.

The damn man couldn't even wait until we got on the road. Then at least I could be distracted by the racing trees as they blurred through the darkness outside my window. Not struggling to breathe in this insufferable atmosphere inside the crew cab of his pickup truck.

"I don't think there's much to talk about now, is there?"

"I think there's a *whole hell of a lot* to talk about."

"Look, I already know what you're going to say. You're gonna tell me that the kiss was a stupid mistake that you made in the heat of the moment–"

Jamie's hands hit the steering wheel, causing his truck to let out a strangled honk. The man was suddenly red with frustration, much like in the early days when I had to teach him a new dance move. The man was rather intimidating, especially in closed spaces. But he stayed clear on his side of the truck.

"Dammit, Cadence!" I froze. "Will you just listen to me for once?" I'd never heard the man this much at his wit's end. And I tried to teach him a fucking step ball change with disastrous results.

"But I–" Nothing, and I mean nothing prepared me for what fell out his mouth next.

"You're the damn reason I keep coming *back*. It took me forever to realize it. I want to play baseball but instead, I show up at a stadium that I loathed being assigned to, just to see what color your matching workout clothes are, to see the smallest hint of a smile from you." There was a pause before his voice and furrowed brow softened. "You're the highlight of my work day. I'm trying all these stupid ass fucking dance moves because they make *you* happy. And trust me, I've been at odds with myself over the stupid fluttering in my chest every time I see that smile on your beautiful face."

I–

I just…

What in the ever-loving fuck.

My heartbeat was so loud that it was the only thing I could hear, even with my panting breaths. The words tumbled out of him with such overwhelming force that I was having trouble getting my brain to focus on any of it. Did he say he liked my smile? That…that I was *beautiful*…?

"For fucks sake, please say something." Jamie breathed out his plea as he stared at his white-knuckle grip on the steering wheel. That was a hell of an information overload. I was having a difficult time processing it all. Let alone try to find words to coherently answer him back.

Was it worth throwing my mess of feelings into all of this? What if all this was just a fleeting thing for him? How the hell could I tell him that my heart and body *ached* for him? That each and every day I had to see him made me hurt from the inside out because he acted so cold towards me. And despite all of that…

I still couldn't get him out of my mind.

"The reason…" *Fuck this was going to be difficult.* I sighed heavily in a vain attempt to pull my shit together as I ran a hand down my face. "The reason I've been weird around you is, well… For the last few years, I've had like a…*gigantic* crush on you. I didn't know how to handle it when you joined the Sillys. I tried everything in my power to be professional, but in the end, I've just been a pathetically awkward, grouchy mess."

All I could do was sit there and cringe over the fact that my deeply seated secret was out in the open. A confession to the man himself, no less.

"You've had a crush on me…?" Jamie stared at his hands as he murmured to himself in disbelief. "It all makes so much more sense now."

"I-I'm sorry. I was such an insufferable asshole to you. I didn't exactly do it on purpose. It was more like…a *weird protective reflex.*" The silence dragged on along with the uncomfortable air in the cab of his truck. The word vomit was coming as I was unable to calm down. "I just couldn't get the thoughts of kissing you or taking you to bed–"

"Oh…" *Oh no. I fucked it up I knew–* "It wasn't just me then." Jamie's voice dropped down to a husky whisper of relief as he slowly turned in his seat to drink me in. The pure, intense fire in his eyes made me press my thighs together.

Jamie lunged across the front seat. He reached out, grabbed ahold of the back of my neck, and brought my mouth to his. We collided in a shower of sparks. Letting out a noise of relief, I melted into his leather seats. At that moment I knew one thing for sure.

Our earlier kiss against the lockers was *no* fluke.

How could this be real life? I was passionately kissing my grown-up crush, in the front seat of his truck, and it was the greatest fucking thing on the motherfucking planet. The only thing I could concentrate on was how Jamie's lips made my body feel like a stadium full of fans cheering for their team after a comeback win. My common sense was knocking at the back door of my consciousness, but I ignored it. That was a problem for tomorrow's Cadence. Today's Cadence didn't give a flying fuck.

Because today's Cadence wanted to *get fucked*.

In the *good way* this time.

"Dammit, I want you, Cadence." He mumbled against my mouth before diving back in for another taste. "This conversation only cemented that fact." Goddamn if my body didn't have its third flashover for the day. That was a new record for an actual man. Fictional men excluded. Although Jamie was on his way to dethrone them all.

"Well…let's round the bases, Slugger." Jamie stopped his kisses for only a fraction of a second before he burst into laughter. Of course. I had to go and fuck up the searing hot moment with one of my poorly timed, sexually suggestive baseball puns. Why couldn't I just be normal? Why did I have to be so unbelievably cringy and awkward?

A deliciously wicked grin curled his lips.

"Game on."

I think my panties *actually* spontaneously combusted.

Cadence **14**

ELECTRIC TOUCH

TAYLOR SWIFT

"**Y**our place or mine?"

I blinked at Jamie as if he was speaking another language. Did he really just ask that question? Did I black out after dinner? Was I dreaming?

"Shit." His exclamation made me blink again and pulled me from my thoughts. Oh no, was he going back on his invitation? "I'm being presumptuous again."

"Jamie, if you don't have sex with me tonight, after all of this mind-boggling teasing, I will absolutely explode." The words fell out of my mouth in one tumultuous breath. It was now his turn to gape at me for a moment before a slow grin curled the edges of his mouth.

"*Fuck, that's hot.*" He muttered to himself as he started up his truck. Clearing his throat, he fully addressed me. "Does your place work? I'm good with whatever." He cringed as he put his truck into drive. "I told you I'm no good at this, okay? Fuck. I don't even know where I'm going."

His sudden and overwhelming juvenile-like fluster made me erupt into a giggle. Jamie's blue eyes glanced in my direction quickly before his shoulders

146

bounced with his awkward mirth. The sexual tension was still palatable in the air, but the laughter cleared a bit of the humidity that was certainly stemming solely from my thighs.

"Go straight. Take the next left. Then right at the light." I offered in between my chuckles. It was such a wonder to see him much more relaxed. The man had the ability to be goofy and fun. He took the whole Sillys dancing thing too seriously. Which was the one thing you couldn't do in the ELB. The point of it was to just play and have fun. The crowds fed off that. Hell, they were feral for it.

I offered up the final few directions which left a few miles ahead of us with no turns. My breathing was shallow, excited for what was to come. In the bedroom would he be as timid and shy as he was outside of his icy demeanor? Or would he be firm and intense as he was behind home plate in the majors? Or perhaps…a bit of *both*?

Jamie's strong hand found my thigh. A wildfire wreaked havoc throughout my body from the simple touch. I chanced a glance at him only to find his heated gaze reflecting mine. A car's horn sounded. Jamie cursed under his breath, turning his eyes back to the road. But his hand lingered. I focused solely on the feel of it against my thigh. Anything to keep me grounded to this moment instead of floating away.

His big truck found its way into a visitor's spot at my apartment complex. His hand only moved from my thigh to put the vehicle into park. My hands gripped my purse to stop them from shaking. I was so distracted with getting my breathing under control that I was oblivious to Jamie jumping out of his truck to race around to open my passenger side door.

He reached a hand up to help me down from his lifted truck. There was an ulterior motive for his chivalrous move. As soon as the door slammed shut behind me, he pressed my body against the panel of the crew cab. There was no time to even suck in a breath of surprise before his mouth was breathing new life into mine.

There was no denying the searing heat between us this time. My arms tangled around his neck as his hands gripped ahold of my sides and assumed a position very much like the one in the locker room. Only without my legs hooked around his waist. The next time I attempted that feat, there wasn't going to be a lick of clothing between us.

We needed to get inside, stat. It was late enough that there probably wouldn't be questioning eyes. But I didn't exactly want to be the scandal on the front page of the sports tabloids. If that even existed.

"You were saying something about being horizontal earlier…?" I managed to gasp out as his mouth worked its way down my neck. My pulse was a riot of rhythm beneath his lips. Jamie swore hotly under his breath.

"I got distracted. Stop being so goddamn tempting." Pulling away, he grasped onto my hand. "Please don't tell me it's a far walk. I'm this close to throwing you over my shoulder and making a run for it."

My brow cocked at him as my cheeks flushed with heat. For some reason, I couldn't get it through my head that the man was desperate to have me. *Me.* Out of all the billions of people on this planet, the guy I had a crush on actually, maybe, felt the same way.

I put a pin in the being "thrown over the shoulder" thing for later. My other boyfriends had been scrawny. They could barely give me a piggyback ride without exerting a lot of effort. Jamie could throw me over his shoulder without breaking a sweat.

Pulling on his hand, I led him in the direction of my building. It was only about fifty or so feet away from my parking space and up a flight of stairs. It wasn't far. But when your arms were full of groceries or you were leading the man that you hoped would fuck your brains out, it was like walking across the Tunisian desert in the dead of summer.

It was an arduous walk, awkward almost. But since that was the overall theme of the evening, it was rather fitting. I wanted to get behind closed doors as soon as possible. Because I wasn't sure either of us could stand starting up something just to stop it. Again.

Unlocking the door to my apartment, I tossed my bag and keys to the slim entry table I used as a drop zone. Neither of us waited long enough to see if they hit the table. As soon as the door latched shut, Jamie had me pressed against the wall for yet another searing kiss.

For some mind-blowing reason, the kisses had only gotten hotter. Maybe it was because all of the uneasy pretenses were out of our system since we'd come clean to each other. Or maybe it was because we were finally and officially in *complete* privacy.

Pulling his signature move yet again, Jamie shoved my body up the wall to cup his hands under my ass before coaxing my legs to hook around his waist. He couldn't help but cop an appreciative feel of my body as he did so. I needed to be dragged to my bedroom and stripped. *Immediately.*

"Bedroom?" It was as if Jamie could read my mind.

"Second door on the right." I managed to mumble against his lips mid-kiss.

Adjusting his hold on me, he pulled us away from the wall. Blindly gaining his footing, he juggled me in his arms as he set foot in the right direction. Despite his earlier sobriety check, maneuvering an arm-full of me made him clumsy.

He took out my thigh with the corner of the entry table before jamming my side into the awkward bar top that stuck out from the half wall in my kitchen. I swore under my breath from the jarring pain but cracked up in laughter. We ended up knocking my one living room chair askew before he finally managed his way into my bedroom with both of us in a fit of laughter. It was amazing to hear him laugh so freely.

"Maybe you aren't as sober as you thought." I snickered, jabbing at him playfully for his earlier exploits of maneuvering around blindly.

"It's a lot harder to walk when you have someone hanging onto you like a spider monkey." Jamie groaned against my bottom lip. His hands adjusted their hold on my hips so he could press his hard bulge right into the junction of my thighs. I couldn't help the visceral moan out of my mouth as he did so.

"Please tell me you're not going to quote *Twilight* now."

I gave him a wicked grin as he tossed me onto the bed with a soft bounce. Jamie huffed out a perturbed laugh as he whipped off his ball cap and shirt in one go. Seeing him shirtless in front of me was as if someone turned my AC unit to the temperature of the fires of hell. The sheer vision of him topless made me woozy.

The sculpted V of his hip bones was like a neon sign pointing straight to the hard lump in his dark wash jeans. I had to move my tongue around the inside of my mouth to stop myself from drooling out of the corner of it. He was only half naked but what a fucking goddamn *vision.*

His piercing blue eyes undressed me as if he was slowly going over every possible outcome of how this night would progress. If it didn't end in at least two sessions and a few Os, I was going to be completely ruined by this whole fantasy I already had in my head. The man looked like he enjoyed a challenge.

Kicking my shoes off, I managed to prop myself up on my elbows for a better view before Jamie dove in to meet me. Despite the intensity in his eyes, his hand gently reached out to my face. A tender caress traced along the apple of my cheek. He cupped my jaw and tangled the tips of his fingers in the loose hair behind my ear. His mouth followed only seconds later, capturing my lips in a soul-possessing kiss.

Fuck it. My soul was his.

The man could certifiably pop the seams on a baseball, yet he touched me as if I were a priceless artifact. His touch started out so timid but grew more confident as he eased himself back into this seduction tango that we were both out of practice in. It was almost like getting on a bicycle again after so many years.

My hands shot out, hungry to devour him from my touch alone. He was outstandingly hard, in every sense of the word. There was an approving rumble deep in his chest under my fingertips.

Nudging off his shoes, he crawled up onto the bed as he continued to kiss me. That's when I heard the jingle of his belt. I wished disintegrating clothing was a thing. Although from the sheer flashover my body had, I was surprised they hadn't melted off my hot skin already.

Fumbling with the hem of my t-shirt, his hands drifted down to assist. The force with which he tugged off my shirt almost gave me fabric burns on the tip of my nose. But the quick release of air from the man seeing me topless for the first time, made me forget the minor pain that lingered.

Cupping my breast with his hand, he pressed the orb up and almost out of my bra. My head fell back to the mattress with a gasp. I lost my train of thought for a moment.

Typically, by this point, I was uncomfortably self-conscious about what my partner was thinking about me. But not with Jamie. He seemingly couldn't hold back his unquenchable desire for me. It was literally my sexual fantasies brought to life. That helped me lose myself in the moment for once in my life.

On one side I wanted to strip down immediately and ride the man until tomorrow's sunrise. But on the other hand, I wanted to take this at a snail's pace and absorb every damn millisecond. Commit it to my core memories. So, if this wild night was only a one-off, I could get off to it until the day my vagina dried out.

Which, at this rate, wasn't going to be for another millennium.

"Jeezus, fuck, Cadence." Jamie breathed against my neck as he dipped in for a taste. Not one part of him was timid anymore. He was a breath away from sinking his canines into me, sucking me dry as he sampled the skin along my throat. "Can you stop being irresistible for like five seconds? I'm about to bust another one."

Especially if he kept saying shit like that.

"Like earlier?" I mumbled out stupidly. How the hell was I capable of making my crush jizz his pants just by our hot-as-fuck make out session? I felt him wince.

"I was really hoping you didn't notice. I promise I can last longer than a few seconds." His other hand joined in to massage and mold my breasts. Jamie groaned as he stole a few kisses along the edge of my bra. "Although at this rate, it's going to be impossible with you. You've been driving me crazy from day one."

He gasped against the damp skin of my throat as his hands went on a possessive rampage up and down my curves. My brain flatlined with that admission. "At first, I thought it was just a pissed-off crazy. Turns out…" His mouth recaptured mine. This was the most spark I'd seen in his eyes since before his surgery. "I really just needed to fucking kiss you. Because damn… Kissing you feels like the whole world makes sense now."

My arms tangled around his neck, pulling him firmly against me. His body felt like the sun, and I wanted nothing more than to burst into flames because of him. With me being this all out of sorts and flustered, there was no help for what spewed from my mouth.

"Do you have any idea how many times I've fantasized about you? In this very bed?" I gasped out in between kisses. The words left me without going through the proper filter channels. This was the only time my word vomit had been acceptable. We were sharing inner secrets and all. Jamie suddenly stopped moving and let out a groan of utter frustration.

"You do remember I'm trying *really* fucking hard not to cum as it is, right?" Who would have thought that I'd have to get the gruff man into bed for him to open up and have a conversation with? Although classifying it as a conversation was a stretch.

"I should say I'm sorry…but I'm really not." After that warning, I was almost afraid to touch him. But I needed to see what was under the rest of his clothes. Although if I didn't give him a breather, it would be a damn shame to have another orgasm go to waste in his pants.

"Oh, I'm not either. This should be fun for both of us." Jamie shot me a rakish grin as he fumbled with my bra clasp. "Hopefully I don't disappoint. It's…been a while." He sheepishly admitted.

"How long is 'a while'…?" I cocked a brow as his fingers paused. There was a long moment before he answered.

"Five years."

I coughed on my inhale. "Five years?!" And I thought I was in a dry spell.

"Look, I told you, I don't like to sleep with a woman unless I see long-term potential with her."

Thank fuck he distracted me by finally unfastening my bra. I barely had time to dwell on his admission. I let out a sigh as the fabric gave way.

Jamie let out a low breath as he drank me in before he dove in for a taste. His mouth on my nipple was a straight lightning bolt to my vagina. My hips shot off the bed and right into his. It drew a hearty moan out of both of us. There was no going back now. Especially not when he admitted that this, all of this, with me, could be something like forev–

Don't get carried away now, Cadence. One fluster fuck at a time here.

Right.

I couldn't ponder the seriousness of this entire situation because I was fairly certain I'd start awkwardly screaming with a mixture of shock and excitement. Jamie was being so suave and delicious, albeit a bit shy. Meanwhile, I was trying to keep my collective shit under control and not fangirl all over myself.

As a distraction, my hands slipped down between us, more determined than ever to reveal more of his fabulous body. I'd watch him squat or lunge behind home plate, flexing his thighs as his uniform stretched over the muscle. Even when he was at bat, there was a twist on the follow-through that made his biceps and thighs bulge in the most drool-worthy way. Now I finally had a chance to see, *and feel it*, firsthand.

Jamie helped himself to a second helping of my breasts as my fingers opened his fly. Despite their trembling, I eased the denim over the curve of his ass before I double fisted a handful of cheeks. I knew it was unusual, but I was definitely an ass girl. A plump ass on a man was seriously top-notch.

A breathy chuckle against my nipple caused it to harden as my breath hitched. Okay, so I may have been a bit overly enthusiastic about massaging his glutes. But damn, I was ready to ask for copper molds of them as bookends for my bookshelf.

Shifting above me, Jamie's mouth returned to mine. This time the kiss was longer, deeper. All-encompassing.

Deep within the kiss, his hands shifted to shimmy out of his jeans. Kicking them aside, all that remained were skin-tight boxer briefs that left little to the imagination. Especially when he was sporting one hell of a mouth-watering hard-on.

Once he disposed of his pants, he came for mine. I clumsily attempted to assist in his endeavor. Which only resulted in both of us erupting in laughter due to the stubbornness of my skinny jeans. Suddenly I felt both completely exposed and yet stubbornly clothed.

It was a breathless few minutes, but once we were down to our final piece of clothing, there was a noticeable slowdown. Jamie eased himself down into the slot my body heartily made for him. Now skin-to-skin, curve-to-curve this suddenly became a lot more intimate.

He only added to it as he tenderly brushed a wayward strand of hair off my cheek and behind my ear. The endless pools in his eyes coaxed me into their wicked depths as we both caught our breath.

"I can't believe I finally get to know what you feel like." The whispered words left my mouth before I could stop them. My body tensed with my uninhibited admission and what Jamie thought about it.

"So many nights I've laid awake wondering what these treacherous curves would be like to grab ahold of."

Jamie's response made my breath catch. It was paired with a long, admiring sweep of his heated gaze up my body as his hand moved south to toy with the waistband of my panties. Dipping his fingertips under the elastic, he eased the last piece of clothing down my legs. I swallowed dryly.

My hands moved to cup his sculpted jaw. I could feel the sandpaper scruff that had grown back from his morning shave. He was real. His body was warm and solid under my touch. This time, he wasn't a ghost of a fantasy when I closed my eyes.

I needed to enjoy the awe of it because there was a chance all of this could disappear tomorrow.

Jamie's hand cupped over my heat, relishing in the aura of it. Curling his pointer and middle into position, his thumb moved to gently caress against my clit. That was just the distraction he needed before two of his fingers eased their way inside me. The man let out the sexiest fucking growly groan in the history of ever. As my brain short-circuited, I was simultaneously trying to comprehend the fact that, the man I had a crush on for the past few years, was now knuckle-deep inside my soaking-wet vagina.

With a sharp inhale, Jamie dove in for another kiss. He was seemingly fit to consume every millimeter of me. My moans were just the appetizer. I could feel his hard cock as he rocked his hips against my thigh in time with each thrust of his fingers. He was turned on by how much I was turned on.

Holy fuck I needed him inside me.

"Jamie…" Goosebumps exploded across my skin as I mumbled his name against his lips. He pulled away with a smoldering gaze but continued to work magic with his fingers. It took all of my willpower not to crumble at that exact moment.

"Shh…" The hush set off sparks down my spine. "Give me at least one, Cady. I need to see what you look like when I send you over that wall in the outfield." It was a hell of a time for a baseball reference. But what a metaphor. "I need to see your face, hear your sounds. I want to have the feeling of your body around mine so fucking ingrained in my brain that I think of nothing else."

The only answer I could muster was a tangle of my fingers in his hair before pulling him down into a hard kiss. His fingers and thumb worked me into such a fevered frenzy in the blink of an eye. I could hear the squelch of my desire as his fingers thrust into it.

I couldn't decipher where his grunts of pleasure met with my moans of delight. It was a hypnotic symphony of our shared sensuality. Those strong digits, that worked the innards of his catching glove, had no trouble flexing inside me to bring me to a fucking *spectacular* climax.

With just his fingers.

This time I didn't keep quiet. I didn't whisper his name in fear that the fantasy would disappear behind my eyelids. His name shot from my mouth and reverberated off my bedroom walls. A rhythmic chant of whimpers of moans of my favorite two syllables. Just hearing it leave my lips, and knowing that Jamie, and not my usual silicone toy, was the reason my body was in utter ecstasy, made my orgasm all the more stronger.

Jamie was panting almost as heavily as I was as I finally fell back to earth and back into his arms. There was a light sheen of perspiration along his forehead. He had to be doing everything in his power not to lose it.

"Fucking worth it." He huffed out as he leaned down and kissed me. "Every damn second. I can die a happy man now after hearing you scream my name like that as I finger fucked you to orgasm."

Jeezus.

Not only was I in bed with the man who'd been the star of my fantasies for the last few years, but he also had a filthy mouth and just made the most epic confession I'd ever heard in my entire life. My hands shot down between us. I needed him naked. I needed him balls-deep inside me.

The bonus would be if he ended up screaming *my* name. Because holy fuck, I was going to do everything in my power to make that happen.

A heated groan grazed the skin of my throat as he tucked his head in the crook of my neck to brace himself. From the feel of him through the fabric, he was deliciously girthy and ironically close in scale to my suction cup dildo that hid in my bedside drawer.

The man seemed like he was ready to blow his load at any moment. I needed to go about this delicately before we had to stop for an interlude. This might be my only chance to sleep with the man of my dreams. I wanted to make it count.

Careful to ease off the throttle just a bit, I grazed my fingertips along the straining outline of his cock through his boxer briefs. My other hand reached out to ease his boxers down over the obstacle in question. It was no easy feat, but I managed to do so without teasing the man any more than I needed to.

A sharp hiss whistled through his clenched teeth as the cool air of my bedroom hit his bare skin. I was so tempted to dip my gaze down to look at him, but I stopped myself. I wanted to see him completely naked before I took in that vision. Thankfully he assisted me in divulging his body from his last piece of clothing and chucked it into the dark void of the room.

Jamie adjusted himself back to his previous position to cage me beneath his toned body. It was then that my eyes fluttered open and dipped down to enjoy the view. But little did I know that he was doing the same thing to me.

"Fuck it, Cadence. I need you. I can't wait another damn second to be inside you." Jamie gasped out before he claimed my mouth for yet another soul-sucking kiss. It was a bunch of flusters all at once. My eyes were still open in shock as he made me melt into the bed from the touch of his lips alone. "Condoms?"

"B-Bedside drawer…" I managed to get out as the jumble of cartoony hearts invaded my vision. Reaching over, I had a front-row seat to the flex of his bicep as his arm stretched out to open the drawer.

With him considerably distracted for the time being, my eyes slid further down his stretched body to drink him in. I let out a slow breath as my gaze caressed down the hills and valleys of muscles along his torso. All before my eyes stopped on his glorious dick that was only inches away from the skin of my inner thigh. I couldn't help myself.

"Oh my god."

"I…take that as a good thing…?" It wasn't until Jamie's response that I realized I had said the words out loud instead of under my breath as I originally thought.

"I…uh…" *Fuck it, too late now.* "Holy fuck, you're gorgeous." Although my words may have been misconstrued as I was staring directly at his fully erect and glorious cock instead of his face.

The empty condom wrapper fluttered through my line of vision, pulling me from my stare. Easing himself back on his knees, Jamie sat up and gave me the most utterly beautiful sight. He was in the exact position that he typically was in behind home plate. Only in all his naked glory, straddling my bare thighs with both of us in *my* bed.

I could never watch another game without imagining him like this. All sinew and strength as he commanded over me. Which was only made hotter as I watched him roll the condom down his dick. There was a breathless smile on his lips.

As if of its own accord, my hand shot down between my legs to graze along my clit. With the nude visual of Jamie Rheems kneeling above you, what woman wouldn't want to get herself off to it? The move resulted in a desperately hungry groan from Jamie as he fell onto all fours above me.

His hand grabbed my jaw, pinning me right where he wanted me while the other dismissed my hand from its duty to take over himself. I couldn't help my needy whimper as his fingers dipped back into my slick heat. The rest of the noises he swallowed up as he reclaimed my mouth.

"There's nothing hotter than a woman who can't help but touch herself."

"It's all your fault." I gasped out in between kisses. The only response I got at first was a rough exhale as he used the coating of my desire on his fingers to lubricate the condom. The fact that he was now stroking himself to the same extent did not escape me.

"So, you've said." I would have said some smart-ass remark in reply, but I couldn't exactly fault him for being correct. Or be mad at a man for actually listening to me for that matter. "And fuck if it's not my favorite thing I've ever heard."

There was a bit of a commanding husk to his voice as he nipped at my jawline. My hands couldn't stop moving across his body. I needed to memorize it all.

With a subtle shift, his hips dropped down. A delicious, heated shiver moved from the tips of my toes to my scalp. The head of his cock brushed against my inner thigh as my legs adjusted to accommodate him. I needed him deep inside me more than anything I'd ever wanted in my entire life. I wanted to feel what it was like being intimate with Jamie, just once. Because so far, he was already batting a thousand on the sexy hotness seduction scale.

The searing heat turned into a tender simmer as Jamie's mouth and hands moved to soft caresses as he adjusted his hips to line himself up. My hands slid up his body to cup his face. The pads of my thumbs brushed across the stubble on his cheeks. I needed to see this. I needed to feel all of it. To ground every part of myself to this moment.

Jamie's eyes caught mine. My heart skipped a beat which sent a cascade of goosebumps down my arms. The moment his gaze softened and he gave me a tender smile, it was all over.

Sealing our union with a kiss, he used the distraction to ease himself inside me. I was not at all prepared for the literal fireworks that exploded behind my eyelids. My bottom lip broke the seal as an unexpected, shaky whimper spilled forth.

With the broken connection of our mouths, Jamie let out a ragged breath. My eyes flashed open only to be met by his just-as-surprised steel-blue gaze. What in the fucking history of baseball was going on here?

"*Fuck...* You feel it too?" He gasped out hoarsely. I stared at him blankly for a second, unable to comprehend the fathomless question. What did I feel? Nothing? Everything? That the feeling was too overwhelming to even describe?

Yes.

"*Yes...*" I breathed out with a quick nod. For some reason, he didn't have to explain it further. I just knew. *He knew.*

A boyish smile brightened his face. The soft lines at the corners of his eyes creased as his cheeks rose. I admired his features close up before he cupped my face and kissed me so hard that my toes curled. He sucked the oxygen clear out of my lungs. All I could do was tangle my arms around his neck and hold on for dear life.

The thrusts began slowly. They were drawn out and I could feel every inch of him leave me before my body enveloped his entire length with hungry abandon. Rounding my back, my hips curled up to meet him as I threw my legs around him. Now his body was locked in against mine.

Of all those hours imagining what it would be like to sleep with Jamie Rheems, I was utterly unprepared for what it would *actually* be like.

Because I'd never had sex like this.

Like ever.

Our bodies rocked together as our heated breaths intermingled in the fraction of space between us. Hands were seemingly frantic, desperate for a touch or to hold onto a piece of the other before being thrown out into the nether regions of space. I wanted to feel him everywhere. For him to envelop me whole and keep me locked in the strength of his embrace.

Jamie kept me in the present moment with his frenzied caresses. A squeeze of my breast, a grip on the jut of my hips, hooking his hand under my knee, aiming it at an angle that had my eyes rolling back in my head. He never neglected me for a second. It was a heady way to keep my innermost thoughts in the moment, even when I was looking at the back of my skull.

But I wanted to watch him. I wanted to see every flicker of emotion that pulled at his face. The way his brow furrowed and relaxed. The way his skin sparkled from the exertion. The way his jaw set with the clenching of his teeth before his lips parted in a huff of air. He was so fucking beautiful.

There was something deeper here below the surface. If my brain wasn't in Jamie fantasy overload I might have sat and pondered over it. But about 98% of my brain cells were solely focused on the man atop of me and the electric connection our bodies had from where we met in the middle.

The man left me breathless between rich kisses. I kept up with his rhythm with the answering call of my hips. I wanted to go all night. I didn't care if I couldn't walk or even stand upright tomorrow. Because holy fuck it would be worth it.

Jamie was incredibly intense. He desired constant closeness. It was a bit surprising for how stand-offish of a personality he had. Most of the men I'd been with could barely kiss and thrust at the same time. Perhaps it was his skills on the ballfield that enabled his talents in the bedroom.

The thought of it made my cunt flex around his thrusting cock. Which only made him groan in a way that he sounded like he was close to the edge of restraint. From there it was just a continuous circle of our bodies responding to one another in silent conversation. His thrusts waxed and waned, desperate to make this last as long as possible.

With both hands on the jut of my hips, Jamie added a sharper uptick to his own as he held me still. My inhalation stopped dead in my esophagus as I felt that delicious gooey warmth bubble up deep in my belly. I was close. And the noise from him that followed made me aware that his body *knew* I was on the edge.

"I want nothing more than to feel you lose yourself, Cadence." Jamie huffed out, not easing back on the throttle at all. If anything, he went harder and deeper into me. "As many fucking times as possible."

Never in my entire life had a man asked for my orgasm or was so determined to get me to have *more* than one. Guys seemed to be winded after just getting one and then needed ample time for a round two.

Jamie had the endurance to go for the gold. Multiple times over.

My hands shot out to grip the corners of his jaw. Tangling my fingers into the strands of his mussed hair along the nape of his neck, I mentally prepared myself in the last few seconds before chaos erupted. He had me so tantalizingly close to the precipice, almost as if he enjoyed watching me struggle as I teetered on the edge.

With a heated grunt, Jamie angled his hips followed by an extra bit of speed that had me careening straight into the blissful abyss that was catcher Jamie Rheems. It felt like literal universes were colliding inside of me all at once. The sheer intensity made my body arch clear off the bed. I wouldn't be surprised if I pulled away with two fistfuls of his hair in the vice grip my fingers had in his locks.

A reiterated litany of his name escaped my mouth. It was soundless as I couldn't inhale from the orgasmic spasm that had a vice grip over my entire body. I could feel his nails digging into my skin as his hands raked up my body.

"Louder, Cady." Jamie gasped, breathless from his exertions but more determined than ever. "I want the whole fucking world to know what I'm doing to you." The man was holding onto his restraint by the thinnest thread. It was evident from the edge in his voice. He wanted to see me orgasm first.

Finally able to inhale properly, I let myself give in to his pleasure. Screams, moans, whatever expression I could give to release at least some of the explosion of feelings. Goosebumps erupted across my skin as I chanted his name over and over again as another orgasm quickly took me. Good god was this man bad at anything? Oh right. Dancing.

With an aggressive kiss, Jamie shifted his body slightly. As my eyes fluttered back open, I saw a rather delicious underside view of his flexing bicep as he white-knuckle gripped my headboard as his hips slapped against mine. Fucking hell, did I even dare ask what was in store for me next?

His free hand scooped under my bottom to roll my hips up, effectively pressing me in half. Adding to the new delicious angle, I hooked my ankles higher up his back His cock went deep, and I inhaled so sharply the air was cold down my esophagus.

The man gave an approving moan as his eyes fluttered closed on the threshold of delectable chaos. I did my best to watch the utter bliss soften his face and enhance his noises of delight as he raced to the end. That visual alone was going to fuel my solo sessions for the rest of eternity. Honestly probably clear into my next life.

"Cadence..." The grit in his voice had such a dream-like quality that it took me by surprise. It only lasted a fleeting moment as, yet another orgasm snuck up on me as Jamie found the beginnings of his release. "Fuck yes…give me one more. Take me with you." The words were a breathy plea. I couldn't deny the man. *"Please..."*

"Jamie..."

With one hard thrust, my arms and legs locked around him for dear life as we were both sent careening over the edge into the blissful beyond. A lengthy groaning moan punctuated by his continued thrusting dispelled my noises of enjoyment as Jamie exploded inside of me. If I thought the orgasms before this one were mind-blowing, it did nothing to prepare me for the utterly world-ending big bang that was a mutual climax between us.

A mutual quiet soon settled between us as our bodies eventually slowed to a stop. The only sound was our breaths as they slowly eased back to a normal rhythm. I was in bliss, floating in the expanse of the space-time continuum. Was this…real life…?

Whisper-soft kisses tickled my cheek pulled me back from wherever my brain had yeeted itself to. Heat rose to my cheeks as Jamie's gaze found mine. Never in a million years did I ever think I'd have this post-coitus visual of the most handsome man on the planet completely blitzed out of his mind after an orgasm *I* gave him.

"Wow."

The same exact word came out of both our mouths at the same time. We both only held it together for half a second we broke out in laughter. Well, I guess that settled that. At least it was a mutual feeling for…*whatever* this was.

Mid-laugh, Jamie snuck in a quick but heated kiss as he slipped out of me. My body let out a whimper against his mouth. I wasn't ready to be separated from the man, but condoms threw a wrench in the potential for sensual cuddles afterward.

Wait. Shit. Was Jamie even a cuddler? We went about this all backward.

My heart raced watching him pull away to deal with the condom. He was just as pretty from the back as he was from the front. A specimen like that should be admired from all angles.

Part of me was terrified that this was it. He got what he wanted and was now headed out. Anxiety rose like the bile in the back of my throat. *Cadence, calm the fuck down. You wanted this chance and didn't care about what happened afterward.*

Right.

However, what happened afterward was not even in the wheelhouse of what I expected. Jamie reappeared from my bathroom with a satisfied confident grin on his face. He dove back into my bed, stopping for a kiss before pulling me against him. Rolling us both over, I felt like a ragdoll in the crook of his arm as he tugged up the sheets. His bicep curled around me as I settled against him with my cheek on his collarbone.

My body was tense for a hot second as I tried to take it all in. Letting out a slow breath, I relaxed against him as his fingers lazily stroked up and down my arm. This was bliss. Utter bliss. As much as I didn't want to admit it, Jamie Rheems just made me fall even harder for him.

I DID SOMETHING BAD

TAYLOR SWIFT

I had to have been dreaming.

For fucking certain, I was dreaming.

Because this wasn't my actual real life that I currently existed in. That's all I could think about as I stared at professional baseball catcher Jamie Rheems, the biggest crush of my entire adult life, sipping coffee, in nothing but a towel wrapped around his waist, as he looked out my patio door into the early morning.

It was like every impossibly delicious wet dream I'd ever had about the man.

Except it wasn't a dream.

I leaned against the doorway of the kitchen, admiring how the lingering beads of water sparkled from the sun along his sculpted skin. The man was literally a god. A god in a baseball uniform. Er, well, my bathroom towel at the moment.

If only my 14-year-old self could see me now. I was ready to burn my cringe-filled teenage diaries of all the lame-ass shit I complained about with boys. I wanted to thank that naive young woman and give her a high five for manifesting this.

"Morning." Jamie looked over at me with a smile that could coax even the most extinct volcano back into erupting. My brain short-circuited. He was...*happy* to see me? He didn't think last night was a mistake?

When I woke up this morning and saw that the bed was empty, I assumed he left. A major league player who got his kicks, ready to bed his next willing fan. I was already calculating how long it would take to get a ride share to pick me up and make it to work on time since my car was still there.

A flicker of hope reawakened within me when I heard the clatter of a coffee mug in the kitchen. I managed to tip-toe into the kitchen for a peek, dressed in nothing but my short silk robe. It was the easiest thing to throw on in a hurry.

With the way Jamie slowly stalked over to me as his eyes scanned me up and down, I knew I had made an excellent choice. I felt like a rabbit as it stared down a hungry wolf. The coffee cup in his hand tinked against the counter as he set it down. That was the only signal of warning I had before he grabbed hold of me, caressing a lingering kiss against my mouth.

"Morning..." I breathed out in reply as he pulled away. His smile was reminiscent of a cat who had cream for its supper. He was content. Happy. A side of Jamie that was exceedingly rare to see.

"I hope you don't mind that I helped myself. I didn't want to wake you." Kisses interspersed with his words as his touch possessively lingered on the jut of my hips.

This was heaven. It had to be. I must have died in some sort of horrifically awful fashion on the way home last night to get to this point.

"You can honestly help yourself to anything." *Holy fuck was that an actual uninhibited flirtation out of my damn mouth?* I was the most awkward flirt on the planet. Maybe it was Jamie's sultry look of delight with each of my flirtations that was somehow training me to be more off the cuff.

"Is that so?" A brow cocked on his forehead as his cerulean eyes dipped to the gaping V of my robe. In my haste, I didn't tie it all that well. "Because I haven't had breakfast yet. And I was in the mood for something *sweet*."

My mouth dropped open to retort, but Jamie silenced me as he lifted me with effortless ease and plopped me on the edge of the kitchen counter. My brain hadn't even fully registered what was happening before Jamie was on his knees, coaxing my thighs apart. The darkened gaze he shot me as he leisurely kissed his way up my inner thigh made my blood come to an immediate roiling boil.

All I could do was grip the edge of the counter before the entire breadth of his tongue dragged straight up my slit. He was doing his best to devour his breakfast in the most delicious slow and methodical fashion.

Me.

I was his breakfast.

I was stuck between not being able to breathe and gasping sharply for air. The heady sensation left me dizzy.

"You are so wet already. Were you fantasizing about me while you were watching? That's a good girl." Jamie gasped out, his lips glistening with the evidence of his exceedingly incredible oral talents. "Come on, Cady. Your body wants this. *Beg for it.* I want to fucking hear you." My bottom lip dropped open, but no sound came out. He dove back in with a vengeance, eager to make me comply with his demand.

The moans tumbled out quickly, completely uninhibited since he *asked* for them. I couldn't overthink at this moment. I just had to throw caution to the wind as yet another one of my fantasies about the man was about to come to fruition. I could finally scream out his name in ecstasy and he would actually *hear* it. Again.

"Jamie…! Fuck yes, I want it, you… *Ohmygod…*" Oxygen burned my lungs on the intake as I inhaled sharply as he coaxed two fingers into my slick cunt. He angled the pads of his fingers to hit my G-spot. My words caused a vibrating moan against my clit from the man. There was no stopping the noises of pleasure now.

"Yes! *Fuck yes!* Jamie, *yes*… I'm cumming…*fuckfuckfuck*…!" My eyes clamped tightly closed as I thought my soul was going to shoot straight out of my body through my eye sockets. Bless him, he didn't stop the work of his mouth or fingers. He kept me perpetually over the edge of utter euphoric bliss until my vaginal walls were spent.

I was fit to collapse on my counter but the sultry move of Jamie as he rose to his feet, all while sucking my release off his fingers, had me ready to keel head over heels. A hum of delight reverberated deep in his throat as he cleaned each finger clear down to the third knuckle. My brain could no longer process thoughts.

"That was delicious but…" Jamie murmured as he boxed me in, a thick bicep to each side of me. A lazy kiss grazed along my jaw. "I think I need seconds…of *everything*."

"I don't have any condoms in the kitchen." I blurted out. Because what lonely-as-fuck single woman in her early 30s would have condoms in her kitchen? A smart one. I, apparently, was not at all smart. Or efficient.

"That's fine. We can go where the condoms are." With a rakish grin, his hands wrapped around me. In one smooth move, he tossed me over his shoulder. My bare ass grazed along the scruff of his jaw, chafing the mostly untouched sensitive skin there. I would have squealed if it wasn't for the fact that all air had vacated from the premise of my lungs as I found myself staring at his glorious bare ass.

Somehow in the scuffle of my first orgasm of the morning, his towel had worked its way loose. I pouted a little bit that I only had a bird's eye view of his ass instead of getting the entire top-to-bottom vision as he strutted past. *Weird thing to whine about, Cadence.*

Jamie dropped me onto the bed but didn't give me a moment to adjust myself after the first bounce. Grabbing me by the ankles, he dragged my ass to the edge of the bed. The move was aided by the silk robe that had completely slipped off my body into a crumpled mess beneath me. One wrong move and I would have tipped forward and over the edge of the bed onto my ass. He wedged himself between the V of my thighs to stop me from doing just that.

He stood like an utter god above me. The morning sunlight gave him an ethereal glow with his golden skin, tan from many hours on the ball field.

While I laid back admiring him, he did the same thing to me with his intense stare.

What did we come in for?

Oh right. Condoms.

With one hand, I reached out and managed to finagle my bedside drawer open. Dipping my hand inside, I fished around for the box of condoms. However, at that moment, Jamie thought it was a perfectly acceptable time to distract me.

His fingers gripped the underside of my thighs, pushing them open for his hungry gaze. The pads of his thumbs dipped into me to open my slit like one would the petals of a rose. With a swift uptick of his hips, he slid the underside of his thick cock through my slick. My entire body shuddered with the glorious sensation as the box of condoms slipped through my fingers and back into the drawer.

Holy shit this man had no chill.

The condoms were left forgotten for the moment. I could feel the intense heat from his hard cock as the underside of it teasingly slipped through my folds. With one subtle buck of my hips, my body could swallow him whole. That thought process was dangerous. I'd rather be safe than sorry, no matter how badly I wanted to feel him bareback.

"Dammit, Cadence. I'd give anything to bury my cock deep inside you. You're *drenched*. And only getting wetter by the second with my cock against your clit." The grit to his voice was fierce as it filtered between clenched teeth.

"You're a major league ball player. I've heard the stories. Who knows where your balls have been?" I gasped out. "If you want to hit a home run, you'd better suit up." I didn't want him to stop. He seemingly wasn't going to stop. It was almost as if we were both hypnotized.

"That was too many sexy baseball puns. And I'm not like other players." I shot him a look and caught his panty-melting grin. Good thing I wasn't wearing any panties for his hot-as-fuck gaze to incinerate. "You really are something..." Jamie hummed as he finally stopped the teasing thrust of his hips. Instead, he bent down to kiss me as his hand went fishing in my bedside drawer.

"Gotta keep things interesting." I shot back, surprised I was able to manage this much smartassness first thing in the morning without my usual jolt of coffee. Because Jamie was certainly a *hell* of a shock to the loins.

"I like interesting..." Shooting me a playful grin, he quickly ripped open the foil packet. I could see the shiver of delight ripple up his body as he fisted his cock and rolled the condom down his shaft. Goddammit, I wanted him again.

Reaching down, he coaxed my legs to bend and come back towards me a bit. Once within reach, his pointer and thumb cuffed around my ankles. From there, they found a seat of power, perched against his shoulders.

I just...*whoa.*

I was typically a missionary girlie. This position was a freaking unexpected wild card slot late in the season. My head was spinning. Because damn, he looked like a literal god staring down at me from the heavens. And I was his newest acquisition.

His hands wrapped around the front of my thighs like a vice, clamping them together. I felt the delicious press of his armored cock. My breath caught and shuddered to a sudden halt.

I needed it. All over again. To remind myself that last night did actually happen and we were deep into game two after a blowout performance from the home team.

I felt the tickle of his hair as it brushed against the tips of my big toes. It was the oddest position which left me completely exposed to him. I wanted to cover myself up from the intensity of his gaze. But there was something in his look that stopped me. His usually icy irises had a fire within the blue depths. A fire that was ready to engulf *me*.

Jamie's bottom lip dropped as he buried himself to the hilt inside me. The position of my locked legs gave my cunt a tighter seal around his cock. From the quickened rise and fall of his chest behind my calves, I could tell he was trying to keep himself from falling apart in that moment.

His hands cupped around the front of my thighs as he pressed my legs tight against his torso. With a breath, the sultry slap of his hips against my ass permeated the room until it became a constant rhythm. My arms shot out to grip onto something, anything. Because this man was taking me for a hell of a ride.

"Fuck…Cady…" Jamie gasped out as he parted the sea of my thighs to press me into my mussed bed. His groan followed because I couldn't help the spasm of my cunt around him as his words absorbed into my skin. As soon as he was within reach, my arms tangled around his neck. I needed that tangible feel of him somewhere other than between my legs.

He reassured me with a hungry kiss, his mouth slanted against mine with utter abandon. With the change in angle, it gave a stronger force to his thrusts. His hands coasted up and down my curves as he moved. My own followed suit through his hair, down his back, and around his biceps in one seemingly endless loop.

I wanted to savor every second of it. But in the back of my mind, I knew the workday loomed. Jamie's big premiere was today. If only we could spend the rest of the day in bed, tangled up with one another.

Between the talent of his mouth and the sheer power of his hips, I felt my climax racing towards me like the bright light at the end of a tunnel. From the noises Jamie was making, it sounded like he was right at my heels. I wished I could hit record or bottle it up because, for as quiet as this man usually was, he was the complete opposite in bed.

I screamed his name as I felt myself shatter beneath him. My body arched as the waves of orgasm overtook me, stealing my breath away. It was a delicious and heady suspend in the middle of a swirling galaxy as utter shockwaves radiated out from my thighs.

Jamie gave one last desperate race to the end, rocking my bed from the sheer impact of his hips. My orgasm was still in its full impact throes as he followed suit with a satisfied grunt that morphed into a moan against my mouth. Even though our climaxes waned, his physical affection towards me did not.

"Now that's a hell of a way to start a game day."

16

AOK

TAI VERDES

After a quick second shower for Jamie and a morning shower for me, we were able to get on the road on time for work. As handsy as we were in the shower, and very quickly headed towards yet another round, we managed to stay *mostly* on task. But Jamie's toned body under running water was a delectable vision I wasn't prepared for.

Shifting in the passenger seat, I drew my thighs together to quell the heat. It pulled Jamie's gaze back to me. An amused smile played across his mouth as his hand reached over to clasp onto mine, splayed on my thigh. Moving his eyes from the road, he glanced at me as he pulled my hand to his mouth and brushed a quick kiss across my knuckles.

Straight-up fire shot down to my core. The touch was sweet, tender. Not exactly something that should invoke such a visceral sexual reaction in my body.

He continued to keep a hold of my hand as he settled them between us on the center console armrest. That's what people in committed relationships do. Not something in the aftermath of a one-night stand.

As much as I melted from the gesture, I didn't want to get my hopes up. It was only one night. This could all change in an instant. He could up and forget about me.

This was why I didn't want to get tangled up in this sort of mess with a ball player in the first place. What would happen if Philadelphia called him back up to the majors? The schedule was more demanding, and the travel was daunting. Not to mention the Sillys had their schedule I had to follow. We'd never see each other during the season.

But why did he have to be so pretty?

Just enjoy it for what it's worth, Cadence.

Okay, fair. But damn, if this ended poorly, I wasn't sure if I'd be able to recover. It might literally kill me if I had to stop watching my beloved baseball team. Seeing Jamie at the games would only remind me of tender moments like this. Then they would come crashing into a heaping pile of flaming shit because I was thrown to the curb by their overly luscious catcher who had a fabulous cock *and* a body to power it.

"Hey, you okay?" Jamie's soft words pulled me from my dark tumble of thoughts. Blinking, I glanced at him and was fully unprepared for his tender look of concern. The stone-cold catcher was secretly a softie at heart.

I wasn't prepared to answer him. I was barely holding in a sobbing plea for him not to break my heart. But that sort of reaction would be utterly psycho.

"I'm worried about you."

"Me?" Jamie glanced over at me with a huff of a laugh. "Why?"

"Well… It's your big premiere tonight with the Sillys. Do you think you're ready?"

A long moment of silence passed before I noticed his subtle nod. "Considering I've started in a few World Series games? This should be a piece of cake."

I cocked my brow at him. He wasn't wrong, but he had a hell of a lot of animosity leading up to this game. The sudden about-face in his mood was suspicious.

"Yeah…but dancing…?"

"I'm not worried." This was so not the Jamie of yesterday. There was a playful flicker in the blue of his eyes as he looked over at me. "I'm feeling pretty good after those *private dance lessons* last night. I think I picked up a few pointers." With a cocky little grin, he turned back to the road.

My free hand shot out to grip the handle on the truck door. The cab of the truck was spinning, and my crotch just had a category five rager of a hurricane soak my panties. *Breathe, Cadence. Just breathe. So what if the gorgeous man you have a crush on just made a sexual innuendo about you.*

There was something else that was eating away at me inside since I remembered that he was the one who drove me home last night. Another *complication.*

"Oh uh…yeah. Well, that's good." I awkwardly cleared my throat. "I'm also…worried about well, if the team *sees* us…you know… Roll up together."

"Fuck." The swear bitterly fell from his lips. "Right. I forgot."

"You can just drop me off at the gate before anyone sees." I offered as I shifted uneasily in my seat. Jamie's hand still held mine tightly in his grasp.

"What?" Jamie exclaimed as he shot me a side-eye. "That's stupid." Perhaps no one would even see. I wasn't exactly looking forward to the questions or teasing from the guys. Or worse, what they would do to Jamie if they thought he took advantage of me?

"No…no. It's fine. I don't mind walking." I half-heartedly assured him. My eyes drifted down to where our hands were still clasped. Utter confusion knitted my brow. Was this something he always did with women? Did he see this as something…*more?* I wanted to ask him a zillion questions all at once, but I also didn't want to scare him off or overwhelm him with a jumble of assumptions.

It was still early when we arrived at the stadium. Some of the essential prep staff were there getting the place ready for the game. The Sillys guys weren't exactly the promptest people on the planet, so the main staff area of the parking lot was still vacant, safe for my car.

I waved to the security guys who let us in after flashing our Sillys ID badges. The maintenance staff was already getting things underway. The food stands were doing their usual prep work. In just a few hours the park was going to be full of spectators ready for another chaotic game of Entertainment League Baseball. But time before all the crowds was my favorite. Where the sleepy ballpark slowly woke up. Fans were what gave it life.

We walked into the players' area and team offices. It was always quiet down in the den, even with the stadium full of people. Well, before the nonsense of the team showed up. I liked having my peace before the chaos that was the entire Sillys roster came barreling through into the locker room to gear up.

Jamie's hand suddenly grasped onto mine and I turned to look back at him in question. In a blink of an eye, he had me twirled around and pressed up against the painted cinder block wall. It was cool against my back as a fire quickly licked its way throughout my body from where Jamie had cupped his hand around the curve of my neck. My eyes met his for only half a second before his mouth was back on mine.

Fuck.

Something was happening between us. Whether it was love or lust, it was still too soon to tell.

We were literally seconds away from being caught and the man's tongue was giving me a tonsillectomy. Not that I was complaining. Although the hallway to the locker room wasn't exactly the most ideal place to make out. At this rate, we were going to kiss everywhere in the stadium before the end of the week.

"It's going to be so fucking difficult to keep my hands off of you when you're this close," Jamie whispered against my jaw as he dipped down for a taste. His hand still had a firm hold of the other corner of my face. I was left at his mercy.

"Actually, you brought me this close." I immediately huffed back. Goddamn my attitude. Why couldn't I just take the hot admission from the equally hot catcher and let it fucl the fire Jamie continued to stoke?

Jamie's husky laughter against my neck was my reward. A few more heated kisses followed suit as his free hand coasted down my curves. Even though I wore my usual Sillys branded t-shirt and skinny jeans for game day, he was able to find the lines that made me a woman. The lines that he spent a lot of time worshiping over the last twelve or so hours.

"You really are a wildcard slot, Cady." The murmur was as if in disbelief as he pulled away a bit to look me over. "And I like that about you."

I could have fried an egg on my face from the sudden flush of heat that hit my cheeks. In all of the time that I'd gotten to know Jamie, he'd barely said anything to me. Now he was spewing words left and right as he shared his feelings in such an intimate fashion sandwiched with sexy baseball puns.

Voices reverberated off the walls down the passageway. With a grumble, Jamie pulled away and gave me a moment to compose myself. Although the color of my face would give me away if any of the fellow Sillys happened to be onto us.

"What are your plans for tonight?" The look I must have given him made him feel like he needed to elaborate further. "I mean…I had fun last night." *Oh fuck, I was afraid of that.* But perhaps "afraid" wasn't the right word? Apprehensive? "Especially dinner." He added quickly with a sheepish tip of his jaw.

His crystal blue eyes looked at me, hopeful and expectant. As far as I was concerned, he hadn't asked me a question. Was he waiting for me to agree? Invite him out?

"Jamie Rheems…" I started cautiously. His name on my lips still gave me goosebumps. "Are you asking me out on a date?"

I watched as his bicep flexed while his hand rubbed the back of his neck nervously. He couldn't meet my gaze. There was also a telltale blush on his cheeks. Gosh, he wasn't kidding. He really was rusty. Not that I had any room to talk.

"Uh…yeah. I guess I am." Now it was my turn to be flustered all over again. Of all the fantasies I'd had starring this man, I never thought in a million years I'd actually see it firsthand. I must have taken too long as he quickly added, "Look, I told you I was no good at–"

I silenced him with a kiss. It took him only a single second before I felt his body melt. His arms wrapped around me in a bear hug. He smiled against my mouth.

"Let me drive my car home at least. Maybe we can grab a pizza after the game…? Just, shower first." My words were breathless as I finally pulled away. Jamie's smile and chuckle in agreement only cemented the fact that I wasn't going to breathe for the next few minutes.

"At your place?"

Holy shit he was *eager*. If he was up for a repeat performance of last night, I was more than ready.

"Uh yeah, that um…sounds great. There's an awesome pizza shop around the corner from my apartment."

"Perfect. Text me the details and I'll pick it up on my way over."

"I–"

"Fuck, right. I need your number." Blinking, I pulled out my phone and handed it to him. His strong hand brushed mine before his calloused fingers glided across my screen to put in his digits before he texted himself.

Holy shit I had Jamie Rheems' number.

Holy shit I had an actual date with Jamie Rheems.

Holy fucking shit I was probably sleeping with Jamie Rheems. *Again.*

I was left in a happy daze for warmups. The guys kept giving me curious looks since I was a bit more aloof than normal. Maybe also a bit sore in some places. But it was totally worth it. Did they suspect something?

Thankfully Jamie kept his distance. But there were plenty of looks from him in my direction. Not that I was staring at him at every free moment in utter disbelief.

We were walking into dangerous territory here. How dangerous remained to be seen. Mine and Roman's dating life was too short to even bring it to the attention of HR. Jamie wasn't even technically a permanent member of the Sillys roster. The fact that he was in the majors might overly complicate things. But this was only day one. Er, well, technically day thirty, but day one post-coitus, if we were being technical.

Did adults even ask to be partners with someone anymore? High school was easy, you just sent them a note with "Will you date me, circle one: Yes or No". Or was nothing assumed until you moved in together?

For fucks sake, Cadence. You're barely twenty-four hours into this. Stop overthinking it all.

Right. I was supposed to be watching the game to make sure Jamie hit his dance cues. But how could I concentrate on visual nonsense when there was so much mental nonsense going on inside my skull?

My view of Jamie's butt as he squatted over home plate was as good of a draw as any to bring my focus back on the game. Thanks to last night, I'd seen that delicious ass firsthand. For fucking fucks sake, I really needed to get the naked thoughts of Jamie out of my brain or else the combination of the summer heat and my fluster was going to give me a heat stroke.

I did notice that Jamie looked a little more enthusiastic tonight with the Sillys. Not a single grumble. His leg would pop out with dramatic emphasis when Ender would let a creative pitch sail over the plate.

Despite his overall reluctance to this whole dancing thing, Jamie's head bobbed to the music in between batters. For this debut game, he wasn't going to be in any of the big dance numbers. I wanted to ease him into being front and center with the Sillys. To see how he did in front of the crowd with a few signature moves. So far, he was going *above and beyond* what we planned on. Which was honestly nothing.

The moment he tossed off his catcher's mask to catch a pop fly stopped my heart. He'd done it dozens of times when playing in the majors. But there was just something about a luscious man wearing a backwards ball cap in baseball uniform, after having an epic night of sex, that made my body tingle. His electric yellow pads only added to the chaos. Who knew yellow could be so sexy?

He looked like his old self again. Maybe with a bit more of a spring to his step. The knee wasn't giving him any issues. Yet I held my breath. He still needed to bat. That was the biggest point of contention as to why he ended up with the Sillys.

Chewing on my lower lip, I sat on the edge of my seat as he stepped up to the batter box for his first at-bat as a Silly. The man had the absolute audacity to look in my direction and *wink* at me with a tip of the brim of his batting helmet. It was like a direct shot to my heart and inner fangirl.

The ladies around me must have been fellow Jamie fans, as there was a chorus of shrill cries of excitement. Part of me knew it was just for me and yet the other part was still in disbelief that I had a fucking date after the game with Jamie *fucking* Rheems. Hell, I had sex with Jamie *fucking* Rheems *twice* in the last 24 hours.

I really needed to stop picturing the catcher naked.

I tried to suppress the overwhelming heart palpitations as I watched him take his stance next to home plate. *Come on Jamie, you can do this.* I repeated the mantra in my head until I heard the ball hit the catcher's glove.

STRIKE!

Dammit.

The man was eager for that ball. He had to be careful and wait for the good pitches. His cleats shifted in the dirt. He was antsy at the plate. Nerves had settled in. He took a step back to do his usual calming routine: hit the tip of his bat on the toes of his cleats before he adjusted his belt. Dear god, why was all of this so much hotter with him in a Sillys uniform?

I knew the Sillys crowd was a bit different than the raucous and judgy majors crowd, but he still needed to keep his head down and concentrate.

Another pitch.

A sharp crack pierced the crowd's ambient noise.

It gave way to hearty cheers as Jamie made a beeline for first base. My ass popped up off the plastic stadium seat as my heart slammed to a stop in my chest. *Oh, please let him at least get a base hit.* If his hit ball was caught or he was tagged out, it wouldn't move his batting average in the right direction.

I only exhaled when I saw his bright yellow cleat hit the dusty white bag of first base. My eyes stayed glued on his form as he did this unexpected but fun one-footed spin on the bag before he continued to the next base. I shouted at him to stay at second. The ball had bounced its way into the green grass of the outfield but was quickly making its way back in-field.

Jamie arrived at second and stopped at the bag just seconds before the ball hit the second baseman's glove. The ump did a little booty wiggle before he waved his palms in opposite directions to designate "safe". I bounced up and down and screamed my damn head off.

Oh my god, the man did it.

Jamie did this little happy thing with his feet across the base. Wait, did the man just *frolic* on the bag? The man didn't have a graceful bone in his body when it came to dance moves.

Baseball, yes.

Dance, no.

Wait…was that an actual *grin* on his face? Was he actually *finally* having fun at this "stupid excuse for baseball", as he called it? I felt the corner of my mouth quirk up before my jaw suddenly dropped. His blue eyes sparkled when they met mine as he did…a *shimmy*.

He did a fucking shimmy at second base. The man looked at me and shook his non-existent titties, okay so they were hella toned titties, in celebration. In celebration of his first hit playing for the Philly Sillys. Despite his constant reluctance in my attempts to crack through that grumpiness, something must have sunk in. Or maybe it was all the horizontal dance moves we did before the game. He just did an *unrehearsed and unprompted* dance move for fucks sake!

I couldn't help but puff my chest with pride. All those hours of frustration and a forced smile to counteract his monotone personality. They finally paid off. Especially if the crowd's response had anything to say.

The Jamie Rheems Shimmy.

It had a nice ring to it.

And he looked *hot as fuck* doing it. My god, he's handsome. Maybe he could pull this off after all.

17

CADENCE
FRACTURES

I felt like a giant weight had been lifted off my chest. The moment I kissed Cadence was as if everything in my life clicked at once. Which would have been ideal, except for the fact that I wasn't where I wanted to be in my life. I wanted to be back with the team that I loved. Back in the locker room that felt like home and not some 2-bit inner city cinder block bomb shelter.

But then I wouldn't have met *her*.

Cadence.

From the fateful moment we met in the Sillys locker room a month ago, there was just something about her I couldn't put my finger on. She cowered anytime I got within ten feet of her. Which only brought my attention, and curiosity, back to her over and over again.

Despite her intriguing me to a frustrating end, the dancing aspect of this reassignment had made her an unforgiving thorn in my side for the past few weeks. The fact that I'd been just as stubborn as she was with this dancing nonsense, making us butt heads, only made the situation even more bonkers.

Never in my life had I met a woman who met me toe-to-toe. One who didn't immediately fawn all over me because they recognized me from television or jumped in my lap after I mentioned I played major league ball. The funny thing was that she thought I was hot all along and had *no* idea how to act around me. Instead, she avoided me like some 16th-century European plague or gave me two tons of attitude.

It was…*cute*.

Okay, fuck cute. It was the biggest damn turn-on. She had been an unsuspecting tease the entire time. I thought it was just my mind-blowing frustration over a woman who made it her life's work to annoy me to death. Had I been good at dancing, the whole experience might have gone along a bit easier. She could command a room full of loving assholes and yet she had no idea what kind of power she wielded.

Cadence was…*different*. A good different. An amazing different. She was carefree and goofy. Not to the extent that most of the team was, but she didn't take life too seriously. Each day was a different adventure with her. And when she was passionate about something, it showed.

After my breakup with Vanessa, I felt lost. She and I were supposed to be forever. But the fact that she didn't want to leave San Diego to follow me to Philadelphia spoke for itself. Trades in the majors were bound to happen. I needed a partner that would be by my side to support it. Or at least make the effort to figure out a solution to new living arrangements. Vanessa didn't even want to *try*.

I had to make the cross-country move all by myself. It was a big ask of her, I knew that. But had Vanessa followed me, I would have asked her to marry me. As much as it hurt to bring a years-long relationship to such an end, perhaps it was just fate's odd way of letting me know that I avoided a lifelong mistake.

The longer I spent in Cady's presence, the more I realized that Vanessa was just…safe. She was a safe choice with a steady job. We went on dates and the sex was fine. But there was no earth-shattering chemistry. I thought that was a myth. Which maybe was why I had no idea what to do with my feelings towards Cady. I'd never felt them before.

Once I got to Philadelphia, the team made it feel like home almost instantly. I never had a deep connection to San Diego. I was there to play and live my major league dreams. The thought of being traded from Philadelphia made me sad. I wanted to stay here. Hell, I'd be ecstatic if I retired here. When I came to Philadelphia, I wasn't looking for the city to have such a strong hold on me. Let alone find love.

Whoa, love?

Hold onto your fucking horses, Jamie Rheems.

I spent one night with the woman. Knowing something serious like that after one night had to be impossible, right? Maybe I was only eager for a second evening with Cady. Now that we had the weird pretenses behind us, it made everything so much easier.

She was so easy to talk to. Easy to joke around with. More so than even Vanessa had been. Me throwing the "L" word around was something I didn't take lightly. Although it did scare me shitless to even consider it.

Was that why I couldn't get Cady out of my head? Even on the days that I wanted to punch the wall in frustration with my predicament and because of her attitude. She was the last thing I thought of when I went to bed and the first thing I thought of when I woke up in the morning.

During the game, my eyes couldn't keep off of her as she sat in her usual staff area by the side of the dugout. She needed to hover close by so she could assist with the bigger performances with props or effects and whatnot. But for the most part, she got to sit back and watch the team make total asses of themselves during the games while the crowd cheered on and yelled for more.

It was probably a blessing that she was out of my direct and peripheral vision during the game or else I wouldn't have been able to pay much attention to anything else. Which would have completely fucked Ender over. Even though these guys played for much lower stakes, they played this insane version of baseball with all of their heart and soul. Maybe even a little more so since they had the freedom to express themselves.

Cady was a gorgeous inspiration while I was out on that field during the game. My thoughts drifted to her and the wish to impress her. She inspired something within me last night.

She was athletic and lithe with her dancer body, filled out in all the right places. She was carefree and gave no fucks. With her short stature, she certainly made up for the loss of inches in outright attitude.

Damn. And that woman in bed? Completely unmatched. She was wholeheartedly into all of it. No faking. She was the furthest thing from a pillow princess. No bedding me for bragging rights. The fact that the woman listened to my every desire and then *begged* me for it still had me all out of sorts.

My hand shot down to my post-game joggers to adjust myself. This drive after the game was taking forever. Especially with my thoughts running away like this. If I couldn't get shit under control, I'd be picking up the pizza with a hard-on. At least I'd be able to balance the box hands-free.

After showering and getting my locker organized, I called ahead with an order as soon as I left the ballpark. The more efficient I made this trip over to Cady's apartment, the better. She texted me the number and address of her favorite pizza joint, along with her favorite toppings. As delicious as the pizza smelled, my hunger was for something *else*. Namely, a petite spitfire that was hopefully waiting for me.

Despite it being only the second time I'd been at Cady's apartment complex I drove there as if it was an old habit. I took the stairs two at a time in my impatience. By the time I knocked on her door, my heart was in my throat from excitement and nerves. For fucks sake I felt like a dumbass overeager teenager all over again.

The door opened so quickly that it sent a soft tendril of her hair flying off to the side. With the rosiness of her freckled cheeks, she looked like she had run up the flight of stairs right along with me.

"Hey."

I could have melted into a puddle right on her doorstep with the dreamy smile she gave me. If only there wasn't a pizza box separating us, I would have kissed her right then and there.

"Uh…" I cleared my throat to work on my best delivery boy impression. "Special delivery for a

Cady?" Her amused snort made my chest puff out a bit.

"Well, you took forever." She over-dramatized her words with a playful roll of her eyes as I stepped inside. Without even an ounce of hesitation, she played into my little role-play game. "You can forget about your tip."

"Oh, I have a *tip* I can give you."

The strangled noise that came out of her made me stop in my tracks as the door slammed behind me. It wasn't like me to sexually flirt so unabashedly. I swear this woman had somehow removed my filter.

Her hands twisted into the hem of her oversized T-shirt as she eyed me up. I wasn't going to lie. My gaze immediately strayed to the hem of it to see if she was wearing anything underneath. From the looks of it, no. The way she pulled her lower lip into her mouth and chewed on it was the last fucking straw.

Haphazardly tossing the pizza box on the bar top in her kitchen, I scooped her up into my arms. I silenced her squeal of surprise with a hungry kiss as she wrapped her arms around my neck and held on for dear life. I wanted to devour her in midair.

"Do you have any idea how crazy you drove me that entire game?" I gasped out when I had my fill of her for the moment. Somehow, I had meandered the both of us over to the couch. Her arms didn't unlock from my neck as I dropped the both of us on the cushions.

"Me...?" Cady panted, looking thoroughly confused.

"I saw you in the stands. Watching me. Cheering me on." Propping myself up on my forearms, I took in her delightfully pink face. It only enhanced the smattering of freckles across the bridge of her button nose.

"Oh… Um…sorry…?" I loved seeing her flustered. Especially when it was my fault. And from her admission yesterday, I knew it was always one thousand percent my fault.

"Don't ever be sorry."

"Even if I was checking out your ass?" There was the no-filter Cady I adored.

"Especially then."

"Sorry, it's a habit." Her eyes went wide as more unfiltered truth came bursting through her flushed lips. "Shit. Sorry! And I'm sorry I said sorry. Sorry!" I couldn't help but laugh. With one rough kiss, I reluctantly got off of her.

"Maybe all of your ego-boosting of late is the reason I hit that double today." My heart was pumping firmly in my chest. There had to be some correlation here. Cady brought my security walls tumbling down.

"Me…?" Gesturing to herself with surprise, she slowly sat up. Running her fingers over her mussed hair, she tilted her head in question.

Kicking off my shoes by the front door, I wandered back over to her on the couch with the pizza box. I for one wasn't a fan of cold or reheated pizza. The quicker we ate, the quicker we could continue where we left off this morning.

"Yeah…" I quietly admitted. I distracted myself by opening up the box and drawing out a slice for each of us. With everything going on in my life, I hadn't shared what was going on behind the scenes and why I ended up with the Sillys in the first place.

The words burned in my throat, wanting to escape. I hadn't felt connected with anyone enough to share this part of my life. But Cady? I felt like I could tell her all of my inner workings and utmost secrets without judgment. "I haven't hit a ball since my injury."

"Really?" Her voice softened as she took the plate of pizza I offered.

"Yeah." Normal me would have stopped there. Cady on the other hand gave me the feeling that she was a safe space to talk about my career and she would understand. "It's why I ended up with the Sillys in the first place." The words tumbled forth and were surprisingly easy, even with the subject matter.

No going back now. I already put it out in the open. Suddenly, it clicked. Me being more relaxed, me having fun at the game, and getting that hit. "The only thing that changed was you. Us. And well…everything that happened last night."

Cady choked on her pizza. It took her a moment to safely finish chewing and swallowing.

"What…? That…" Her lashes fluttered as she went deep into thought. The pizza hovered halfway to her mouth as she pondered what I said. I still was trying to figure it all out myself. "No…I'm sure you just figured your shit out." She shook her head as she delicately took another bite. "It always takes time with a new team."

I finally managed a meager bite of my pizza. She could be right. Perhaps I did finally find my stride. The ache in my knee had waned enough that I didn't feel it when I was playing anymore. But something deep down inside me told me that it was due to the pretty little, short stuff seated on the couch next to me.

"Well, maybe…"

Or maybe it was a mixture of everything that made up Cadence Andrews in a glorious hurricane of sexiness and chaos.

"Or maybe," The words felt foreign in the quiet air between us as Cady finished off her slice. She still avoided my gaze but now I was more determined than ever to get this out in the open. Maybe I could finally sleep tonight after denying this for so long. "Maybe I *really* like you."

The single noise of laughter that came out of her mouth surprised me. To my dismay, she rose from the couch and began pacing.

"Jamie…" Her wavy hair tickled her cheeks as she shook her head. She paused for a moment. "Look, last night, well…and this morning, it was fun. A hell of a lot of fun to be honest." She was rambling in her nervousness as her fingers wrung together. "But you don't have to do this."

My brows rose as quickly as I stood. "Do what?"

"Whatever *this* is." She stubbornly continued to avoid my gaze. Even when I blocked her anxious pacing with my body. I cocked my pointer finger beneath her chin to draw her attention back to me. "The pretty words, the flirtations–" My knuckle gave her jaw that one final uptick. That was when her eyes finally met mine.

"But…" The oceans in her irises glistened as her lashes furiously blinked. "They're all true." My thumb traced along the ridge of her cheekbone. She was so soft under my touch. "Like I said. I *like* you, Cadence Andrews. I don't exactly understand it myself. But…I want to get to know you better. To take the time to figure all of this out.”

There was an undeniable tremble that went through her body which ended at her bottom lip. Her hands slid up my sides, timid at first before making themselves at home right above my hip bone.

“After one night?” Her voice dropped to a whisper with her incredulousness. “This kind of shit just…*doesn’t* happen in real life.”

“What?”

“You know…where the female lead’s crush admits feelings for her in return.”

“It doesn’t?”

She shook her head and bit her bottom lip.

“Well,” Leaning in close, I brushed the tip of my nose against the side of hers. “Then consider this a first.” Her breath halted. I felt every hearty beat of my heart. Despite me being seconds from a wild admission, it felt right. More than anything I needed to get it off my chest. “Because I, Jamie Rheems, have a crush on you, Cadence Andrews.”

The moment lingered so long that I could taste it, savor it. I didn’t want to move a muscle to break what we had between us. All I wanted was for her to say this was okay. For her to admit that she wanted it too.

“Really…?” She breathed out, her voice dreamy and sultry all at once. I was trying to be a righteous and respectful man, but fuck was she making it difficult.

“I mean it. Look, I know it's crazy. We barely know each other. But you feel it too.” My voice was raw and breathy as I ruminated over the events of yesterday. “I saw it in your eyes the moment I slipped inside you last night.”

Cady's nails curled into the fabric of my T-shirt. The silence was almost suffocating. I needed her to say something. To agree with me or even to disagree. Maybe I was the daft one in all of this.

"Forgive me." My heart immediately sank. "But… it's just…difficult for me to believe." I opened my mouth to protest but her words continued. "I've spent years dreaming about you. Wondering what you were like in real life. And now…you're here, blowing my mind two different ways to Tuesday."

I tried to suppress my laughter, but it wasn't humanly possible. Not with someone like Cady.

"That's good, right?" I asked, just to be sure.

"Very." Her eyes demurely lifted to mine. "Do you think you can blow my mind again?"

It was as if her words were the match and my body was the wick. Despite another round of laughter, heat rushed straight from my head down to infiltrate every extremity. A telling little smile drew my eyes to her lips before she leaped into my arms.

Oh yes.

This was perfect.

The woman seemingly read my mind and I was all too happy to oblige. Scooping my arms under her ass, I made a beeline to her bedroom. My feet knew the way this time.

I felt her grin as I kissed her. We tumbled onto her bed, grabbing at each other's clothes in a more heated frenzy than last night. But this time Cady got the upper hand and had me flat on my back as she straddled me.

She worked me faster than a batter stealing second base. There was a fiery look in her normally cool eyes as she looked down at me. The way her butterscotch waves tickled her cheek and jaw as she tipped her chin to drink me in, I was swooning all over again.

My eyes drifted to her cleavage. Her breasts were fitting to burst straight out of her bra. She didn't fuss with overly complicated lace contraptions, which made it all that much easier to get her out of them. This sports bra had a front clasp that I unlatched with a flick of my thumb.

The creamy mounds burst forth in their newfound freedom and tumbled into my eagerly awaiting hands. Her nipples were already hard, aching for my attention. Sitting up to embrace her, I humbly obliged. She answered back with a sharp arch of her back, pressing her breasts into my mouth and hands.

With our one night together, I was already addicted to her flawless response time to me. It was like she took my pitch calls in stride and never doubted the call. With every new at-bat, I was becoming more and more infatuated with everything that was Cadence Andrews.

She took my tumble of thoughts with her as she pulled away, shrugging off the remains of her bra. I was so hypnotized by the bounce of her breasts that I had no idea what her next move was until her fingers were already tugging down my pants. My cock sprang free, and I let out a hiss with the contraction of the cool and heated air between us.

A happy little hum from Cady made it twitch, which only enticed her further. She had me pinned to the bed by sitting on my thighs. I was strong enough to flip the odds in my favor but fuck, I was eager to see where this was going.

Cady didn't leave me in rabid anticipation for long. Her hands reached out and wrapped around my straining cock. My head fell back to the bedding as my breath caught. *Fuck.* I had a whole game plan to claim this woman as mine again. Yet here she was, turning me into a single-brain-celled organism with one stroke.

Slender fingers danced around the circumference. There was something about the delicate way she went about it that made me sit back and watch her wonderment. This woman was something else.

Tucking an arm under my head, I was able to tip my chin down enough to watch her work. My cock ached to no end, and she had barely touched it. It took everything in my power not to grab ahold of her and do what I wanted. To hear her scream my name over and over again.

Pre-cum dribbled from my tip at the thought. The woman was vocal and the fact that she got off to thoughts of me drove me fucking insane. Talk about a hell of an ego boost. More than any home run or grand slam hit I've ever done.

Even better than–

Holy motherfucking shit.

While I was mid-thought she dove headfirst to my cock. Those pretty pink lips of hers parted. Behind my eyes, I saw an inky blackness with sparkling stars for a moment. I didn't exactly expect this sort of thing. But fuck it was an amazing bonus.

Once I managed to get my thoughts back in order, my eyes refocused on her. In the dim light of her bedroom, with the flicker of the city lights through her window, she looked otherworldly.

I watched in disbelief as she swallowed inch by inch until her lips brushed against the base of my cock with a wet gag. Jeezus, she was going to set me off at any second.

"Fuck, Cady…" I gasped out as she slid her mouth off only for it to be replaced by her slowly pumping fist. The taut skin of my cock glistened from her spit and made a proper lube. I couldn't help but buck my hips up into her grip. I needed more. I wanted more.

She didn't answer me, instead, she bowed once again to me, drawing the swollen head into her mouth while her hand continued its work. My head fell back to the bed with a gasp as my vision whited out. The woman was going to be the death of me. An outright delicious death if there ever was one.

"Cadence…*fuck*…fuck *yes*." The words spilled from my lips, a thankful reverence to the woman that had bewitched me mind, body, soul, *and cock* at this point.

Reaching down, I caressed my fingers across her cheekbone before tangling them in the loose locks of her hair. An approving rumble vibrated around my cock, and I inexplicably thrust my hips up. The motion shot my cock down her throat with a choking sound in reply. My body froze, afraid I'd hurt her.

Instead of pulling away, she continued with a sexual hunger which left me reeling. Her hand quickened its strokes as her mouth became even more eager. This wasn't some wannabe porno hand/blow job. Cady wasn't only talented at dance, but in her oral skills as well.

She took her time. She savored it. And fuck if it wasn't amazing.

"You'd better slip those goddamn panties off and sit on my face if you know what's good for you, Cady." I gasped out. Her mouth on my cock was making me lose all my inhibitions. Hell, she in general was making me lose them.

Cadence gagged on my cock on her way up. Her face was delightfully flushed as she gasped for air, filling her lungs as her breasts thrust out with her inhale. Sitting up a bit, her hands moved from my body to address the panties in question.

She was such a good girl to listen to my request without question. I let out a breath of relief from the break of contact as I was very close to coating the back of her throat. As much as I wanted to do that, there was a laundry list of other things I wanted to get through first.

A vivid pink continued to stain her cheeks as she wriggled out of her last bit of clothing. Now that she was gloriously naked, my mouth began to water. She eagerly crawled her way back up to me, straddling my torso as she went. But instead of moving her hips up to my awaiting mouth, she did a sudden twist and dropped her lips right back on my cock where she left off.

I choked on my next inhale. The woman was a force to be reckoned with. Instead of me having my turn with her, I now had a front-row seat to her soaking wet cunt as she worked my aching dick.

Did her giving me a blow job make her all wet and needy like that?

Because *fuck*.

Because fuck *fuck* **fuck**.

It took me a moment to focus on what I wanted to accomplish as her worshiping mouth had my eyes going crossed. Remind me why I thought this was a good idea? How the hell was I going to concentrate on making her scream when her mouth was busy working utter magic?

Reaching out, I eased her legs into position. Her knees found a spot on either side of my cheeks while the top of her thighs rested against my shoulders. The scent of her was heady and sent me reeling.

With the pads of my thumbs, I parted her folds, relishing in the absolute vision of her flushed, bright pink skin. She glistened in the dim light as if she glowed from the inside out. I dove in.

Nectar of the gods she was. All sweet and hot. Because of me.

"For fucks sake, Cady. You're gonna be the death of me." I gasped out against her slit. I watched as the creamy skin along her ass pebbled with goosebumps from my hot breath.

Her essence thoroughly coated my lips and tongue and yet I couldn't get enough. She could only reply with a sharp inhale around my cock that was swiftly followed by a moan as my mouth closed over her swollen clit.

That little bundle of nerves was begging for attention. I felt her thighs tremble to either side of my cheeks as I applied ample suction. I knew I was getting somewhere when her mouth began to falter on my dick.

Grinning to myself, the pads of my thumbs dipped into her slit to open her up even more. Stretching her out, I dove in like a starving man. My tongue slid in to swirl around her searing hot channel. I dragged the surface of it from her slit straight up her perineum.

That did it.

Ripping her mouth off my cock, her back arched sharply as she cried out into the room. Dipping my chin down, my tongue returned to her cunt before drawing her clit back into my mouth. I suckled on it for a moment, my noises of delight piercing her cries. Moving my bottom lip gave me room to flick the tip of my tongue back and forth against the protruding skin.

My god she was heaven. On all fours she deliciously responded to my every move, pleasuring her in return after she had done the same to me. Easing off my oral attentions just a bit, I slid two fingers slowly inside her.

Her body welcomed me like an old friend. At this rate, we were some semblances of that. I was doing my best to commit each and every curve of hers to memory. To memorize what touch and intensity made each sort of noise that fell from those luscious lips of hers.

My fingers disappeared with ease. I wanted to do everything in my power to consume this woman from head to toe. Starting with her creamy center was as good of a place as any.

With the talents of my fingers and mouth, she had abandoned her efforts south of my border. Which made this a hell of a lot easier for me to get her back to screaming my name. Adding another finger, the threesome did a subtle twist inside her that had her mewling into the night air.

I found myself getting lost in her epicenter. Each thrust of my fingers sent her cunt flexing around them. I had a front-row seat to the rush of desire that dripped out along my digits. No words made it from her mouth, only utter nonsense as she couldn't string a coherent sentence together. I felt myself getting harder and harder with each hot cry from her mouth against the tip of my dick.

Latching my lips around her clit, I made magic with my tongue, fingers, and lips. A tag team effort to get her to climax. With each withdrawal of my fingers, I felt her wetness pepper my cheeks. She was getting more soaked by the second.

Cady's thighs trembled against my cheeks before a piercing cry of my name hit the air. Her cunt squeezed around me as a gush of her sweet cum trickled over my lips as they still worked her clit. My mouth opened, drinking her in and savoring every last drop.

Everything all at once with Cady's orgasm unexpectedly sent me over the edge. Moaning and enjoying my bounty, liquid hot desire pooled deep in my belly before shooting straight out the tip of my cock.

Shit.

Fuck...

Her body jerked back in surprise as I lost my mind for a few seconds, blacking out as I emptied the carefully curated contents of my balls without a single touch from her.

All over her face.

Once my brain came back online, my head shot up off the bed as Cady adjusted her body to sit her ass down on my chest. Swiping my hand down my wet face, I reached out to apologize but stopped dead in my tracks. Settling in, she tossed me a look over her bare shoulder.

With a smug curl to her lips, her pointer finger slowly slid along her cheek. I watched with utter fascination as she collected my cum with the digit, coaxing it along her skin to her lips.

And lapped up the pile of cream with a delighted little hum.

TREACHEROUS

TAYLOR SWIFT

"Jeez Jamie, you must have really gotten into those dance moves last night at the game. Cadence must finally be rubbing off on you." The words filtered in through my open office door and I glanced up with a dry swallow. "You're hella tense, old man."

The trainer's words were truer than he could ever realize. Considering that last night Jamie was the first man ever to make me squirt, I certainly *did* rub off on him, all over his gorgeous face. He gave me the kind of oral that had me speaking in foreign tongues. Languages I didn't even know. I was surprised my neighbors hadn't called a priest to exorcise the demons from my apartment.

My eyeballs still had trouble settling into their proper forward-facing position in their sockets after the man rocked my world multiple times last night. The fact that the man shot cum all over my face, without me having my hands or mouth on him at the time, unlocked a shiny, brand-new kink for me.

The sexiest man on the planet had been *face-first* in my cunt and *climaxed* because of the orgasm that *he gave me*. Jeezus fucking All-Star game, Batman.

After last night, Jamie Rheems had officially ruined all other men for me.

I froze as Jamie's eyes caught mine from across the training room. Thank fuck I was in my office. If anyone happened to look in my direction, they would have seen my cheeks erupting in red-hot flames of embarrassment. The man gave me a hell of a confident smirk from the trainer's bench.

He wasn't sore because of the game last night. I mean, maybe it started there. But it was *definitely* from the three different sex positions he twisted me into last night. Okay, technically two. I was at fault for the first round.

As mortified as I was, the man should be proud of himself. He was the reason I was walking so bow-legged today. Everything that happened last night had been well overdue for my downstairs. I shouldn't be ruminating on our liaisons last night as much as I was. Especially at work.

This was literally the worst.

…or was it the best?

Things still remained to be seen.

Even if he was the man of my literal dreams, we were colleagues. Coworkers. I was pretty sure that this wasn't at all kosher. To say that I was a little hesitant about this whole unexpected turn of events was the understatement of the year.

But damn that man could *fuck*.

It was difficult to concentrate on anything in my office when Jamie was being stretched out by one of the team's physical therapists. No wonder he had me bent like a Philly soft pretzel for most of last night. He probably got a few of those ideas from therapy.

My eyes strayed to the clock at the corner of my work computer. Time was ticking by at a glacial pace. I needed to get out of here just so I could sit at home, in private, and ruminate over everything that had happened in the last few days.

Jamie had stayed the night again, although we learned from our first night together. He left early to shower and change at his place before heading to the stadium before practice. If we kept showing up to work together, people would start to ask questions.

The guys had their usual morning choreography practice and were now winding down from their fieldwork with Topper. That meant time in the weight room, physical therapy, massages, and ice baths.

I was trying to ignore the fact that they were gearing up to go on the road for a week straight to three different cities. Due to this year's budget constraints, only essential staff traveled with the team. Which meant I wasn't able to go on the road with them this season.

Up until Jamie showed up, road games were a blessed reprieve of a break in the vigorous ELB schedule to have some peace and quiet from the Sillys. Travel games meant that we recycled old routines. If they played opposing teams that weren't close to each other, they did the same set for each away game. They had anywhere from three to five routines each season to cycle through.

Being on the away team meant that there was less spotlight time. The home team had the advantage. Which was fine. The guys needed the break on top of all the hours spent traveling.

With Jamie traveling with the team, would things still be the same after he got back? Would everything we did in the last few days be forgotten? I did have his number now. We could text. Would he even want to text?

There was a subtle knock on my office door. I jumped before my head shot up only to find Jamie sexily leaning up against the door frame. His strong arm flexed as he braced it on the wood trim next to his head. Just like all those viral videos of women getting their men to do the "sexy door lean". Fuck me within an inch of my life. The man was a constant fluster on my body.

Biting down on my lower lip, I pressed my thighs together under my desk. I was ready to soak my panties then and there. Which would have only made a rather awkward conversation when I headed home for the day.

"Hey."

"Hey." I breathed out as my eyes finally flickered back up to his face.

"I figured it was time to court you again." A warm smile matched his overall swagger. I had to stifle back a laugh. He really was stuck on his C.O.C.K. guidelines.

But again? We'd spent every night together since that first one. At this rate, Jamie was going to court me once every 24 hours. And then have sex with me at double the rate.

"But you guys are heading out on the road early in the morning." I bit my lower lip even harder to stop the pout that was desperately trying to break through.

"That's why I'm asking you out to dinner. A week is a long time."

Feeling the heat in my cheeks, I rapidly rose from my desk chair and walked over to him. This wasn't a conversation that we should be having with teammates and staff being so close. I came to a halt as close as I dared without giving anyone a reason to ask questions. My eyes darted off to the side to see if anyone was watching. Thankfully the room behind him was clear.

"Dinner?" I murmured, afraid to make my voice any louder.

"Maybe a movie is more your thing?" He was toying with me. My body was tingling. Dammit, I wish he could kiss me. Hell, I wanted him to take me on my desk. *Stop accelerating, Cadence.* "Although, I was hoping we could talk more. I'd love to get to know more about you. In whatever method that involves some kind of *intimate* conversation."

My face blossomed with a fresh blush. Over the last 48 hours he had more intimacy with certain parts of my body than my brain. But in between we managed some rather delightful pillow talk. My body wilted a bit. *Okay, stay cool, Cadence. Your crush wants to get to know you better.*

"Dinner would be great." I breathed out.

"Are you good to go out somewhere?" His voice went much softer but damn his eyes were heated. "Because if we go back to either of our places, I think I'll find myself a bit *busy* and accidentally miss curfew and report time."

I did everything in my power to swallow back my fluster. The man exuded sexual energy. Or was it because I'd conditioned myself to only think about sex and baseball when I saw Jamie?

"N-No. I-I mean I'm fine with that." I finally had the strength to breathe out. Shooting him a smile, I busied myself with tucking a loose lock behind my ear. "Actually, a night out sounds amazing."

"Perfect. Pick you up at 6?" All I could offer was a nod as Jamie slipped me a smile before he wandered out of my office. It was too bad that I didn't know any artists. Smart me would have commissioned a painting entitled "Jamie Against a Doorway" so I could always salivate over the utter vision it had been for decades to come.

It was smart of Jamie to suggest we go out in public. Without closed doors, we could concentrate more on each other, all while being fully clothed. Part of me was afraid that maybe we were only compatible sexually. But given our lighthearted and free-flowing conversation over dinner, this connection I'd been feeling was much more well-rounded. Hopefully, he felt the same way.

"Book lover, huh?" Jamie mused as he tipped back his beer bottle. We had settled on an Italian restaurant in Rittenhouse Square. The overall mood of the place was quiet, a bit more casual, given the upper-scale part of the city. There were trees outside the tall windows of the repurposed antiquated building with marble floors and gold trim.

"Guilty pleasure." I shyly conceded. Jamie's gaze turned a bit heated as my tongue rolled around the words. "I feel that reading gives my brain more of a workout instead of TV." The tip of my finger absentmindedly danced around the curve of the lip of my wine glass. "But I do share your love of movies. Especially the same ones over and over again."

"Let me guess, romcoms?"

"Actually, no." I laughed with a shy shrug of my shoulders. "I love plain old comedies. Romcoms are more for reading. For some reason, the romcom movies are infinitely cheesier."

Jamie let out a warm chuckle as he nodded. "Yeah, I can see that. But you did say you liked *Mean Girls*."

"It's a classic. A regular rotation in my movie watching. But I consider it more of a comedy than a romcom."

"Interesting." Jamie mused as he slipped a forkful into his mouth. Chewing it, our eyes locked from across the table. "So are early 2000s movies the only classics you watch?"

"Oh hell no." I wiped my mouth with a napkin to hide my shy smile. So far, I haven't done anything super embarrassing while eating. But the evening was still young. "I'm also a sucker for Molly Ringwald movies."

The blue hues in Jamie's eyes glittered. "Really? Me too." For a moment I felt like he was sizing me up. Maybe there was some psychology as to which Ringwald movie was your favorite. If I picked *The Breakfast Club*, did that make me a psychopath? "How about on the count of three, we say our favorite?"

"I'm game." I laughed. There hadn't been a dull moment yet. Of course, I'd been nervous at first, but Jamie made it easy for me to relax around him.

With a nod, Jamie counted down. As he mouthed each number, his smile grew bigger. I was so thankful that with each hour we were together, he withdrew from his grumpy, serious shell more and more.

"*Sixteen Candles*!" My eyes widened as Jamie and I said the exact same thing at the same time. We both burst out in laughter, drawing a few eyes towards our quiet table in the corner. I took my humor down to a muffled snigger. "Really?"

"Well…yeah." Jamie shrugged as he looked down at his plate. "I don't know, the part where Jake shows up to Sam's sister's wedding, like a knight in shining armor," His eyes shyly met mine with a smile at the corner of his mouth. "It gets me every time. And the car is pretty nice too." Oh, sweet heaven on earth. That was my dad's favorite part too. Was it a sign of something?

"Jamie Rheems, are you a romantic?" *Please say yes, please say yes.*

"Maybe a little." A warm chuckle warmed me from the inside out. "I do enjoy a good grand gesture. But one that really means something. Something personal. Something that resonates with someone. Not all this bullshit with showering someone with expensive gifts that are pointless trinkets."

Jamie easily had the means to spoil anyone rotten. And yet, with one line, he showed me that he was a down-to-earth guy. Love and caring for someone was so much more than earthly things. It was something you couldn't touch or explain. You just *knew*. You felt it. You showed it.

I had no interest in money. Or fame for that matter. I just wanted to pay my bills and survive without worrying about keeping a roof over my head. Well, and have a few extra bucks for books and baseball tickets.

"I know what you mean. It's not something you can buy. It's what it makes you feel." There was a sparkle of delight in Jamie's gaze as he nodded.

"These guys in the majors, and the women that chase after them, it's like all they want is the spotlight. Between pressure from social media or greedy women, it's…it's not even about love anymore."

I felt my cheeks light on fire. Jamie Rheems just dropped the "L" word in casual conversation. It's not like I hadn't thought about it myself. I'd thought about it a lot and had the high heart rate alerts to prove it. But that was the last part of this entire insane delusion I was currently living through. The part that I was so certain I would never see. And yet…

"At least we're alone here and not bothered by the paparazzi or public or whoever feels like invading my personal space on any given day." Jamie's additional words interrupted my thoughts. Brushing away the fantasies of forever, I leaned back onto the table instead of being adrift in dreamland.

"I take it you're not a people person." I teased. I already gathered that in our time together. This was only the second time we'd been out in public. Like him, I preferred the quiet of either of our apartments.

"Not in the slightest." He busied himself cutting off a piece of his grilled chicken. "Well, I get along with my team just fine. But some days they are the max capacity of people I can tolerate."

"I feel the same exact way. The Sillys…they're a *lot*. As you now know." I chuckled with a shake of my head. God love the guys, but they were always a bit much.

"I can't tell you how refreshing it is to have someone say that." Jamie's steely gaze looked at me in earnest. Heat rose to my cheeks. I took a quick bite of my steak salad in a vain effort to quell it. "Aside from my family and some childhood friends, it seems that everyone wants a piece of the spotlight. It's like they see me on TV and automatically think it's their ticket to stardom. That I'm now their best friend."

"That's honestly the last thing I'd ever want." The words came out a bit muffled as I swallowed down my bite of salad from behind my cupped hand. "I happen to like my quiet life. I don't know how you guys do it. To go out in public and have someone chase you down because they recognize you. Sounds like my worst nightmare."

Jamie let out another laugh as he speared a few sprouts of broccoli onto his fork and slipped it into his mouth. How the hell did he even make eating broccoli look sexy? It made my heart so happy to know that he was the down-to-earth guy I always suspected. He really was my dream, well…*everything*.

"And that's just another reason why I keep falling harder and harder for you, Cadence Andrews." The words were so soft and earnest that I honestly thought my heart would burst at the seams. My eyes darted over to him as I lowered my fork. How the hell could anyone eat at a time like this? "It's like…somehow the universe took every single beautiful thing that I ever loved and created…*you*."

Blinking, I pulled my gaze from his. Tears of excitement and joy stung at the corners of my eyes. My heart soared in my chest. It took everything in my power to remain in my seat. Meanwhile, everything inside me was shooting off like fireworks all set off at once. It was going to take every ounce of strength

I had left to not say something stupid and ruin the moment.

"I think you're more than a *little* romantic, Jamie."

I chanced a look across the table at him only to see him dip his gaze bashfully to his plate as he nudged some food around with his fork. How could we be so explosive in the bedroom and yet dance around each other like timid teenagers in public? Whatever kept us humble, I suppose.

"I think I'm just a simple guy. All I need is my girl wearing my jersey cheering me on and I'm content." *Immediate swoon.*

Sir, I want that too. So much. You have no idea.

Chewing on my lower lip, I hesitated to share a personal story on the off chance that he'd think it was weird. But if I wanted this to be a genuine connection, Jamie had to like me. *Me*, me. Quirks, weird fantasies, and all.

"You know…back in high school, I wanted to date this one football player. He was so cute. Their girlfriends always got to wear their jerseys on Fridays for game day. I just wanted to…you know, be that important to someone."

There was a long moment of quiet between us. I was worried that I made it awkward. But maybe we were getting way too close to a much more serious conversation for being only a few weeks into this. A soft smile danced across his lips.

"You a football fan too?" I let out a slow breath through my nose. Thank god he changed the subject. At least for now. We kept tiptoeing along the water of serious emotions even though I wanted to dive in, head first.

"Who isn't? Go Birds!" I said a bit too loud and enthusiastically to cover my fluster. Jamie outright laughed. A few others in the restaurant echoed my sentiment right back. *Fuck, I loved Philly.*

"Go Birds." He replied with a laughing grin. After all, it was the greeting and response in the greater Philadelphia area during the season. Or whenever you saw someone wearing team gear. It was an unwritten law as a Philly fan.

"I grew up with all the Philly sports. My dad has always been a big fan. I suppose I was reluctantly indoctrinated over the decades." Our laughter mixed and danced in the air between us.

"Yeah, my dad is the same way. Although he's more of an 'all sports' kind of guy. If it's a sport and it's on TV, he's watching it." Jamie added. More than anything I wanted an afternoon of us sitting with our dads watching football in the baseball offseason.

My cheeks were hurting from all the smiling I'd done over our meal. We talked about our likes, our dislikes, our families, and what we liked to do in our free time.

Like clockwork, his hand took hold of mine as he drove me back home. It was a reflex. I smiled to myself as I watched the sleepy city fly by. While the sexual attraction had been rampant the first few days, this was something more tender.

Being the gentleman he was, he walked me to my place. But what surprised me was that he stopped by the main front door instead of escorting me inside to my apartment door. I turned to invite him up, with only innocent intentions. *Mostly.* Instead, he silenced me with a kiss, the first kiss we'd had since he left that morning.

My toes curled in my heels. I was frozen in place from the sheer intensity of it. I felt my knees buckle a bit, but Jamie's hands were right there on my lower back to keep me steady. How was he simultaneously my rock but also putting me on my knees?

"Good night, Cady. Thanks for going out with me." Jamie murmured the words against my mouth as I tried to get my brain back in order after that kiss.

"Don't you want to come up?"

Jamie smiled before trailing slow kisses from my mouth to tickle against my ear. His words sent a heated prickle down my spine. "As much as I would give up my favorite catcher's gear to do so, I'm afraid I wouldn't leave until you're a...*puddle* in your bed."

Pulling away, he sighed. "It's a 4 AM wake-up call to report for the bus. It's better...it's better if I cut the *temptation* off here before I throw you over my shoulder. Being away from you for a whole week is gonna be *really* fucking difficult."

I stood there in my stupor for a hot second. Did my super-hot crush seriously just say that he was going to miss...*me*...? Thank fuck that he still had a hold on me because I would have wafted away with the summer breeze. It gave me a sudden burst of confidence.

"I'll tell you what." My voice dropped to a husky murmur as I pressed back in close to him. "I have an idea. A bit of motivation while you're on the road. To make sure you stay on this hitting streak of yours."

It was a rather devious idea, but perhaps it might continue this little streak of his even though I wasn't there. My hands slowly smoothed their way up Jamie's crisp dress shirt.

"Every base hit you get while you're away, you get to go to the corresponding base." His eyes widened as my voice turned sultry. *"On my body."*

The way Jamie reacted to my words only empowered me further. His fingers curled into the sides of my dress, crumpling the fabric in his fierce grip. I was worried that his first few games had been a fluke. He was on the verge of being his old self again.

After that first night in my bed, Jamie had the best week of baseball since his injury. If I gave him something to look forward to when he got back to Philly, then maybe it would give him something else to fight for. A *sexy* motivation.

"If you get to first base…" Leaning back in, I brushed the barest hint of a kiss against his bottom lip to emphasize my point. My hands made their way down his arms to grasp ahold of him. It was like he was frozen there, hanging onto my every word, ravenous to see where I was going with this. I felt so nervous taking dirty to him, but I had to give him that extra little incentive. "You can cum in my mouth."

"Second…" My lips hovered along his jaw, close enough that I could feel each of his heated breaths. Taking his hands into mine, I brought his palms to my breasts. There was a subtle groan deep in his throat. My breath hitched as he took the open invitation to touch me with suppressed glee. "You can fuck these."

"Third…" My voice was almost nonexistent as I gathered all the courage I had to put on my sultry best. My heart was racing. I moved his hand to slip into the V of my thighs. With our bodies so close together, I could feel that he was already fit to burst through his dark dress pants. Hopefully, this was going to make a lingering impression. "Maybe we break out some toys?"

"And a…" With my now free hand, I teasingly danced along the waistband of his pants. "…*home run*." With that, I firmly cupped my palm around the tip of his diamond-hard cock that was straining against the unforgiving fabric. His hands shot to my waist and pulled my hips tight against him. "Or…runs." I gasped out. He was nearly foaming at the mouth to hear what the final prize would be. "Feel free to stick your *bat* in *any* hole."

19

ARE YOU EVEN REAL

TEDDY SWIMS & GIVEON

My phone buzzed with a message notification. Normally I'd ignore it, especially when I was engrossed in a book. But if I was being honest, I could barely remember anything that I'd read in the last week. Not when I was on the edge of my seat in anticipation waiting for a text or a call from Jamie.

The messages and calls had been infrequent, but when he did manage to contact me, I found it difficult to get the outrageous beating of my heart under control. Having my sexy professional baseball player crush actually text me was so much better than any romance book out there.

I tried my darndest not to look at the scores or game stats while they were on their road trip. Because if I looked, I was sure I'd end up texting him, asking for all the details. I didn't want to overwhelm him right now. Besides, part of me was still worried that he would fall off his streak and I couldn't take the heartbrcak.

Desperately grasping for my phone, I lifted it to see the alert only for my raging heart to stop.

You owe me

Big time

I blinked at the message, trying to wrack my mind as to what he was alluding to. After a very hot few days with Jamie, a week with him and the team on the road had been torture. Normally I loved the quiet of road trips. But with this one, I'd been counting down the hours.

But I also owe you

You owe me?

What for?

That sexy deal of yours

I gulped. Hoo boy. Those promises I made were about to be the stupidest thing I'd ever done.
Or the smartest.

What's the damage?

Should I break it down per game or...?

PER GAME JAMIE RHEEMS?

I relished in the pitter-patter my heart vibrated with as I typed his name. How the fuck was this real life right now? Jamie could have completely cut ties when he went on the road, instead, he kept it as is. Where was Jamie when I needed that ass pinch of a reality check?

With his smart-ass remark, I smiled. My sexy promises, or his luck, had worked. Letting out a relieved breath, my phone vibrated again.

Yes

Like I said I owe you for this Cady.
Knowing I had you to look
forward to helped a lot.

A lot

Chewing on my lower lip, I tucked my legs underneath me. Was I hallucinating? Was I still reading my book and this was the book boyfriend being utterly perfect? Because for sure there was no way that Jamie Rheems just texted me that.

I'll have you know the biggest hit
of this away series was a triple

So I get to go to your third base

My mouth has been watering at
the thought of you spread out for
me to feast upon

Or is it my third base to have
your lips on my cock again?

I don't know how this works

For as many smutty books I'd read, nothing, and I mean fucking *nothing*, could have ever come close to the words on my phone screen and the immediate inferno that engulfed my insides. I mean…*fuck*. I'd left the third base promise a bit ambiguous, but I was more than happy with either choice he asked for.

My hand shot down to my lap and I pressed my fingers against my searing hot center in a vain attempt to quell the ache. If that was Jamie's siren song, my body definitely heard it.

All thanks to you and those delicious promises

So I owe you

Name your price

Anything

The man was asking me what I wanted? My body tingled with the implications. He left it open, so it didn't have to be something sexual. As much as I really wanted it to be, I had something tame, but firmly in my kink column, in mind.

You in your uniform next time we hang out

Done

See you in 20

Wait, 20? As in *twenty minutes*? I knew the guys were due home today. They had a report time of 8 AM tomorrow for practice. But were they that close? If so, I was woefully unprepared.

My heart began to race. Shit, I wasn't in any state to intimately entertain the hottest man on the planet. I hadn't shaved my legs in a few days, and I was probably a day overdue for a shower. Scrambling off the couch, I did a whirling dervish quick clean of my apartment on the way to the bathroom.

I did laundry a few days ago, so there were fresh sheets on the bed, but the rest of the wash hadn't been folded yet. Depositing the haphazard pile of laundry into my closet, I shut the door behind me and moved to quickly make my bed. It wasn't the tidiest job but at least it didn't look like I spent most of the day in it.

Making a beeline for my shower, I did a rapid scrub down from head to toe. I took my time shaving my legs as I didn't exactly want tiger stripes of blood running down from careless nicks. I was just about finished with blow-drying my hair when I heard the knock at the door.

Cursing, I nearly tripped on the cord as I made a mad dash out of my bathroom. Realizing I was still naked, I grabbed one of my oversized tees from my dresser and shoved it on. As much as I would have been completely fine with answering the door in only what I was born with, I didn't want to have *that* embarrassing conversation later with my neighbors if they caught me.

Quickly combing my fingers through my hair, I answered the door as my breath halted in my chest. Jamie was a fucking vision before me. Some women loved a man in a dress shirt with the sleeves rolled up.

My kink was a man in a baseball uniform.

The heat and intensity of Jamie's gaze almost sent the cotton of my t-shirt up in flames. The man hadn't even touched me yet, but he devoured me with his eyes alone. I subconsciously pressed my bare thighs together as I felt the heat in my cheeks.

"Hey."

"Hey." Our signature timid greeting. This was the first time after a week of not being together. Would we just fall back into our dirty habits, or would we have to start all over again with this delicious push and pull?

I didn't have to wait long to quench my curiosity. There was only a moment of quiet before Jamie sucked in a quick breath. His hand shot out, grabbing the side of my neck as he pulled me to him for a searing quick kiss. Stumbling back, still locked in our kiss, I wordlessly allowed him access to my apartment before closing the door behind him.

"I missed you, Cady." His sentiment was barely above a breathless whisper as he hovered close to me. "Games just…aren't the same without you by the dugout. And the nights were too quiet without you moaning in my ear." The words warmed me slowly from the inside out, much like a mug of hot coffee on a cold day.

"Now that you're back I'm sure I'll be annoying you in no time." I breathed out, still in utter disbelief that this beautiful specimen missed me.

My quip gave us a breather from the sexual tension that almost suffocated us in my tiny entryway. Jamie chuckled as his hands moved away from dangerous territory for the moment. It gave me a chance to catch my breath after my awkward sprint to answer the door followed by the mutual eye fucking.

"So…where do you want me?"

I was still salivating over the glorious sight before me and hadn't exactly thought the rest of this fantasy through. It was going to take me even longer to properly formulate words. While I hadn't made a preference as to which uniform of his I wanted him in, somehow Jamie Rheems wearing the Sillys uniform was a thousand times sexier than I could have ever imagined. Maybe because it was the *real* Jamie and not the Jamie from my fantasies. This Jamie was mine. *All mine.*

"Well, since we aren't in the locker room…" Jamie's brow arched high on his forehead. That fantasy was something to bring up to him later. Even though our locker room kiss was the hottest thing that ever happened in my entire life, I didn't exactly want to lose my job because I was caught banging the star catcher on company property. But maybe in the off-season…

My eyes quickly darted around the room for another plan. Considering it had been a week since I'd slept with the man, the closest surface was preferred. "The kitchen table works."

A smile reminiscent of the Cheshire cat's slowly made its way across Jamie's mouth. I didn't give two shits where he took me, as long as he was wearing his uniform and letting me *fucking* have it.

Jamie took a stalking step forward to close the gap between us. His hands went to my hips. There was just something so easy about this, so delicious. Like I had finally won the most epic lottery of my rather sad love life.

While this tryst was hot, it wasn't just about sex. I mean, it was sex. *Great* sex. Okay, fucking fantastic sex. And a whole lot of it. But the best part was this sparkling connection between Jamie and me right beneath the surface.

I no longer shied away from him. Instead, I tipped my chin up to catch his heated gaze as he edged me back to the table. There was such intensity there. His playful smile never wavered, simmering the desire deep in my belly. Just seeing him show up at my apartment, exactly as I asked, had me barely keeping my feral side in check.

"So...*just* the kitchen table?" His smile curled into a wicked little grin. How was he on the same fucking wavelength of fucking as I was? Since he arrived, I'd already fantasized about half a dozen other places where I could enjoy him in uniform. A girl needed all the angles.

"To start." I quipped back breathlessly. A sordid chuckle let me know that Jamie was in delicious agreement.

His hands grabbed onto the jut of my hip bones as he lifted and plopped me down on the edge of the table. The man didn't want to move more than an inch from me as he wedged himself in between my thighs. Sliding his hands under the lifted hem of my oversized T-shirt, I sat in wait for the little surprise I had, by chance, left for him.

Jamie's eyes went wide for a second before his gaze darkened as he found, or well, didn't find a certain piece of clothing between my thighs. With a deep growl in his throat, he crushed my hips to his. A gasp left my mouth as I felt how hard he was already. There was no cup to cage his erection. For a moment

I was worried about how much of a creamy mess I just made all over the front of them.

With dizzying speed, his one hand grabbed the corner of my jaw to hold me right where he wanted while the other furiously worked his belt open. This man could multitask like no other. Our mouths met hard and fast after our rather calm flirtatious interlude leading up to this.

I heard his belt buckle jingle as it fell loose after his other hand joined the first to make quick work of it. The back of his hands graced my bare inner thighs as he quickly worked the fly open. God love this man. He understood the assignment perfectly.

My hands shot down to greet his erect cock as he shoved his uniform pants and boxer briefs down just far enough for the zipper to not be a bother. Fuck, he was going to be such a fucking vision fucking me. I could only manage a one-track mind at the moment.

With one hand, I admired the taut silken skin while my other flailed behind me in my haphazard search for the protection I'd secretly stashed away. The lid to the sugar bowl clattered onto the wooden tabletop. The noise startled Jamie enough to pull himself, breathless, from my mouth.

Tilting to the side a bit to see the chaos behind me, his eyes fell onto the now topless sugar bowl, filled with colorful condom wrappers. Needless to say, I thought it was a rather clever hiding spot for something so filthy. Jamie's laughter made me grin.

"I see you learned from last time."

"What, that we should *always* be prepared for unexpected sexy times, no matter where? Duh."

"You know… I've been doing a bit of fantasizing myself." Jamie gritted out as I put the condom-hiding spot to good use. Ripping open a purple one, I had to pause midair as he slapped his hard cock a few times against my already-throbbing clit. It made such an unholy wet sound. The noise that came out of me as I jumped from the stimulation was not human. Foreplay was not going to be necessary for either of us. "The thought of taking you bare. Coating your insides. Claiming you as *mine* in every way possible."

And it definitely wasn't going to be necessary for the next century after saying shit like that.

He emphasized the point with a few slow swipes of the underside of his rigid dick up and down my slit. The ache between my thighs was unbearable. I knew I was readily slick and prepared to take him with little to no effort. If he kept talking and looking like that, I was more than prepared to take him multiple rounds without a break in between.

Technically, going condom-free would be kosher. With an IUD in, I didn't have to pay daily birth control any mind. On Jamie's side of things, I knew that the guys needed clean bills of health to play. And considering his confession of years since his last partner, I didn't feel like I had much to worry about.

But that was a conversation for another time with much cooler and less horny heads. He was already gloved up and ready for action. Why let it go to waste? Barely getting my brain back online, I finished rolling the rubber down his shaft.

Taking action, I hooked my ankles together around his ass and pulled him in close. Immediately, he got the point and took over, grabbing my hips as he took aim and thrust inside me with an almost bruising force. The mutual moans that shot out of our mouths reverberated off the walls of the kitchen. Oh, fuck yes. I needed this.

Jamie waited until I relaxed around him enough that he wouldn't hurt me if he moved. There was an initial testing thrust before all hell broke loose. Grabbing two fistfuls of his uniform shirt, I held on for dear life as he began a relentless pace. That was exactly what I needed to pair with the visual of him in uniform.

I could feel the table rock beneath my ass cheeks. The downstairs neighbor was not at all going to be happy with the rhythmic noise of the table legs practically vibrating against the tiled floor. Considering it wasn't an ungodly hour, maybe they'd forgive me.

My eyes hazily drifted over the utter vision in front of me. My knuckles were white from the grip that I had on his jersey. The Philly Sillys logo was crumpled into sharp hills and valleys of wrinkles as they fanned out from my curled fingers.

"Oh, fuck, Cady." Jamie gasped out as my eyes found his. They were dark and intense, almost as if they were staring into my soul. "This is fucking heaven." The words and tone of his voice were an utter aphrodisiac as they slipped, hot and breathless from his parted lips.

My wildest fantasy come true.

"Dammit, you're so wet. Such a good girl. All pantyless and waiting for me." Jamie groaned as my cunt fluttered around him in response. "Were you fantasizing about this before I got here?"

I couldn't dignify him with a proper response. Technically, I pregamed in the shower with my removable shower head, but only for a teasing minute as I hosed off my undercarriage. Tossing my head back, I cried out as the orgasm hit me in full force. The sheer intensity and sudden onslaught of it left me completely shell-shocked as nothing but jumbled moans of ecstasy escaped my mouth.

Jamie took that as his cue to grab hold of my hips with a fierce vice grip as he chased his release. Gasping from the almost constant orgasmic pulses, I collapsed back onto my table, sending the sugar bowl clattering to the floor. He followed suit after me, caging me in against the wood without missing a thrusting beat.

His hands fumbled with my shirt, shoving it up to my armpits so he could feast upon me. Murmurs of hungry delight vibrated against my skin as he pressed open-mouth kisses to my breasts. Holy fuck this was too much.

"That's my girl. *That's...fucking...it...*" Jamie rasped out as he used this new angle to continue his onslaught. My mind was already reeling from the fact that we were sinfully wrecking my table and yet my brain had to fixate itself on two singular words of his: *My. Girl.*

My eyes flashed open to see Jamie's intense ice-blue gaze staring back at me. A breathless smile smoothed away the intensity. I needed to touch him. To hold onto him and never let go.

Reaching up, I grabbed his face and pulled it down. Jamie sensed the shared urgency and met his lips to mine. The embroidery of the team's logo on his jersey scraped along my erect nipples, sending my body into a renewed frenzy.

Jamie's groan reverberated throughout my body as I descended into orgasmic chaos once again. Holy fuck, at this rate I didn't think I'd ever be able to stop climaxing. My second orgasm of the evening brought on Jamie's. He buried his face in the crook of my neck, moaning with each slowing thrust of his hips.

We lay there for a while as we let our breathing slow and almost become one unified inhale and exhale. My back was beginning to riot. Being smashed under Jamie's hard body against my wooden kitchen table wasn't exactly an ideal place for a cuddle. I couldn't help it. I started to chuckle.

"My body thanks you, but my back does not. I think we need to find somewhere softer." I murmured against Jamie's ear in my mirth. He immediately followed in laughter. But godfuckingdamn I was not complaining in the least bit.

"It was so worth it to make this jersey my lucky one."

20

FIGHT THE FEELING
ROD WAVE

"You're fucking him," My head whipped around to see Tiffiny standing behind me with a smug-ass grin on her face. "Aren't you." I let out a dismissive snort and turned back to fussing with the prop closet. Nervous sweat immediately beaded along my brow.

Tiffiny was my best friend. It was tearing me up inside keeping this delicious secret from her. I knew she wouldn't blab about it, but it was just safer to keep it from her. As far as I knew, Jamie and I were doing a decent job at keeping, whatever we were doing, quiet. It needed to stay that way. Remaining cool under my friend's interrogative stare might act was going to be difficult.

"What?" Holy fuck I didn't sound the least bit convincing. "Come on, we both know I'm not that lucky." I kept my gaze firmly on a spot in the closet. I knew if I looked at her, I would crack like an egg in a bodybuilder's ass cheeks.

"Girl you've been walking on air, smiling, and looking freshly fucked. *Daily*. And it's been ever since Jamie started in his first game." Why did my best friend have to know me so well?

"Maybe it's from a new dance routine I'm working on–"

"Yeah, the horizontal one with Jamie Rhe–" I immediately stormed over and hushed her with my hand over her mouth. The cement block walls of the stadium reverberated sound like nobody's business, which, in turn, made it everyone's business. Jamie and I had found that out the hard way when he cornered me after a game the other day. That was too close.

"Oh, my fucking god, will you just shut up?" I hissed at her as I nervously glanced around. Her brows, raised from surprise, knitted together on her forehead with judgment. I hesitantly pulled my hand away.

"Look, I'm just collecting all the obvious evidence here." Like me, Tiffiny enjoyed her true crime podcasts entirely too much. "Because Jamie suddenly had a miraculous change in batting talent two days after you two danced at the bar." My eyes darted away. Which apparently was my guilty tell. Tiffiny screeched in triumph. "I fucking knew it! You guys went from mentally fucking each other to eye fucking to just general fuc–"

"Holy shit, do you truly have no filter?!"

Tiffiny crossed her arms in front of her as she cocked her hip out. "You and I both know the answer to that question."

I rolled my eyes.

"At least use code words or something if you insist that we talk about this *at work*."

"Oh yes. I *absolutely* insist."

"Fine." I huffed before rolling my eyes once again. But there was a small part of me that was just as smug as she was. I was living every fangirl's dream, sleeping with my favorite baseball player. But how the fuck can we talk about this at work without someone overhearing us and knowing exactly what we were talking about? "Yes, Jamie and I are...*running the bases*."

This was not going to work. At least not around anyone who had as dirty of a mind as Tiffiny and me. Because who the fuck picked baseball to be the sport where the terminology is sexually suggestive? My friend had to swallow back her snort as she made a poor attempt to hide the amusement on her face.

"*All* the bases, huh?" She asked, trying to make it seem like this was just a casual conversation about the sport.

"Multiple *home runs*," I added as I tried to hide a satisfied smile. Her brows lifted in surprise for a fleeting moment before her gleeful little smile quirked at the side of her mouth. Being my best friend, I was just waiting for her to gloat.

"Told you so."

"Oh, come off it, Tiff. You could have given me at least a full minute before you rubbed your smug shit in my face."

"I'm sure that's not the only thing being rubbed in your face." I made a strangled noise before I chucked a mini disco ball from the prop closet in her direction. She let out a squeal and ducked out of the way. I heard it tink across the concrete. "Hey! At least I didn't say 'dick'."

"Besides," I sighed with the weight that I'd been carrying around. "It's so much more than *that* with Jamie. I don't know. We just...*clicked*. Like, immediately." A smile drifted to my lips. "Maybe those romance books were right about one thing."

Tiffiny avoided my gaze as she mumbled something. Cocking my brow at her, she looked like she was suddenly sweating bullets herself. What the hell was up her ass lately?

"Did you say something, Tiff?" I smirked at her. It was about time she got a taste of her own medicine.

"I-uh said…" Tiff cleared her throat, avoiding my gaze at all costs. "All this talk of *bats in holes* making me sick." I snorted.

"If you want to have a raunchy conversation about this serious situation then you should have cornered me via text message like a normal person."

"And miss watching you sweat out the interrogation? Absolutely not."

"You really need to get out more. I can't be your only form of entertainment."

"Nah I have dirty books, remember?" I let out a snort as she retrieved the discarded disco ball. Tiffiny had distracted me from my mission in the closet. Whatever that was. I couldn't rightfully remember. Even *talking* about Jamie fucked me up. "Speaking of book boyfriends," Tiffiny's voice dropped to a hush as she straightened her spine, a vain attempt to look innocent.

Tossing the ball into the abyss of the cluttered room, I leaned around the door to see Jamie and the guys heading in our direction. Now that Tiffiny knew my little spicy secret, I wasn't sure if I could keep a poker face around everyone at once.

"Please, don't say anything." I hissed at her. "If this gets out, I'll be in shit so deep it will be up to my eyeballs." Tiffiny rolled her eyes.

"Why the hell would I say anything? You're the only sane person here. I'd bite off my left hand to keep you here. But…" Her eyes darted to the approaching group of players. "It is rather fun to watch you squirm–"

"Hey Tiffiny," Ender interrupted our whisper fight as he curiously glanced between the two of us. His eyes lingered on my best friend a bit too long to not arouse suspicion. My eyes narrowed as I watched Tiffiny suddenly take the hot seat.

"Ugh, doesn't my brother teach you manners along with pitches?" Tiffiny grumbled under her breath. "Cadence is here. You should say hello to her too."

I narrowed my eyes to judgy slits. Something was super odd about how she'd been acting around Ender lately. Ender was one of the sweeter, more level-headed of the guys. This was the second outburst I'd witnessed. Maybe she was giving me so much shit because she was just trying to deflect?

Ender was cute. Like the boy next door, kind of cute. Always had a soft smile on his face. He was the opposite of the tall, dark, tattooed, looming hunks from her dark romances that Tiffiny read religiously. Maybe he pissed her off more than normal?

The rest of the guys played along with Tiffiny's demand. They all said hello to me in unison. Their voices vibrated off the walls and I cringed at the off-key singsong of my name. I was trying my best to focus on the uneven air between Tiffiny and Ender, but I was distracted by the feel of Jamie's gaze hot on my skin.

With a laugh, the guys headed off to the lockers. Glancing over to my friend, she and Ender were having some sort of heated conversation, but I couldn't hear it over the commotion of the guys.

A hand appreciatively cupped my ass, sending me up on my toes in surprise. I choked on my sharp inhale before turning to look at the offender.

My racing heart calmed down for the surprise but ramped back up when I realized that it was Jamie who copped a feel. Not that I should be shocked, but my crush just went out of his way to feel me up. *In public.*

"Is Tiffiny always that mean? And I thought you were testy when we first met." Jamie murmured in my ear. I could hear the smile in his tone as my skin prickled with goosebumps beneath his warm breath. His hand didn't move from its spot on my butt. Which was fine, we were technically alone for the time being.

"I believe you're going to have to define 'mean'. Tiffiny has different levels of it. Now that you mention it, these last few weeks it seems that her anger is all stemming either towards, or from, Ender." It was then I chanced a glance up at Jamie. I could see his sweaty skin prickled with his five o'clock shadow. There was some red field dirt flecked across each strand. "Has Ender been acting weird too?"

"I don't think so? But I don't know the guys like you do. Except now I know a hell of a lot more than I ever wanted to. None of them seem to have a filter."

I snorted in laughter. "It took you that long to figure that out?"

"No, just stating the obvious so we can commiserate in our mutual misery."

"Jamie Rheems," I breathed out, rather impressed. "You've said some pretty hot shit, but that might be the hottest thing you've ever said." Jamie's laugh was loud, causing me to glance around and see that Tiffiny and Ender had disappeared. So, for the moment, we were alone.

"Hmm, that sounds like a challenge." He also realized we'd been left to our own devices. Jamie's hands slithered down my sides to hook into the belt loops of my skinny jeans. "A challenge to see if I can *outdo* myself."

"Your place or mine tonight?" I shot right back. He didn't have to ask me twice.

"Yours. I haven't had a chance to look at that leg on my bed."

I bit my bottom lip, stifling a laugh as I reminisced about the fun we had last night after the game. Things had gotten so wild that his mattress went all cockeyed in the middle of it. We had to finish each other off on his bedroom floor. Sleeping in a not-broken bed tonight sounded ideal.

"Eww, you guys are gross." Tiffiny's voice cut through our simmering sexual tension. I grumbled as Jamie stepped away from me. Where the fuck did she come from? "If you're gonna do that kind of gross shit in public, at least find a closed room. Preferably behind a door that locks."

Jamie had said far filthier things to me and yet he was the one blushing like a priest in an adult toy shop. He shot Tiffiny a wary eye before glancing at me.

"Tiffiny figured out that we didn't *hate* each other." It took Jamie a moment to realize what I implied. When it dawned on him, he couldn't keep a straight face. His shoulders relaxed with a laugh.

"Right." With a nod, he cleared his throat before adjusting his workout gear and the budding erection I felt just moments earlier. "Cady and I were just–"

"Cady, huh?" Tiffiny quirked her brow in my direction, and I crumbled under her scrutiny. Oh, I was going to hear all about that later. I gave her a drunken little smile of pure happiness. "You two are at the pet names stage? It's even more disgusting than I imagined."

Jamie and I both glanced at each other, looking guilty as fuck. He was "Slugger", and I was "Cady".

Holy shit, this was bad, wasn't it?

With a smirk, Tiffiny walked past me on her merry way to bring her unhinged chaos elsewhere. She gave my shoulder a nudge on her way past before flashing Jamie a "thumbs up". It wasn't until she turned the corner that Jamie relaxed.

"The weirdness here even extends to the mascot."

"Honestly she's the weirdest one here." His head snapped to me with a question in his steely blue gaze. I laughed. "The fact that you haven't realized that means she hides it as well as she thinks. Tiffiny grows on you though."

Jamie glanced at me with a tinge of worry to his gaze. "She won't say anything, right?"

"Of course not." I dismissed him quickly. I knew she wouldn't. Not only because she was my best friend but her speaking to just about anyone was her least favorite thing to do. She wouldn't go out of her way to make herself miserable.

Looking at Jamie, I felt my heart swell. As much as I was living the fangirl dream, I was doing my best not to fall in love with the man. There were too many things that could go wrong with dating an athlete and a revered athlete at that. But hell, he was making it more and more difficult to keep to keep my apprehension at bay.

"Good." Jamie's hand slipped down to grasp mine. "Because…" Lifting my hand to his mouth, he brushed a tender kiss across my knuckles. I was ready to melt into a puddle at his adoring feet. "I think we have a good thing going on here."

21

NUMBER ONE GIRL

ROSÉ

It was working. This stupid stunt was working. Well, not exactly in the way the franchise imagined. I didn't think "getting railed by the coach" was on their bingo card when they dropped me in the Sillys' lap.

Maybe it was a bonus?

Or maybe it was something that was going to change my life.

Sillys ticket sales had soared. Sell-out crowds showed up daily. Apparently seeing me dancing was doing just what they wanted, filling seats and making this crazy investment worthwhile. Not only were my dancing skills getting better, but my batting skills had greatly improved.

When I arrived here, I thought it was a death sentence for my career. But with each day that went by, I found myself more and more at home with the Sillys. The more I thought about going back to the majors, the more I dreaded it. The pit of despair in the bottom of my stomach opened wider and wider.

Maybe this was where I belonged now? My batting average took a complete 180. Cady insisted it was due to the new coaching staff, but deep down I knew it was mostly her. She gave me incentives to play well, *sexy* incentives.

Every day I was in her sunshiny presence invigorated me, both on and off the field. She and the guys on the Sillys taught me how to have fun again. They taught me that, yes, this can be a career, but it doesn't mean that you couldn't make the most of it. You had to find the good in every day.

With my more relaxed attitude, I was more consistent in my hits. The power wasn't all the way there yet, but *trying* to hit all home runs didn't win games. Hits won games. Whether it be over the fence or bouncing down the infield. Sending that white ball skipping across the green field grass got guys around the bases. It gave me hope that my career as a mid-30s major league catcher wasn't quite over yet.

I had to admit, I was scared of "the end". Baseball had been my life since before I was in grade school when Mom and Dad signed me up for T-Ball. Years of grit and determination got me here. I didn't know anything *but* baseball. So, what happened once it was all over?

My thoughts strayed to Cady.

Up until now, baseball was everything. I didn't feel the need to find happiness elsewhere. I was content.

Ever since I met Cady, my mind had been on her more than my career. She was incredible, how could I not think of her? Witty, flirty, sweet and caring. Everything about her was a dream come true. Baseball was as much a part of her life as it was mine. She understood the stressors of the sport and took them seriously. She was the first genuine woman in my life who meant more to me than a career in the majors.

Someone I could see myself spending forever with.

I glanced down at her, nestled into the crook of my arm. We were back in her bed, a favorite pastime of ours now. It was a safe space, a place we could relish in the quiet of just the two of us. No bright lights, no announcers, no cameras.

Sure, the sex was incredible, but it was all the tender times in between that made me feel like molten goo inside. On one of our early dates, she'd asked if I was a romantic. I never really thought of myself as such. The extent of my romance had been watching corny romcoms. But maybe that was because I hadn't *felt* overly romantic towards anyone before.

Nor had I had this much sex before. It was almost as if her own personal fragrance was an aphrodisiac. A drug that I needed to keep breathing in deep that exploded in an orgasmic flora around me whenever I was inside her. It kept me wanting more.

This feeling was intense. The more time I spent with her, the more I felt like that all of the time. How could one live without it after having a taste of it? I was unabashedly addicted to her.

I was only half paying attention to the movie she put on. My mind was a hapless mix of flashbacks of our earlier intimate session and this never-ending churning bubble of feelings inside. My hands had been full of her asscheeks only an hour earlier as I claimed her from behind as she buried her face in her pillow. She must have enjoyed herself immensely since I could hear her, clear as day, even with a mouth full of cotton and feathers, buried in her pillow.

A familiar tune jarred me from my reminiscing. Which was good timing as I was already on my way to another erection. All I needed was one thought of the woman and I was ready to bend her over the nearest surface.

Finally nudging my brain away from my dick, I recognized the music. Cady, like me, grew up with Disney movies. She told me she put them on as background noise when the world was too quiet. Something familiar, something comforting. Something she knew the ending to. It helped her relax.

Hopefully, she didn't think I was getting a boner from Rapunzel singing her heart out with Flynn Rider. The princess was pretty, but she was no Cady. Although Rapunzel with her hair cut did have a striking resemblance.

As I watched their duet, an idea hit me. Cocking my head to the side, I ruminated over the two characters singing. Had the Sillys done a musical number from a movie before? I knew the licensing for a song from Disney would be nearly impossible. But perhaps another musical? Maybe even a Broadway show?

"I didn't think cartoons were your kink." Cady hummed as her hand drifted over my thigh. My cock wasn't exactly being subtle at this point. Her question, and the blazing trail of her hand, stalled me mid-thought.

"They aren't." I shot back as my hand lazily began to stroke her bicep, trying to deter her attention so I could get out my thoughts before she blew them from my mind. "I was thinking of a certain woman whose bed I'm currently in."

Cady let out an amused noise. "Smooth. Real smooth."

"Well, actually I was thinking about something else. But that didn't cause this…" I cleared my throat as I gestured to my bottom half. "*Problem.*"

For fucks sake, her sucking on her lower lip was going to be the death of me. It was an automatic reflex now to anything I said or did that was even remotely a turn-on to her. Which only made it a never-ending fluster between the two of us. I really needed to get on with this conversation before I forgot what I was thinking about.

"So…" She glanced up at me as my brain slowly rebooted after her enticing visual. *Shit, get on with it man, before she mounts you again.* "Any chance you take requests?"

"Requests…?" Her brow quirked on one side. I knew it was a question out of left field. And it was a rather open-ended question.

"Yeah, songs for routines for the games."

The look on her face was one of shock and awe before it turned a little bit sultry. She scrambled out of my arms and sat up so fast that she seemed to swoon from the sudden blood rush.

"Did you fuck my brains out entirely or did you really just ask me if you could request a song for the Philly Sillys to dance to?"

My eyes went wide. There was too much in that sentence for me to dissect at once. All I could do was cough out a laugh.

"Um, I would hope, *both*." I managed to get out after the fluster of her words. With a grin, I ran my fingers through my disheveled mess of hair. She had me in the hot seat, but I noted her squirm. I wondered which one of us would break first.

"Well, so…yes." She stuttered, bringing the sheet up to her bare chest as she tried to hide her smile. "I take song requests. Within reason. No foul language and we have to get permission and whatnot. I had to put those parameters in place after the guys asked for some rather *questionable* ones."

"Okay, well…don't laugh." I had no idea what she would think of the specific song that I had in mind. Her brow arched in curious question.

"Cross my heart." She placed her palm over her breast for emphasis. Why did she have to draw attention to her chest? I was trying to stay on the subject for once. We were never going to get through this important conversation at this rate.

"Well…I was thinking…" Hanging on my every word, Cady leaned forward a bit. "How difficult would it be to do a song from a movie? Or a Broadway musical?"

"Oh," She mused, licking her lips as if she were trying the flavor of my suggestion. Or salivating over it. "You are definitely speaking my language." Her stormy eyes flashed up to mine with unbridled anticipation. "Which one did you have in mind?"

"*Wicked.*"

Cady was quiet. I froze as she did. Something was moving the gears inside her head, but I didn't know if it was in my favor, or against it. Her face was impassive.

"Fuck me sideways." The words left her mouth in breathy disbelief. "Jamie Rheems you're gonna make me fall in–" She cut herself off immediately as her eyes went wide. Was she going to say what I thought she was going to say? My heartbeat quickened. Was this the moment? "I-uh…um, make me fall in love with that *idea*."

Oh.

"So uh, *Wicked*, huh?" Cady shifted the conversation forward while my mind was still reeling. If I was a braver man, and if we weren't only weeks into this, I would have pressed it further. Instead, I pivoted right along with her.

"Yeah." My voice sounded as strained as my thoughts. I cleared my throat. "Every time I hear 'Dancing Through Life' it's just asking to be a Sillys dance routine. Hell, there's already a whole dance routine that goes with it."

"You…are absolutely not wrong." Cady slowly looked back up at me with a grin. Leaning in towards me, I could feel the aura of her warmth against my bare skin. "And you're fucking brilliant. It's an awesome idea. I'll pitch it to ownership tomorrow."

With a laugh, my hand shot out, wrapping my palm around the back of her neck as I pulled her in for a kiss. Brushing the pad of my thumb against her cheek, I took that moment to admire her. She was glowing, cheeks flushed, with a smile that made her eyes sparkle.

Even if she couldn't say it yet, I was pretty sure I was in love with Cadence Andrews.

22

I SEE THE LIGHT

MANDY MOORE AND ZACHARY LEVI

Holy fuck.

Was I completely out of my gourd from that last orgasm or did Mr. I-Hate-To-Dance just ask me if he could *request a song* for a Sillys dance routine? It was completely out of the blue. Even more so for it being a Broadway musical song. The man continued to surprise me, both in and out of the bedroom.

The man had a gift in the bedroom. He was selfless and attentive. Each time he slept with me it was as if he unlocked another secret to my desires. He took the time to figure out what made my body tick. At this rate, he was going to know more about my sexual needs than I had in my 32 years on this planet.

Right now, his kisses were sending me right back down that path to orgasmic euphoria. It was an off day for the team. Jamie and I planned on movies and books, among *other* things. And the "other things" had certainly taken precedence over everything clsc. The man had a hunger like no other and a bounce back that rivaled a teenager who just found the Victoria's Secret catalog.

His mouth and hands always sent off a barrage of fireworks in my brain. Thoughts and feelings were going every which way. It was chaos yet, quiet. Maybe it was more like my brain set off fireworks in celebration of how this man made me feel.

Just what did Jamie make me feel? It was something that occupied my thoughts more and more with each passing day. I never thought I'd have this conversation with myself over a fantasy that was actually tangible. Aside from the shit schedule of a ball player, the rest of him was amazing.

As much as I enjoyed the sex, it wasn't just about the sex. Sure, those first few days it seemed like it was only that. But once we got the weeks of dancing around the searing hot sexual tension out of our system, we spent more of our time talking or hanging out, enjoying each other's company. It was becoming common practice for me to forget that I initially thought he was the unattainable major league ball player of my fantasies. That maybe, he was someone I could spend forever with.

My breath stalled, along with my thoughts, as I felt Jamie's hand slip between my thighs. A happy little hum of approval vibrated against my skin as his mouth and tongue lazily made their way along my collarbone. My body arched towards him, wholeheartedly inviting him in.

That was the other thing that took me by surprise with this man. Typically, my body was unimpressed with the acts of seduction by men I'd been intimate with. With them, I spent most of the intimate process mentally making a to-do list or working on what I needed from the grocery store. With Jamie, all semblance of thought dissipated. All I could focus on was what his body was doing to mine. It was like a mantra, a meditation, something that hypnotized me and made me forget about the world for a while.

His finger slipped inside me with his hearty groan just as I heard the crooning between Rapunzel and Flynn during my favorite scene of the movie. As romantic as it would be to have sex to the song, I wasn't exactly looking for the romantic kind at this very moment. Not with the man practically growling in my ear from pure and utter need to have me all over again.

"You know," I managed to breathlessly get the words out as Jamie's lips moved along my collarbone. "I think we should turn the TV off. I don't exactly want Rapunzel to watch me get railed."

Jamie stopped his actions as his hot breath of laughter coated my bare breasts. There went my mouth, dropping word vomit like I made money off of it. He looked up at me as he withdrew his fingers. I pouted.

"Ah, smart. I definitely don't have the voyeur kink." Now it was my turn to laugh. Despite the superheated moment just seconds ago, we could still laugh at each other. It was nice. It made sex more fun and put less formality on it.

With another laugh, Jamie rolled over and reached for the remote on the side table. I'd tossed it there earlier since I had a bad habit of losing it in the bedding when I watched television. I was surprised that, with my terrible aim, I actually made it on the tabletop instead of the open drawer. It was still open due to our haste to get condoms earlier.

"What's this…?" Propping myself up in bed, I glanced over to see what Jamie was referring to. Only for my heart to completely bottom out in my stomach. In his hand was my brightly colored vibrating wand. If he found that, then he had to have seen the *entire* silicone toy treasure trove. It was stuffed in the same drawer as the box of condoms that we'd been depleting at an alarming rate.

Slinking down, I avoided his eyes. Those damn toys had been my pseudo-Jamie, or whatever fictional man I'd been reading about at the time, for the past few years. I initially had hoped he'd forgotten my mumbled sultry admission about that in the throes of passion.

"Is this what you use when you think of me…?" Jamie's gaze darkened as he stretched back out next to me. He was like a feline who had caught its prey and was content just to play with it. So much for him forgetting.

"I…yes." I swallowed dryly as I found myself brave enough to catch his gaze. "But you don't vibrate." What the actual fuck was it about this man that made my mouth just say whatever my brain was thinking?

An amused smile sensually caressed across his lips. They were still swollen from the rather heated make-out session. I wanted to hide under the plushness of my bedding. But they were shoved into a crumpled mess of mountains at the foot of my bed from our earlier romp. All we were left with were my jersey sheets. Which did wonders to show off his god-like body but did nothing to hide my embarrassment.

"Show me?" Jamie's voice dipped low and husky as he flipped the switch, bringing my best buzzing friend to life. His brows peaked on his forehead as he studied the toy. The little fucker did have quite the kickback on it. He clicked it back off. "Please? I want to see how you pleasured yourself when you thought of me."

A red-hot fire ignited in the apples of my cheeks. He couldn't be serious, right? The man had spent the better part of the afternoon giving me so many orgasms I lost count. There was no way that he wanted *more*.

His body slid in closer, and my breath hitched. My oxygen remained in purgatory as Jamie's mouth wreaked slow and delicious havoc against my neck. It was fair to say that the man just had to look at me and I'd get on my knees. Now he wanted me to show him how I *used* to get myself to orgasm.

There was a subtle upthrust to his hips which tugged the precariously perched sheets down and off his cock. It was already aching for another round of attention. *Holy fuck.* Did the thought of me masturbating to the idea of him turn him on that much?

"O-Okay…" I managed to squeak out as I bit down on my lower lip. Oh, holy shit was I actually considering this? He did ask me nicely to demonstrate. Perhaps the thought of all of this was a bit of a turn-on for me as well. "But I need a few of its friends."

The look on Jamie's face was going to be ingrained in my brain forever. There was shock and awe in his handsome features. So maybe he hadn't found the rest of the adult toy bounty in the drawer?

"Which ones?" The question was mixed with delight and curiosity as he stretched back over to peruse the choices.

"Um…the one that looks suspiciously like you." There was a bounce to his muscular shoulders as he chuckled. The hefty and realistic flesh-colored dildo appeared in his fisted hand from over his shoulder. "Ah yep," I said uneasily with a nod. "That's the one. But um…also the metal one with the pink jewel." I added sheepishly. What can I say, I liked meeting *all* of my needs, in every *outlet*. He did say he wanted to see *exactly* what I did when I thought of him.

Jamie rolled back over with a look of delighted curiosity as he placed the toys next to me. It was unnerving to have someone watch with such fascination. Although the visual of his body and erect cock took some of the awkwardness out of the entire situation.

"And the lube," I added with a bite to my lip. Jamie gave me a long, appreciative look before dipping his hand back into the drawer to produce the white bottle. He handed it to me as I settled in more comfortably against the pillow, tossing the sheet away. The sharp, appreciative hiss of air Jamie sucked in through his teeth gave me the last bit of confidence I needed to get started.

Closing my eyes, I attempted to concentrate on the already overheated nature of my body. My hands did their usual slow seduction of a tease across my skin. I was already in some wild mix of desire and shyness from the situation. I never had anyone watch me before.

With every teasing pass of my fingers near the apex of my thighs, Jamie let out some muffled sort of noise or a sharp breath. This was delicious torture for him as much as it was for me. The implications of it egged me on.

A low, satisfied groan sounded the moment I swirled my fingers around my clit. The pads of my fingers brought my desire up and around the swollen bud. I let out a sigh as I attempted to focus on the feeling instead of the sexy hunk who was watching me with rapt attention.

Blindly, I reached out with my free hand to grab my trusty vibrating wand. The head of it resembled the convex tip of a cock. The shape wreaked delicious havoc on my clit. My thumb found the integrated switch. I pressed it three times to get to the max level of constant-on.

I couldn't help the little breathy moan as the vibrating tip made contact with my already sensitive area. Between our sessions earlier, and the fact that I had the man of my literal fantasies next to me in bed, only added top-notch gasoline to my already roaring fire. The bed shifted a bit, and I cracked one eye open to see a glorious sight.

Jamie leaned in towards me, propped up on an elbow, to get a better view of the delights between my thighs. His fingers absentmindedly caressed his cock in lazy circles as he watched. Me pleasuring myself not only turned him on, but he was eager to get off on it. My hips bucked at the thought, which only made the man groan again. Dammit, I needed more. So much more.

Using my thighs to hold the wand in place, I grabbed the bottle of lube and the shiny metal torpedo-shaped butt plug. Jamie eyed it with interest as my fingers spread the drops of lube along the chilled exterior.

Adjusting my position, my body arched a bit to the side so I could reach down with one hand to slowly work the bejeweled plug into place. I took a few slow breaths as I worked magic upon my clit with the wand. The pleasure helped relax my body enough that my ass finally puckered and swallowed the toy up.

Jamie made a noise and shifted enough to get a better view to watch the pleasure unfold. The veins on the back of his hand bulged as his fisted hand pumped his cock with purpose.

"Are you…comfortable…?" Jamie asked with some measure of concern as he took one last look. Stretching back out beside me, his questioning blue eyes found mine. I couldn't help but let out a breathy little laugh. The bounce of laughter made the butt plug shift a bit, causing me to bite my lip.

"It's…interesting," I admitted as I opened my thighs back up for full access with the wand. "It adds a certain something when I'm really turned on. Sometimes I don't bother. But sometimes…my body *craves* it."

I let out a slow breath with the unbridled stream of admissions. There was never going to be a damn secret between us at this rate.

A soft, encouraging kiss brushed against my shoulder as Jamie's body settled in parallel to mine. As good as the wand and butt plug felt, I was paranoid that I'd have performance anxiety. But considering how eager the man was to watch, perhaps I could pull off an orgasm lightning round.

The velvet tip of his cock grazed against the outside of my thigh and a new wave of needy heat blossomed through my body. It left the ghost of a sear against my skin. I immediately grabbed the more phallic-looking toy from the bed.

I could feel his gaze on me as I managed to aim the silicone tip of the fake cock against my cunt. It flexed in delicious anticipation as I pressed the mushroomed head inside. It offered a small bit of satisfaction to quell the incessant ache, but only for a bit as I moaned out in relief. From experience, it was going to take the entire length of the toy to quench the need.

Jamie's muscular chest pressed against my bicep as I worked the toy the rest of the way in with ease. With all of the near-constant teasing, my body was overly slick and eager. The only hang-up was how tightly my cunt was squeezing with excitement.

There was a deep groan from the man next to me as I felt his teeth graze along the apex of my shoulder. Having a second party in this, usually a solo endeavor, was oddly delicious. Not to mention the soundtrack he was providing was almost enough to get me off.

With the silicone dick in my right hand and the vibrating wand in my left, I slowly began to thrust the toy in and out of me. Biting down on my lower lip, I felt a little self-conscious about making any noise. Once I felt Jamie's eager hand caressing up my thigh, I couldn't help it. Having that unexpected but reassuring touch made a huge difference.

My eyes shot open as I heard the gurgle of the lube bottle next to me. Jamie squirted some in his palm and spread it all over his rigid cock. My brain certifiably short-circuited as he threw the bottle aside and began to slowly pump his glistening fist up and down the length.

Oh, fuck *fuck **fuck**. The man of my fantasies was getting off watching me pleasure myself.*

The hand with the dildo quickened as my hips arched into the thrusting toy. I could hear the sound of his hand gliding up and down, the rhythm almost matching my own. This whole situation was quickly becoming a kink I didn't know I had. Jamie said he didn't have a voyeur kink, but he sure as fuck was unlocking one in me.

"Cady, you're such a fucking vision. This is going to give me the fuel to get through those road trips knowing this is what you do when you miss me." There was a delicious edge to his voice. I didn't know if it was because he was close or if it was because this was just as hot for him as it was for me. "I want to watch you cum all night, but I don't know if I could handle watching more than one."

Jeezus hell on earth.

I guess that explained the strained tone of his voice. My breathing hitched as I felt the sparks of my delicious demise begin because of his words. Masturbation was going to have a dangerous new level if I continued to get this sort of commentary along with it.

The speed of my thrusts picked up as I chased after my orgasm. I was so close. I felt the unfortunate burn in my forearm and internally groaned. Of course, it had to cramp at the most inopportune time. With a frustrated whimper, I stopped my movements and went to switch hands.

Jamie's hand shadowed over mine as he abandoned his own pleasure to tend to me. His intense blue gaze met mine for a fleeting moment.

"Let me?"

With a subtle nod, I let his hand take over with the dildo. He distracted me with a fierce kiss as his hand adjusted its grip. Gently, he found his rhythm. He groaned at the ease with which the toy moved within me. This was the first time a partner had ever used toys on me. It was so fucking mind-blowing.

He took his time, listening for cues and watching my body language. It was difficult to figure out what angle or speed worked when you weren't on the same receiving end as the pleasure being administered. His gaze was intense as he watched. Each little flicker of his pupil drank in the erotic sight before him. I could feel myself melting quickly from his attentions.

"Yes, yes… Jamie, *right there…*"

It was too much. Between staring at Jamie devouring me with his gaze alone, to him thrusting the sex toy in and out of me, the fluster of it all bundled into one huge hot ball of desire in my abdomen. With one inhale I let out a shuddering breath as his mouth slipped over mine and joined forces with his thrusting hand to get closer to sending me over the edge.

"Oh my god, don't stop! More…more…!" I whined as I begged against his kissing lips. My body arched off the bed as my free hand reached out to tangle in the sheets. Strangling the cotton fibers in my fierce grasp, I cried out. The orgasm came on hot and heavy. A certifiable tidal wave of delights coming from all angles.

"Oh *fuck*, Cady… Such a good girl. Such a *fucking* good girl." The animalistic growl of his words shoved me back off the sheer cliff all over again. My body spasmed with each incredible wave as Jamie continued his thrusting of the toy. The buzzing one in my hand didn't waver, only enhanced each jolt of my orgasm.

My screaming slowly turned to breathless whimpers. I could only see stars in my eyes as Jamie eased back on his thrusts, drawing out the lingering delights. My cunt still reflexed of its own accord every so often, even though the more intense waves had fizzled out. That was the most intense toy orgasm I had in quite some time.

My breathing slowly returned to normal as I was finally able to refocus. Thumbing the control on the vibrating wand, I held it in to turn it off. Jamie took the cue and slowed the dildo to a stop. He slid the toy out of me when I gave him the nod to do so. The whimper that escaped me was a reflex at the loss of feeling so delightfully full.

Reaching down, my fingers graced the edge of the gem of the butt plug to pull it out, but Jamie stopped me, "Leave it." My eyes met his, finding something sultry and pleading there in the endless seas. "That is if you're okay? I'm…*curious*."

Biting on my lower lip, I gave him a nod of consent. The thought made my heart race, but I realized that I'd always wanted to try it. There was a rustle in the condom box before he turned back to me with a sinful little grin.

The talented man juggled kissing me, ripping open the condom, put on said condom, all while slipping himself between my legs. It was an exciting flip of the switch. I went directly from the old-school method to the method I'd always fantasized about. Having sex with Jamie's *actual* body. With a very willing and excited Jamie.

He never made me feel silly or shamed me for what I desired. Hell, everything that turned me on turned him on even more. Sex like this was supposed to be carefree and fun. To feel comfortable enough with a partner that they would be happy to use sex toys and other fun stuff on you. With consent of course.

I welcomed back the heady feel of the weight of his body above mine. A warm cocoon covered me as he wedged his hips between my thighs. I relished in the closeness of his hips, cradled by my legs, while his arms caged me in from both sides. The glorious vision of his smile as he hovered over me was so damn delicious.

Caressing my fingers along his jawline, his lips smiled against mine. The man was the most level-headed person I'd ever met. How could he stay so calm and collected after that? He had to be ready to explode from the sheer pent-up arousal, yet he took time to be tender with me.

The moment he slipped inside me had us both moaning. Goosebumps prickled across my body from the sensation of his cock deep within me as the butt plug flexed along with my cunt. Oh, my fucking hell. How was I going to survive this session? Surely, I was going to combust. Disintegrate into a pile of hot, smoldering, ash.

I was so lost in the fluster of the new sensations that I didn't notice Jamie adjusting his body until his forehead touched mine. My eyes flashed open and met with the most intense crisp blue. His hand lingered along the corner of my jaw, reassuring me. Holding me.

How the hell did something so utterly filthy turn into something that was so intensely intimate? It was honestly overwhelming.

I was drowning in the sensations, overheating me and yet making me feel at ease. His entire cock made its way deep inside me. He held it there, gently guiding me into this new experience. And what a delicious endeavor it was.

Not that I would shove a plug up my ass every sex session, but it was definitely worth a semi-regular rotation. Especially if the plug was joined with Jamie's incredibly talented cock.

He was slow, but deep and deliberate, as he started to thrust in and out of me. My mouth cracked open in wonderment as breathy little noises of delight slipped forth, encouraging him on.

"You okay?"

"Fuck yes." I huffed out with an arch of my hips up into his for emphasis. It earned me a delicious little groan from the depths of his throat.

"Good." Jamie sighed out. "Fuck, Cady. You're an incredible woman."

My eyes flickered up to watch his face. His eyes were closed with his head tipped back. I could see the deep rhythm of his pulse in his neck. My god he was beautiful.

"Are you Team Butt Plug now?" I teased, leaning up to nip at the flutter of his pulse.

"Can't say I've ever had a partner use toys with me before." His hips slowed a bit as his face turned sheepish. Glancing down, he gave me a breathless kiss.

"Ever?" I asked, surprised. "Not even an ex had them or something?"

"I don't think so."

"Well, that you know of." He gave me a huff of a breath in response. "You've been in that drawer how many times?"

"I was a little *preoccupied* every time I was digging for condoms."

There was a tightening along the sharp line of his jaw. My breath caught as I felt him get more intense with each of his thrusts. At this rate, I was only going to get one-word responses out of him.

I was a little surprised by his admission. I'd heard all kinds of wild stories from the guys and their exploits in the bedroom. They hadn't gone into intense detail but some of those baseball groupie girls were rather kinky. Especially the ones that read romance books.

Sexual health has always been an important aspect of my life. As much as I hated to admit it, it wasn't until a few years ago that I took the time to discover what I wanted when it came to sex. I came to realize that I could have most of my sexual needs met without engaging in a sexual partner. It sure as hell took a lot of the desperation out of trying to find a significant other.

But Jamie?

The man was certifiably the whole package. He was wholesome. Sweet. Sexy as hell and a delicious, foul-mouthed beast in bed. Jamie Rheems was everything I'd ever imagined.

Honestly, he was *better*.

My arms shot out to entangle around his neck. I needed him close. I needed him to never let me go.

"Cady…" His strained voice pulled me from my inner thoughts and straight back into the present.

"Fuck, Cady..." There was a desperation there. Almost as if he was begging.

I'd been so lost in my pleasure that he took part in that I neglected the fact that the poor man still needed to get off too. He had sat back and brought me to orgasm all while keeping his release at bay.

Leaning up, I spread suckling kisses up and down his neck. It was just the sort of distraction he needed. Using my core muscles, I rolled the both of us over in one breathless maneuver.

The abrupt change in position made my ass strain with the butt plug, which drew a deliciously needy sound out of me. Jamie's eyes flashed open in surprise to see me mounted atop him. The man had gotten me off. It was only fair that I let him sit back while I returned the favor.

Riding him with the plug was a whole host of new sensations. His hands darted out to lock onto my hips with a death grip. Meanwhile, his handsome features morphed into delicious satisfaction as I picked up the pace.

It didn't last long. With a few swirls and sharp upticks of my hips, I felt his nails dig into my skin. My breath quickened as I watched him slowly descend into the glorious madness of his orgasm. I felt like a powerful goddess seated on the throne of the man that had caught my heart, in more ways than one. Between that thought and the subtle feel of his cock hardening to full strength, I lost myself all over again.

Our cries intermingled in the heated air as we climaxed, one after the other. I didn't stop. I kept up the rhythm, riding him through the throes of his and my orgasms. It was intense. More intense than I thought it would be, especially after getting off only minutes before. If I hadn't alerted the neighbors to what we were up to, I certainly did now.

"Cady…*Cadence*…" My eyes were still closed off to the world as my body continued its intimate rhythm. I vaguely heard my name in the warbled chaos of the aftershocks of my incredibly intense orgasm. The rocking of my hips was almost like a meditation as I slowly cascaded down from my high.

I felt Jamie shift beneath me to sit up and meet me face-to-face. His strong but gentle hands cupped my face, claiming my attention. My eyelids fluttered open. His breathless smile made my heart almost burst through my ribcage.

"*Sweetheart…*" The soft plea with a breathless smile brought me to a stop. "As fucking good as your body feels, you do have to let a man recover." A hot blush flooded my cheeks as a sheepish smile appeared across my lips. "Especially after an orgasm like that. Holy fuck, baby."

With back-to-back endearments and his gentle touch, I was fit to burst from the sudden influx of emotion. An embarrassed bubble of laughter shot from my lips. I muffled it with a savory kiss.

Jamie's hands slid to my hips to gently coax me off of him. We both shared a mutual sigh at our separation before he tucked me back into bed right next to him. I was still in a bit of a daze and tried to get my bearings as he addressed the condom situation. My ass hitting the mattress reminded me that there was still the extra rider aboard.

Grabbing a tissue from my nightstand, I slowly eased the toy out with a gentle pull from my hooked fingers around the jewel end. I let out a huff of air as my body released the thing. If the thing hadn't been just up my asshole, I would have kissed it. That orgasm was top-notch. Although maybe I should give Jamie's cock a kiss too. Between the both of them, it was one hell of a climax that I was pretty sure I'd never forget for as long as I lived. Well, unless there were a few more of those in my future.

"I'm addicted to you, Cady, do you know that?" The words were hot and husky in my ear as Jamie drew me back against his body. Even with all the hours of fantasizing about what a moment like this would feel like, it was nothing in comparison to the real deal. It felt safe. It was warm.

It felt like home.

23

CANNED HEAT

JAMIROQUAI

Once Cady announced to the guys that "Dancing Through Life" was going to be the big song for our 4th of July game, they were all over it. She nearly fell out of her seat when I surprised her with a special, shortened arrangement of the song. With the original song clocking in at nine minutes and forty-seven seconds, I didn't think we had it in us to dance for almost ten minutes straight in the July heat.

Schmidt cornered me almost immediately after Cady had mentioned it, and asked if his DJ friend, Andy, could have a whack at making something custom for us. The hype playlist Schmidt played for warm-ups was 90% DJ Andy remixes. Since the music was fire, I wholeheartedly agreed.

With my specific song request, it was the first time I was able to see Cady in her element. Once she heard the arrangement, she went into full choreographer mode. I caught her absentmindedly working on dance moves any spare chance she had. I lost count of how many times we watched the library scene in *Wicked* so she could commit the dance moves to memory.

273

After I fixed my bed, we spent most nights at my place. It gave her ample space to work out dance moves and placement of the players. I happily shoved my furniture to the side, giving her the full space of my living room and dining room area in my penthouse. My place had been so cold and drab, but when Cady was twirling about, she gave my home the breath of life it sorely needed.

Having Cady join me in my space on more of a regular basis was just so *easy*. She asked for nothing, well, except for another round or two between the sheets, or wherever we ended up. We'd managed to christen just about every abstract surface, horizontal and vertical, in my apartment and hers.

In sharing the same space, I had a front-row seat to those very tasty matching sports bras and bottoms. I may or may not have bought a few sets that were her style and tucked them in a drawer in my bedroom. You know, just in case.

She was irresistible in every which way. I felt myself getting hard just watching her bend over to put her shoes on. It was like I had the stamina of my teenage years all over again. Surprisingly enough, it also spread to my vigor on the field as well. Most days I was giving the Sillys guys a run for their money with the dance routines.

I felt alive. Invigorated. Happy. Much happier than I'd been in a very long time. I thought baseball was all I needed. It wasn't until I met this little spitfire, who was obsessed with me, that I started to take a hard look at my future.

Cady was obsessed in all the right ways. She didn't give a damn that I was in the majors, she didn't care that I got demoted, and she didn't want anything except to spend time with *me*. It was the first time that I wanted to give a woman the world, and she didn't want it.

Fucking hell.

I was in love with her.

I spent so much time avoiding these deep feelings. It was stupid of me to think that something like this couldn't blossom in only a few weeks. When I finally admitted it to myself, it felt like a confession to the sins of my denial.

I could breathe again.

I felt whole. Confident. Confident enough to know that I wanted Cady by my side.

But how could I tell her?

Throwing the "L" word at a person, after not even two months of knowing them, was scary. Even though I felt sure about it, I wasn't completely sure that Cady felt the same way. Would I scare her off if I said something?

I'd caught her appreciative starry-eyed stares in my direction from time to time. Perhaps her feelings were still budding. I didn't want to rush things. Not when they were as incredible as they were.

What would the off-season bring? Long lazy days of the both of us tangled up in each other's arms in bed? Movie marathons on the couch? Enjoy the calm quiet of each other's company? The more I fantasized about it, the more I looked forward to it.

Would the Sillys off-season be less crazy and more prolonged than the majors? Typically, we'd get three months tops, four if we didn't make it to the postseason. I was already enjoying the more laid-back vibes of the ELB season. Away games were easier too. The Sillys played teams on the East Coast instead of all over the US. The only exhaustion was from the days of travel instead of the crazy jet lag on top of it.

"Hey, Slugger, you with us?"

I startled a bit and glanced down to see Cady with a smile just for me. The guys were twirling around me, working on their specific parts for the big dance number. I on the other hand was *somehow* selected to be Fiyero in this scenario. This might have had something to do with the fact that I just so happened to be banging the tasty choreographer. And maybe I dropped a few hints.

"Oh, uh, sorry. Wrapped up in my thoughts." I muttered.

"You missed your cue." Cady bit her bottom lip trying to suppress her grin. I wanted to grab her chin and hold her still while I sucked that damn lip right out of her mouth. Instead of giving in, I lifted my gaze to the field. Noting the music, I grumbled. Damn, how distracted had I been? Ender looked on in a huff with a cocked hip in his impatience.

Since I wrangled the part of Fiyero, the guys unanimously voted for Ender to be Glinda. The match between the pitcher to the catcher was too hilarious for even me to overlook. Poor Ender was a lot shorter than me, so the partnering worked out in that aspect.

"Look, the quicker we nail this routine at home plate, the quicker you guys can get out of here for your lunch break."

"I'd rather nail you at home plate," I mumbled and looked away innocently. Cady's gaze snapped to me. There was a flash of fire in those gray-blue depths, a sultry warning for later. Although now my brain was stuck on a plan to christen my favorite base with her in the future.

"Alright, everyone!" Cady's voice cracked before she cleared her throat. *Mm, she was thinking about that idea too. Excellent.* "Let's start again with Jamie and Ender at home plate."

The guys scrambled back to their starting positions. They were the background dancers fanned out around the infield as Fiyero and Glinda had their little moment while he crooned to her. Well, me crooning to Ender. I think the blonde wig we all suggested would have helped me picture him as Glinda better. But he drew the line there. We managed to talk him into rhinestone jerseys but even that had taken some convincing.

"Dude don't fuck it up this time," Ender grumbled as his eyes darted to something off in the distance. "I have lunch plans." He was a man of few words. He followed my pitch calls without question and was normally much more mild-mannered. Something was under his skin today.

"Yeah yeah, I've got this," I said, not only to reassure him but also myself. This routine was fun. I got to watch it come to fruition, firsthand, in my living room while Cady bounced around in her sports bra. *Shit, Jamie, no. Focus on the routine.*

The music started up again. Furrowing my brows I did my best to focus on Ender and all the dance moves. A spin, a little sashay, a dip. Ender was much more graceful than me, but I was the one who had to lead the dance steps. We pulled off a, mostly, flawless finish.

The music stopped and I immediately heard Cady's excited squeals.

"Holy shit you guys, I really can't wait for tomorrow. You are all going to blow everyone's minds!"

Helping Ender up from our dip, my eyes darted over to Cady as she bounced around to each of the guys to offer last-minute notes. She needed to fucking stop with those double entendres or else my dick was going to have a few things to say about it.

"Okay if you all can manage two more flawless run-throughs you guys can head out early." There was a resounding cheer throughout the players along with a renewed sense of vigor. "I have no doubts you guys are going to wow the crowd tomorrow. They won't know what's coming."

Ender glanced at me, and we shared a nod. Sweat was already pouring down my back from the insufferable July heat and humidity. But the end was in sight. Once again I thanked myself for shortening the song down to something much more reasonable. Ten more minutes in this heat was about all we could stand.

The guys found their first mark and Cady started the music. My heart was pounding with excitement and nerves. Who would have thought that I'd be the star of a musical number? It was enough to make even a major league ball player shake at the knees.

Then I saw her.

Cady was all smiles as she stood back to watch the magic unfold. The chaos inside me subsided enough to let my inner Fiyero out in full force. With each dance step I nailed, her brows went higher and higher on her forehead in excitement. Her encouragement was subtle, but it fueled me. Enough so that it spurred a few extra flourishes of my hands and feet. Cady loved it when we adlibbed. Within reason.

With me super into the song, everyone else fed off the energy. I could only imagine what the stadium would be like tomorrow if we were going to be this on point. To hear the cheer of the fans would make this a production to remember.

By the end of the second run-through, half the guys fell to the grass to have some reprieve from the late morning sun. Cheers and exclamations echoed around as Cady gave us a round of applause. Our afternoon off was well-earned.

"Nice work out there, Slugger." I nearly jumped out of my skin as Cady slapped me firmly on my ass. It was unexpected. But the more unexpected part of it was that I *liked* her spanking me.

"Don't tell me you're going around slapping all the butts of the players," I growled with the thought as I cast a glance at the guys collecting their things off the field.

"No, just yours." She gave me a wicked grin as she bit down on her lower lip. "Although I don't get why guys in sports do it. Who the hell started that?"

"Someone with a spanking kink probably." I shrugged, feeling the tug of a smile as Cady burst out in laughter.

"Who knew baseball could be so kinky?"

"I mean, it is the sport that inspired all those sexual innuendos." My voice dropped to a husky murmur, just for her. Her cheeks went pink as she realized everything that I alluded to with that one sentence. "Speaking of, which base can I slide into tonight?"

24

DANCING THROUGH LIFE
JONATHAN BAILEY (ARRANGED BY JAMIE RHEEMS)

"**S**orry guys, but we're gonna have to scrap the 'Dancing Through Life' routine tonight." There was an overwhelming round-robin groan around the locker room. "Ender had some medical issue that landed him in the ER." A gasp went through the locker room. "He's fine, but unable to make it to the game." I sighed, feeling as disappointed as the guys looked. "He's the only one who could do Glinda's part with Jamie's Fiyero."

It ripped me apart from the inside out to say it. Jamie and the guys worked so hard on this dance routine. While Jamie had been a bit rough, movement-wise, in places, it was obvious that he finally figured out how to have fun with the guys. Rehearsals had been a dream. I'd never seen all the guys collectively excited over something. I made a note to incorporate more songs from musicals in the future. Because there was no fucking way I'd turn down *that* opportunity.

"What the fuck, seriously?" Truitt groaned as he doused his hair and beard with water from a water bottle. It was an overly humid July day. I was ready to jump into a pool with all of my clothes on.

"The pitcher/catcher dynamic was just too perfect. We can't top that. Maybe we can try again next home game. Look, guys, I mean, things hap–" I tried to reason with them, but the Sillys were determined. More determined than usual. Scrapping a dance number before a game wasn't common, but it did happen from time to time.

"It's probably something to do with that chick he's been seeing." Martin offered and I cocked my brow. The guys rarely kept anything from one another, except for Jamie of course, so this was new information to me. Ender was as dedicated to this game as Jamie was.

"But he's in the ER." I attempted to reason with him, but Martin only shrugged. "Yeah well, either way, we can't do it–"

"Cadence," Kellan piped up and the room went silent. "*You* can do it."

Immediately there was a shout of enthusiastic agreement across the room.

"You choreographed the whole thing. You know the dance moves for each of us. Ender's moves are a piece of cake for you." Arlow added. Another murmur floated around as all eyes turned on me.

While he wasn't wrong, I hadn't participated in a routine with the Sillys *on the field* before. Everyone in the stands came for them, not me. My sole purpose was to give the guys a routine to shake their booties to while the crowd cheered them on.

"Not to mention, I think we are all dying to see a little bit of that delicious chemistry between you and Jamie." Benson offered with a wink. I did my damnedest to suppress the look of shock as I glanced in Jamie's direction. He looked just as nervous. How did they know about Jamie and me? The team all agreed in enthusiastic unison.

Shit.

"We all know you two are hanging out outside of work." Tomas offered with a broad grin.

"It is kind of obvious." Arlow rolled his eyes, but it didn't stop the smile on his face.

"I–" Dear god I needed to stop this train wreck before Jamie and I both got into deep shit because of it. We'd been so careful to keep it on the down low from the Sillys. Hadn't we?

"Look," Benson stood up and put a hand on my shoulder. He made a show of glancing between me and Jamie. "I think we all caught you and Jamie sucking face on one occasion or another." My cheeks were hot enough that I could have given myself a third-degree burn from the inside out. We were so toast. Jamie stood up and made a few steps in my direction. "Honestly, we couldn't be happier for you, Coach."

"Yeah, whatever you did to him snapped him out of his bad streak," Tomas added brightly. The rest of the guys burst out laughing.

God just strike me down with lightning. Pretty please? Right now.

"I think we all *know* what she did to get the man back on track." Arlow teased as he stood up and clapped Tomas on the back. The poor outfielder looked utterly confused. "You see when a man and a woman like each other…" The locker room burst out in even more uproarious laughter.

Anytime, God.

The lightning bolt?

Hell, send a few.

Honestly, a plague would work too. Anything to stop Arlow from giving Tomas the "birds and the bees" lesson on my and Jamie's behalf. In front of the entire Sillys locker room.

"No really." Benson pulled my attention back to him as his hand gave my shoulder a reassuring squeeze. "None of us have ever seen you this happy in all the years you've been here."

"You guys totally make a cute couple!" Truitt cheered on from across the locker room. I cringed. He should just announce it to the whole damn franchise while he's at it. "It's about fucking time you guys just came out and admitted it."

But…Jamie and I weren't a couple. Were we? The crush we had on each other was mutual, a thousand times over and we liked hanging out together. Did people even ask to be boyfriend or girlfriend anymore, or was it just assumed? I was clueless.

I felt Jamie's calming presence at my side. While his cheeks were as pink as mine, he was grinning.

"Alright guys, settle down. As for the routine, Cady–" There was a chorus of "ohhhs" and catcalls as Jamie called me by his nickname for me. "…and you all, were able to remind me that baseball can still be fun. Even if I'm on the geriatric side of players. It was a…*team* effort." Jamie's strong hand found mine and he squeezed it. Thank fuck he refocused the locker room on something else. "So, what do you think, Cady? You ready to make an ass of yourself with the rest of us?"

I cautiously glanced around the room at all the hopeful pleading looks. Wait, was Camden getting all teary-eyed? He was always the passionate one, good or bad, of the group. Roman gave him a few reassuring pats on the back as the locker room stirred up an approving murmur.

Truitt's fisted hand shot up in the air as if he were cheering me with a beer in hand. "Fucking right! Let's do this! Come on, coach!" The entire team rose with a roar. I couldn't help but laugh.

"What the fuck is going on in here?" Topper's stern voice made my body turn to ice. He'd been in his open office during that entire conversation. Chances were that he heard every damn thing that had been discussed in the last few minutes. "Why aren't you ballerinas out on the field? It's game time!"

The boys immediately hustled, grabbing their baseball gloves and hats, before making a break for the doors to the dugout. But not Jamie, he lingered by my side and didn't let go of my hand. I couldn't let him go down with me. Especially not when he was finally back to his old self. Hell, he was even *better*.

"Get out there with the guys," I whispered to him as Topper headed in our direction. My heart suddenly felt like a lead balloon in my stomach. "I'll deal with Topper."

"No. This is on me just as much as it's on you." Jamie firmly insisted with a quick kiss on my temple. Well, there was no denying this now. I could only imagine how pissed the franchise was going to be.

"Truitt's right." Topper stopped as he gave the two of us a glance. "You two are a cute couple." My jaw dropped as Topper leaned in towards Jamie to address him. "Take extra care of this one. She's special." With the tiniest hint of a smile, the wizened manager shuffled his way towards the dugout door.

My mouth was still hanging open as Jamie let out a surprised huff of a laugh.

There was a long moment of silence, with just the two of us, in the locker room. Did that mean that Topper wasn't going to say anything to ownership? What was going to happen to us?

Blinking, I turned to head out after the guys, but Jamie stopped me. My mouth opened to say something but his hands rushing up to cup my face made the words disappear. With a grin and a firm grip, he pulled me up to his mouth. On my tippy toes, I immediately melted into his kiss. They were my oxygen of late. My drug. Something I was sure I'd never get enough of.

"No sense in hiding it anymore," Jamie murmured against my mouth as I threw my arms around his neck. "We'd better get out there, Glinda." A snort of laughter escaped me before I even knew what was happening.

"Oh, you know I'm looking forward to this Fiyero shaking his booty." With a smug grin, I reached around and tweaked his deliciously firm ass.

"You know what? Let's dance." Jamie added, in perfect cadence.

Could I love this man any more than I already did?

Whoa…wait.

Love?

I stopped dead in my tracks, but Jamie's grip was firm on my hand. Despite the sudden whirlwind of a possible epiphany in my brain, I found myself being dragged after him up the steps. I had to dismiss the thought and get my stage face on. The "L" word was just was just a slip of my inner monologue.

I barely heard the loudspeaker introducing the Sillys. That was the cue for the dance number. To distract myself from diving deeper into my dangerous thoughts, I quickly reached up to brush off invisible dust from Jamie's uniform. He was so sexy like this, with the boyish glint in his blue eyes to being dressed head to toe in the yellow, aqua, and navy blue colors of the Sillys.

The rhinestones he insisted upon for this Fiyero-approved costume uniform made me chuckle. Jamie was bouncing in his baseball cleats as the musical intro to the song he arranged echoed off the walls of the stadium to wild cheers. The city of Philadelphia apparently was *Wicked* fans too. Despite the long rocky road to get here, Jamie was made for this. He had proved all of us wrong.

"Break a leg, Slugger." With a grin and a kiss on my nose, he ran out onto the field. Damn, if I thought the screams were loud of the first few bars of "Dancing Through Life", they were like mouse whispers compared to the utter roar of the crowd as Jamie strutted his stuff, in true main character fashion, out to home plate.

The routine called for the Sillys roster to form a gauntlet for him to go through before the sexy-as-hell man danced his way from the pitcher's mound to home plate. His happy place. The crowd was eating him up and he was absorbing every ounce of their feedback.

The roar of the crowd was always so addictive. The boys were obsessed with it. From my perch in the dugout, the Sillys guys were feeding the crazed crowd. A few times I was pretty certain I heard a few catcalls as Jamie shook his blinged-out ass for the fans.

Proud choreographer coach moment.

My heart began to beat faster as the lyrics started to point Jamie in my direction. The next part of the routine required him to glide and dip Ender at home plate. I, and the entire Sillys roster, thought it was the funniest part of the whole set. Especially with the lyrics about finding the prettiest girl. The guys could never keep a straight face.

Instead of what we rehearsed, it was now me fussing with a pink version of a bedazzled Sillys jersey. I couldn't believe that Jamie insisted upon such sparkly duds. If it didn't have Ender's last name on it, I would have kept it.

Jamie's intense gaze locked onto mine as he took his variety of, to the best of his ability, flying leaps and spins over to me. I had to stifle my laughter as he looked much closer to an inelegant gazelle than Fiyero himself. But there was such a lively sparkle in his eyes. He was having *fun*.

I was so transfixed with Jamie's gyrating hips and sly smile that I was physically shocked into existence when he grabbed my hand and pulled me out onto the field. The crowd erupted into more screams. I was surprised they weren't hoarse by now.

With one quick tug, my body snapped to Jamie's, in a rather suggestive manner, which wasn't at all like we practiced. But he practiced with Ender, not me. And it was evident in his eyes that he enjoyed me as a partner much more.

Instead of just lip-syncing the lyrics, Jamie's husky voice infiltrated my ears. Making me feel like the prettiest girl as he gave me a whirl. His words drowned out the noise of the crowd and loudspeaker, crooning his way through the more flirtatious part of the song.

I swore my panties caught fire for the whole world to see. He must have been able to smell my fluster as he used the brass section's pronounced beats to gyrate our bodies together in time for the music. Right before he positioned us into a closed partner dance position.

In the remix he made to fit the time slot, Jamie had the song go straight into the duet between Glinda and Fiyero. My heart began to race all over again as he leaned in, nose to nose, with the biggest grin on his face. He continued to sing the lyrics but somehow made them an enchantment that was just for me. And all without missing a step.

I felt the corresponding lyrics leave my mouth. What man, in my entire life, would have ever agreed to sing and dance to a song from one of my favorite musicals? Let alone the man I was dancing with was the man I had a crush on for years. Nothing, and I mean nothing, could have ever prepared me for such a moment ever happening in my quiet yet oddly chaotic life.

My stomach left me as Jamie scooped me up in his arms and spun the both of us. How did this man go from being allergic to dancing to *improvising* dance moves in time to the music?

With my arms tangled around his neck, Jamie took a single step forward as he dropped me back down to earth. His hands lingered, cradling my lower back as he dipped me. He dipped me just like that night at the bar. And come hell or high water, I wasn't going to miss the opportunity this time. I didn't care who was watching.

Leaning up, I snuck in a quick kiss. My heart came to a thudding stop as Jamie looked down at me in a surprised daze. The expression only lasted a moment before he grinned and pulled me back in for a much more suggestive kiss. I was fairly certain the guys were whistling catcalls while the crowd roared but all I could hear, and feel, was Jamie and my hearts beating as one.

25

REAL PEACH

HENRY JAMISON

"**H**oly shit, dude! You fucking nailed it!" Truitt came bounding down the stairs from the dugout into the locker room to give me, yet another, rather aggressive high five. A half dozen other Sillys lined up right after him to do the same.

"Who knew you had all the moves? Shaking that ass." Benson teased as he gave my ass a firm slap with a wink.

"Yeah, Jamie. You were on fire tonight." Chimed in Kellan as he offered a fist bump.

"Hey dude, you're supposed to make us look *good, not* show us up." Arlow razzed me as he elbowed my bicep on his way past. The rest of the guys got a good chuckle out of that.

"Yeah yeah. I just had to show you how it's done is all." I played right into their game. I was awarded with a locker room full of groans followed by a bombardment of sweaty socks, dirty hats, and Benson and Truitt's cooling headbands.

While the opening number was hot shit, the opposing team, the Baltimore Crabbies, was unfortunately hotter. The Sillys gave it their all, but the guys from Charm City had that extra edge. We led for a good seven innings before Kellan missed a bouncing infield hit that rolled under his outstretched glove and into Truitt territory in the outfield, sending one runner home. We couldn't catch up after that once their closing bullpen stepped up to the mound.

Despite all that, I was beaming from ear to ear. I didn't care that we lost, I didn't care one iota. That game was by far the most fun I'd ever had playing baseball. Between Cady granting my absurd request to dance to "Dancing Through Life", to dancing with the woman I couldn't get enough of, to the loudest cheers I'd ever heard in my entire baseball career. I was going to be living on this high for a very long time.

Cady was incredible as Ender's Glinda understudy. A part of me was sure that the crowd probably loved having her out there instead of Ender. But I was never going to tell him that. It was magical, electric, and romantic as fuck.

My heart was still beating a million miles a minute. Because of the added adrenaline and ego boost from the dance number, I played my best game of Sillys baseball ever. Hell, if the rules had been the same as the majors, I probably would have beaten my stats there too. I managed a base hit with each at-bat and even a home run during the bottom of the third inning. So even though we lost, I had a lot to celebrate.

I was on fire, and I had this team to thank for it.

I had Cady to thank for it.

She was such a dream. A *wet* dream. A dream of a woman that was everything I could have ever wished for. All in a cute, petite package.

More than anything I wanted to sweep her up in my arms and bury ourselves in the sheets for the entire night. That was the kind of celebration I could get behind. A quiet, well *not so quiet*, night with just Cady and me.

Two months ago, I was so sure I'd hit rock bottom. Stepping into this ballpark was as if I signed off on my doom. That getting me to do any form of dancing would have been over my dead body.

But look at me now.

I inspired an entire dance number and then *starred* in it.

Was it Broadway-worthy? Absolutely not. Was it my best work in anything I've ever done? Debatably. Did I have an amazing time?

It was...

Incredible.

A round of cheers erupted, and I glanced up from unbuttoning my jersey to see the woman of my dreams waltz down the steps in her white sneakers and pink rhinestone Sillys jersey. I'd seen the woman completely naked and yet this was one of her sexiest looks. My fingers itched to grab ahold of her and not let go.

"Alright alright, keep your shirts on." Cady dismissed the guys and their nonsense with a big ass grin. "Way to kill it out there, guys!" More cheers erupted as the Sillys went back to high fiving each other.

A loss in the majors usually turned the mood of the locker room into one of melancholy. Which, given how many games there are in the regular season, was kind of a moot point. A loss meant it was going to take more games to get to the postseason and the World Series.

But here? It was the complete opposite. The guys were still playful and lighthearted. It was infectious. How could anyone have a bad day here? Now that I had this whole dancing thing figured out, it wasn't a bad place at all

Maybe, just maybe, I wouldn't mind staying.

"Way to shake it out there, Slugger," Cady murmured to me with a playful little smile as she walked past to head to her office. My hands shot out in reflex to pull her against me. I wasn't responsible for anything that happened between us if she walked anywhere near my orbit. She had an irresistible gravitational pull.

Her surprised, but happy, squeal permeated my ears as I pulled her in for a kiss.

"I couldn't have done it without such a badass coach." The color in her cheeks was one that I wanted to bottle up and paint my entire condo with. I was obsessed with everything that was Cady. Today just cemented that fact.

"Get a room you two!" Truitt's voice sliced through the delicious tension between Cady and me. He couldn't keep a straight face or laughter out of his words. A few cat-calls followed from the team for emphasis.

"Oh, I plan on it." I grinned, not bothering to look anywhere else but at Cady. The pink in her cheekbones only deepened before she playfully swatted my arm. The guys went fucking nuts. You would have thought we made the playoffs with how much they were cheering us on.

"You are going to get us into so much trouble…" Cady warned in a volume that was just for me.

"Nah. I can behave in public." Her brow cocked. Okay, fair point. Given our past, especially with this locker room, maybe I couldn't. "But I don't have to behind *closed doors.*"

Cady sucked in her bottom lip. I was transfixed as her front teeth held it down in a subconscious move. Fuck, I wanted to devour this woman. Right now. I didn't know how much longer I could hold myself back.

"Your place or mine tonight?" Her voice was breathy, barely above a whisper. I relished the fact that despite us seeing each other almost daily for four weeks, the excitement was still rampant. Hell, maybe it grew even more intense each day.

"How about yours?" I suggested.

"Hey Jamie, you wanna go get a round with us?" Benson purposefully interrupted Cady's and my private conversation with a cheeky grin. They honest to god were like her protective older brothers. "Our treat." I could hear the guys cheering in agreement with the suggestion.

"Go on, have a round." Cady encouraged me with a smile. "The boys inviting you out is a big honor. That's how you know you've been successfully indoctrinated."

"But–"

Cady leaned in as close as possible, her lips against my ear. "We can do *that* when you come to my place later." The whisper sent a delicious shiver down my spine as I remembered her toy drawer.

With a smug little look, Cady slipped from my arms. I blinked at her in utter stupor as I watched her hips sway, hypnotizing me for a long moment until she was out of view. It wasn't until she was gone that I realized what she meant.

Clearing my throat, I subtly adjusted the sports cup in my pants to deter my erection from getting any bigger. I did my best to adjust my face to something more neutral, instead of one that made it obvious that I was thinking about that jewel sparkling between her chee–

"Well, you heard Coach!" Truitt slapped me on the back as he flashed me one of his trademark grins. "Let's go get some drinks, guys!"

Drinking with the Sillys was just as crazy as I thought it would be. They had their favorite little dive bar just around the corner from the stadium. Some of the fans from the game had migrated over and gave us an uproarious welcome when the guys bounded through the door. They certainly liked all this attention no matter where they went.

Fans recognized me instantly as the star dancer from the game earlier. It was interesting to be noticed for something that wasn't my baseball talent. I found myself smiling. Smiling more than I usually did during a sudden onslaught of fans. If only Cady had come along. She'd probably be laughing her ass off and grinning the whole time. This was such a wild change from where I was a month ago.

Cady.

As much as I wanted to hurry to the promised land of her luscious ass, and the quiet that was just her and I, I was enjoying myself. Being able to blow off some steam like this was rare in the majors. During the season, your free time was either traveling, sleeping to recover from jet lag, or practicing. Letting loose like this didn't happen until the off-season. And by that time, you're so exhausted that you need a good month just to get back to what other people consider "normal".

With the crowd now settled, Truitt hurried over to the bar to order a round of drinks for the guys as we commandeered a corner booth and a few tables to the far side of the bar. I promised myself to stay for one drink and enjoy shooting the shit with the Sillys. Since I was seemingly here for the long run, and the guys didn't hate my clumsy ass, it was high time we did some team building outside the stadium that didn't revolve around dancing.

The clinking of beer bottles being juggled by the armful pulled me from my wandering thoughts. Truitt, Benson, and Camden made their way over to one table to unload the bottles on the tables while the guys' cheered. I stood to make my way to the table to grab the free beer I was promised, but a vibration in my back pocket stopped me.

Reaching down, I slid the device from my jeans and glanced at the screen before hurrying to answer it. Whatever it was, it couldn't be good.

"Yo, Jamie, don't you want your beer?" Truitt looked over at me as I briskly headed for the door. I needed someplace quiet. Pointing to my phone, I slipped outside to escape any further protests.

"Coach," I was breathless as I found a quiet spot by the dumpster. "What can I do for you?"

Topper's voice was even more gruff coming through the phone than reverberating off the walls of the Sillys locker room. And like always, he got right to the point. "Rheems. I just got the call."

The call? I blinked for a moment as my eyes adjusted to the summer sunset out in the bar's parking lot.

Fuck.

The call.

"Your backup is out with a hamstring strain and your backup's backup just got ruled out with a concussion during tonight's game. They need you for the game tomorrow." My mouth dropped open. While I didn't want any of my replacements to get injured for me to get called back up, it was usually the reason why they had an empty roster seat. There was a hint of sadness in Topper's tone as he continued. "And well, the foreseeable future."

In true Topper fashion, he hung up the phone without any further pleasantries. Slowly, I lowered my phone from my ear and just stared at it. This was it. I got my wish. My sentence with the Sillys was over.

So why wasn't I happy?

Despite the urgent phone call, I had to go back in and tell the guys I needed to leave. The majors waited for no man, especially when a team was in dire straits. Besides, knowing them, they probably would think up some hair-brained, elaborate scheme that I'd been kidnapped if I left without telling them.

"Hey guys, I gotta head out," I said quickly, tossing my thumb over my shoulder for emphasis.

"Dude, what the fuck? We just got here." There was concern in Arlow's tone.

"Jamie, man. You look like shit. You okay?" Benson stepped up to me, followed by half the Sillys roster. I didn't want to be confronted by all of them. How were they going to take it?

I swallowed. "I uh…"

Benson eyes widened. "*Holy shit,* you got the call." There was a clusterfuck of murmurs all at once as the guys talked among themselves.

"Fuck, Jamie. You gotta go, man." I looked up at Kellan who gave me an encouraging nod. Taken aback, I looked at the guys one by one. While they looked bummed, I could tell that they knew. If you got a call up from the majors, hell to even level up in the minors, there's no fucking way you turn it down.

There was a resounding chorus of enthusiastic support from the guys. "But, I–"

"No buts man." Camden chirped.

"We will miss you like hell, but Schmidt's been dying to get his full-time star status back," Truitt added as Schmidt shot him a look. I did feel bad taking away the job of an already outstanding catcher. He deserved his spotlight once again.

"But no one can fill the stands like Jamie can." Schmidt reminded everyone. They all grumbled in agreement.

"I'm gonna miss you guys too. It's been fun as hell." My smile drooped a bit. Fuck, Cady. Dammit, how was I going to explain this to her?

"Does Cadence know yet?" Benson asked cautiously, almost as if he could read my thoughts.

"No. I literally just hung up the phone with Topper before I came back inside. I–" The air in the room had gone dry as I tried to swallow back my worry. "I don't know how to tell her. Especially after such a great performance today."

The Sillys clinked their beer bottles together with a murmur.

"You'd better tell her you love her," Martin added nonchalantly, completely out of the blue. The entire Sillys roster turned to look at him.

"Dude, it's been like two months." Benson snapped back. "It's stupid to think that–"

"No," I said firmly. Between Martin and I, we were giving the guys' necks a workout. "It's not stupid. Honestly," I let out a laugh as I shook my head at the incredulousness of it all. "I knew *weeks* ago."

I swear to god Schmidt's gaze turned into cartoony heart eyes. Like Martin, he was the only other married guy in the bunch. They had to have some knowledge of what I was feeling.

"Knew what?" *Oh, poor, oblivious Tomas.*

"That our guy is in looooovveee." Truitt teased his fellow outfielder with his sing-song answer. More cheers followed and I felt myself break into a grin.

My entire body relaxed once I finally admitted it out loud. Now that the words were out in the open, and I was no longer stuffing my head so far up my ass in denial, everything felt right.

But, how to tell her?

"I can't tell her this shit over the phone."

"Hell no." Benson agreed. "You need to do some grand gesture. Women love that sort of stuff."

"How the hell do you know?" Arlow shot at him. Benson rolled his eyes as if the answer was obvious.

"I read those romance books that are all over the internet. Women rave about the guys doing all sorts of shit in those books." The roster of the Sillys burst out laughing, save for me and Benson. "Look, if you guys weren't such a bunch of heathens, you'd learn a thing or two from them."

"Benson's right. Cady likes to read." I agreed as I glanced from Benson's smug face to the rest of the guys' faces who were growing more interested by the second. A few ideas started to percolate in my head. But I realized I would appreciate any feedback from the group of guys who'd known her the longest. "What do you think she would like?"

"You have to invite her to the game." Camden offered.

I hesitated. "Do you think she would come?"

"Cady is the biggest fucking fan out of all of us. If she got a ticket to the game, there's no way she'd ever say no. Plus we're off tomorrow." Kellan shot back. Fair point.

"What about a jersey? Would she wear one if I got her one of mine?" I asked, trying to keep my growing excitement at bay. That vision of Cady in my jersey still swam in my head ever since I told her about it. All the guys shared the same look.

"Having your girl wear your jersey is just about the biggest fucking turn-on ever. Pretty sure all the guys agree with me." Martin added without hesitation. There was an encouraging rumble of agreement. I'd be lying if I said I hadn't fantasized about Cady wearing my jersey. While riding me. Reverse cowgirl style.

"A horse and carriage!" Tomas hollered before slowly slinking back as all of us turned to look at him. "What? I like fairy tales…" He admitted sheepishly. I chuckled.

"I'm not sure how easily I can get a horse and carriage down by the stadium." Tomas did have a good point though. Game day travel and parking sucked. Cady needed an easy way to get to the game. "But what about a car service?" The guys all gave an encouraging nod. Now we were getting somewhere.

"But you have to keep it a surprise." Roman insisted. "We threw Cadence a surprise party once and she still brings it up from time to time." Considering he was the only guy on the Sillys to date Cady, I took his opinion with the highest regard.

"Got it. Thanks, Roman." I gave him a curt nod. "So, game ticket, jersey, car service…" My eyes looked around at the guys. "Anything else?"

"After she gets all that, that's when you tell her you *love* her." Benson insisted with a dramatic flair as if I was an idiot. And maybe I was. I couldn't remember if I had ever told Vanessa that I loved her. Or any other woman for that matter. I hadn't felt anything remotely this powerful and so sure with anyone else. Just with Cady.

"How am I supposed to do that when I have to play? I can't exactly take over the jumbotron."

Truitt blew out a raspberry. "Professing your love on the big screen is so overdone and cliche. You need to keep it classy with Cadence. Classy and low key." I knew that much about Cady. She liked her peace, just like me. Besides, I wasn't overly fond of making a public spectacle of myself. Today excluded.

"Get her seats in the Diamond Club. Maybe by the dugout?" Arlow added.

"Yeah! Then you can talk to her!" Tomas cried out as he bounced on the balls of his feet.

Considering there was only a safety net there to protect the fans from any foul balls or wild pitches, that could work. Although having her so close…wearing my jersey… I was already getting hard at the thought.

"Done." I nodded in agreement. I felt good about this. This was all doable. Well, I was going to have to make a few phone calls first. "Thanks, guys!"

"Go get your girl." Martin fist-bumped my shoulder as the other cheered me on. With an almost drunken grin, I spun on my heels and made a beeline for the door. Before I reached it, I turned around to address the guys one last time.

"If this works, the next home game you guys are off, box seats and beers on me!" A resounding chorus of cheers filled the bar. The fellow bar patrons chimed in, not knowing what they were cheering about. With a laugh, I slipped out the door as I dialed my agent.

"Hey, Tom? Yeah, I heard. Coach called me already. But before I head over, there's a few things I need you to do."

26

I FOUND

AMBER RUN

Jamie didn't show up last night.

He didn't call either.

Instead, he only texted.

He let me know that…he got *the call*.

I tried to tell myself that the majors were different. They had different communication rules. Maybe he didn't have a chance to call me. Maybe all he could do was shoot off a quick text. Either way, it was difficult to hide my disappointment at practice.

I'd grown so accustomed to seeing Jamie's handsome face on the Silly's field. The way his eyes lit up every time our gazes met across the sea of players. Despite his gruff demeanor when he first arrived, he became one of the Sillys in the end.

He poked fun with the guys, laughed at his own mess-ups, and was the one asking me to do another run-through of the dance so he was sure he had all the moves. While he kept his usual seriousness when it came to game time, he rediscovered that spark of fun that he had so long ago that came with playing baseball.

Within the last few weeks, he'd been playing some of the best baseball of his career. The guys in recruiting and management would have had to be blind to miss it. No wonder they wanted him back.

Now that Jamie suddenly wasn't here, it felt as if I'd imagined everything. Were the last two months just a fever dream? Did any of it actually happen?

It's your vagina's fault. It wanted to get into his pants.

Thanks, brain. But not at all helpful.

Whatever. It was a group effort anyway.

I mean yes, sure, I wanted to see what he looked like underneath the uniform. Everything else after that had been a bonus. An *incredible* bonus. A bonus that had me believing that maybe we were something. Or…could be.

"Cadence, did you want to go to the bar with us to watch Jamie's first game back?"

Martin's question jarred me from my thoughts. I hesitated. As much as I would've loved to go with them, I was sure that I'd be an emotional mess. Of course I was thrilled for Jamie, but his sudden departure made me feel as if my life was incomplete again.

I didn't want to damper the guys' mood when they wanted to go out and have fun. All I wanted to do was go home, put on my favorite oversized tee, and bury myself in serotonin-boosting foods. There was entirely too much for me to figure out in the middle of a noisy bar.

"No thanks." The looks I got from the guys made me pause. I never turned down watching a game with them whenever it had been offered. "I mean, I'll just watch it at home. I'm tired after all the prep for the performance the other day. My PJs are calling my name."

When Jamie initially texted, he told me we would talk later. However, my anxiety was not a patient person. Waiting was eating away at me.

"Oh, well…we'll be sure to drink a beer for you." Arlow offered up a lopsided smile to reassure me. He joined the rest of the crew as they slowly filtered out of the locker room. Practice had been less than productive with the guys talking secretively behind my back. It only made me more paranoid.

"You do that." My voice unexpectedly cracked, and I quickly turned away. What the hell? Why was I getting emotional over this?

"Andrews!" I nearly jumped out of my skin as Topper's booming voice invaded my thoughts. He poked his head out of his office. "I hope you're not busy tonight. Corporate car just arrived for you." His face looked as impassive as always. Ownership coming to you for anything was probably bad news. Nobody ever got a visit from their boss when it was good news.

Shit.

Did they know about me and Jamie? Who squealed?

Fuck. Fuck. Fuck.

I had to be in deep shit for ownership to send a car specifically for me. This evening just went from bad to worse.

"Uh…thanks, Coach." I tipped my cap to him as he grabbed the last few things in his office to head home. Swallowing back my anxiety, I grabbed my stuff from my office and made my way out of the little stadium that had become my second home. Maybe this was goodbye.

Sure enough, at the entrance was a shiny black SUV. A looming beacon to my downfall. A hearse to my doom.

My hand shook as I reached out and grabbed onto the handle of the back passenger door. I prayed that I didn't fuck my life up by falling for the blue-eyed catcher that had not only stolen bases but also my heart. If only I had the balls to tell him earlier.

Sliding into the car, I closed the door and buckled my seatbelt. I felt like I was getting into my dad's backseat after he was pissed about picking me up from somewhere I shouldn't be. When my door shut the driver turned to me.

"Cadence Andrews?" My mouth went dry and all I could do was nod. It was then that the driver did something that I didn't expect. He smiled. "This is for you."

My brow furrowed as he extended a nondescript white mailing envelope to me. Timidly, I took it, wondering if I just accepted my termination paperwork. If so, it was a terrifying way to go about it.

As the car pulled away from the Sillys stadium, my hands shook as I stared down at the envelope. It seemed rather light for dismissal paperwork. Might as well rip off the metaphorical Band-Aid and open the damn thing. Then at least this bullshit wouldn't be hanging in the air for the entire ride over to the stadium.

"What the hell is this?" The words tumbled from my mouth before I could stop them as I stared at the envelope's contents.

"I believe it's a ticket to the game."

"From who?"

"That I don't know. I was just sent to give that to you and drive you to the stadium."

For fucks sake.

Was this some kind of cruel joke?

Fighting through the traffic on the way to the stadium was excruciating. My mind had the opportunity to run wild. Why did they give me a ticket to a game? Maybe…this wasn't a bad thing after all?

At least the team car could bypass the headache of parking and head straight to the security gate. My hands shook as I got out of the car. *Calm down, Cadence. If you were in trouble this would be a really weird ass way to go about disciplining you.* Maybe it was one of the guys on the team that set this all up?

My brow furrowed in the most unattractive fashion. This wasn't the main gate. This was the VIP entrance to the Diamond Club. Now I was even more confused. I opened my mouth to ask the driver another question, which he probably didn't have the answer to, but he was already out of the car and around to my door.

These tickets were easily $500 or more *a seat.* Who the hell would drop that much money on me? There had to be a catch. Maybe I won some sort of employee thing? The thoughts tumbled in my head and distracted me enough to stumble from the car and up to the security at the club entrance gate.

I handed my ticket to the person at the check-in desk and heard the reassuring beep. Well, at least it wasn't fraudulent. With a knowing smile, she directed me to the waiting usher to escort me to my seat.

He led me down the stairs and into the main entrance of the Diamond Club. It was a bustle of activity as this was the private restaurant and concession stand for those sitting in the prestigious seats. They were right behind home plate and smack dab in between both of the teams' dugouts.

I timidly made my way down the steps behind the usher in a team logo polo. I could see the guys out on the field doing their pre-game warmups. And that was when my heart stopped. Wearing his catcher's gear, he was hard to miss.

Damn, Jamie looked good in his element.

"Miss…?"

Oh, right. I was supposed to be following the usher guy. With a nod, I closed the gap between us as he gestured to my seat. It was the last plush seat in the front row right next to the home team's dugout.

This was every baseball fangirl's dream. I sank into the plushness of the outdoor vinyl seat. How was I supposed to sit and relax watching the game when I knew exactly what the catcher looked like *naked*?

"Would you like to order anything to eat or drink?"

"What?" I glanced up at the usher, shading my eyes, blinking against the late evening sun.

"It's included with your ticket. Would you like to see a menu?"

"Could you get me a hard cider? Or a light beer? Or hell, wine. Whatever you have, that's sweet and full of alcohol." With a chuckle, he nodded and wandered off to get someone on the wait staff. Thank fuck he left. I needed this moment of reprieve to get my head on straight.

"Miss Andrews?" I nearly jumped out of my seat. So much for a moment to collect my thoughts.

"Oh my god! Yes?" Turning, I was met face-to-face with a white box tied up with a red bow. Surely, he had the wrong person. The fact that he said *my* name wasn't something my common sense wanted to consider at the moment.

"I was told to give this to you when you found your seat." Bending down to my level, the staff member handed over the sizable box to me. *What in the world?*

I gave it a timid shake. All I could hear was the rustle of tissue paper. It wasn't heavy but it wasn't as light as an empty box would be. My pointer and thumb grabbed a hold of the forked end of the ribbon and pulled, loosening the bow. The box barely fit on my lap. What the hell was inside?

Pulling away the lid and a layer of tissue paper, I was greeted with the vision of the gorgeous special edition team hat that I'd been eyeing up all season. I kept my excited squeal internal. *Okay, maybe this wasn't so bad. Employee perks and all.*

I lifted the hat out of the box and quickly set to work adjusting the cap to fit my head. But this was a rather large box for *just* a hat. Glancing down, my heart came to a complete and utter stop.

Carefully folded inside the box was a Jamie Rheems jersey.

My head shot up. Like a hawk after its prey, I found Jamie in an instant, as he caught a hell of a fastball from the pitcher during warmups. Did he do this? Did Jamie orchestrate all of this? Or was it just some cruel prank?

There was also something else tucked in the box. It must have shifted in transport as it was sort of off to the side of the jersey. It was an envelope and what looked like a velvet box.

Skipping any sort of decorum as my hands trembled, I tore open the envelope. The paper had the team's letterhead at the top along with a handwritten note.

Cady,

First off, I'm sorry I didn't call you. Nothing felt right to say over the phone. Instead I thought I would show you how much you've changed my life. If it wasn't for you, I'd still be stubbornly drowning on the Sillys bench instead of being welcomed into such an incredible team. You kicked my ass into shape. In thanks, I had something special made, just for you. A small token from my first game with the Sillys. It was the start of my lucky streak. I have a matching one. You've been my inspiration.

Jamie

P.S. When you see me (and don't want to pound my face in), remind me that I have something I want to tell you in person. I've actually wanted to tell you this for a while, but I didn't want to jinx it.

My brow furrowed as I read his letter over and over again. It was disbelief mixed with elation. Was I dreaming again?

I wanted to hug the piece of paper to my chest and never let go. Jamie and a grand romantic gesture. It wasn't flowers but to a baseball-loving girl, it was the best fucking thing.

Blinking back happy tears, the black velvet box drew my attention next. He mentioned some sort of token from his game in his note. Could this be it?

With trembling hands, I carefully opened the box. Choking back a sob, I covered my mouth to muffle any more embarrassing sounds. I wasn't an overly emotional person, but Jamie certainly had taken me through the wringer with this one.

Inside the box was a necklace. But it wasn't some jewelry store necklace, oh hell no. It was a custom-made pendant. In a frame of white gold was a piece of dirty baseball leather in the shape of a heart.

Then it hit me.

It was his first hit ball with the Sillys. The ball that ended his post-injury no-hit streak. The hit that he claimed was all because of me.

Holy fuck my heart couldn't take it right now.

Sniffling, I gingerly pulled the jewelry piece from the box and fastened it around my neck. My heart started singing as soon as the cool metal hit my flushed skin. I had to deck myself out head to toe with all of Jamie's gifts.

Fussing with the gift box, I shoved it off my lap as I pulled the jersey from the confines. Upon closer inspection, it wasn't one of those cheap knock-off ones, it was a wearable, *embroidered* game-use-only kind of jersey. This had to be from Jamie's *personal* stash.

Fuck.

It even smelled like him beneath the hint of laundry soap. What the hell had I become? And in public no less? Here I was, with a front-row seat to my favorite baseball team, *huffing* my favorite player's jersey.

As I slipped it on, I remembered our conversation at dinner before his first road trip. That he wanted something as simple as seeing *his girl*, wearing his jersey, cheering for him in the stands. The jersey was the equivalent of me advertising the man on a billboard in Times Square.

"Cady!" The shouted pet name hit my ears like a welcoming balm. Cramming the heels of my hands into my eyes to brush away the tears, I looked up. My eyes met the look of pure and utter joy on Jamie's face as he jogged over to my seating area. The rest of the team headed to the dugout to my right.

He leaned over the padded field wall and pressed his face into the safety net. The vision of him turned my heart into a puddle of goo. "You made it! And *hell*," He sighed happily as he drank me in. "You look *fucking fantastic* in my jersey. You found my special gift."

My jersey.

His jersey.

His lucky charm on *my* heart.

"I can't believe you did all this…" I whispered as I met him at the wall. I quickly glanced around, hoping I wasn't drawing attention. Having a player this close to the seats was something reserved for small kids asking for autographs. "Why didn't you call? I've been a mess worried about you and—"

"I know. But I wanted to do a *grand* gesture. The Sillys convinced me." Jamie stopped to catch his breath as his words tumbled out all at once.

"Wait…the Sillys? *My* Sillys?" My hand fell to my chest that was still sporting my team shirt under Jamie's open jersey. My guys had something to do with all this pomp and circumstance?

"They helped." My eyes looked to Jamie as his voice softened. "I should have told you this long before I got called back up to the majors. The truth is…" Leaning in closer, his fingers wiggled through the netting to grasp onto my hand. "The truth is I didn't know how to tell you this. I didn't want to do it over the phone."

"T-Tell me what…?" I whispered, my voice shaking.

"*Cadence,*" The sudden seriousness had me locking eyes with his. He took a step closer, his field cleats against the padded field wall. "*I love you.*"

Jamie said it.

He *actually* said it.

I never thought I'd hear the words, even though I imagined it a zillion times. My brain scrambled. How does someone respond to something like that on the fly?

Before I could manage any kind of coherent verbal response, my body flew into action. I launched myself at him. The net hampered my efforts but with the mutual effort between us, we managed to get our lips locked through an opening in the netting.

"I love you too," I mumbled in between our ravenous kisses. His mouth slanted against mine as he did his best to grab onto me. I grinned and laughed into the kiss while he hummed his delight. It was *magical*.

Well, it *was* magical until I was manhandled off of Jamie by two members of the security team.

"Ma'am! Ma'am! You can't do that!" One shouted as they managed to pull me away. I didn't want to get thrown out of Jamie's first game back.

"Yo, guys!" Jamie's firm voice made them pause. "She's *mine*."

Oh, fucking hell.

Bye-bye panties. It was nice knowing you.

If these guys hadn't been holding me up, I'd be a puddle on the platform.

"Mr. Rheems…?"

"She's my *girlfriend*, guys."

Oh, this was too much all at once for my body to handle. Between the gifts and the "I love you" and now the *"girlfriend"* title? This was a grand gesture of epic proportions. I was just…shocked. With my mouth agape, Jamie's eyes found mine once more. "That is…if you'll have me?"

I used the loosened hold of the security guys to launch myself back at Jamie. His huge grin matched mine as I managed to steal one more kiss. The safety net still kept me from doing everything in my power to tangle my body around him. Only now it was Jamie's turn to be dragged away by his teammates so they could start the ball game.

Oops.

"This game's for you, Cady!" Jamie shouted with one last grin as he dipped into the dugout. I was smiling from ear to ear as I turned to go back to my seat. That was until I realized I had the curious eyes of the *entire* Diamond Club section on me all at once.

With a blush, I avoided every last one of them as I slinked back down into my seat. I couldn't stop grinning. My shit day turned completely upside down in the most unexpected way. Decked out in my *boyfriend's* gear, I was ready for a hell of a ball game. Win or lose. This time I could watch and ogle Jamie and know that he was *mine*. And I was his.

How the hell could I concentrate on the game after all that? Had Jamie not been starting, my eyes would have been firmly fixed on the dugout. Instead, I had a front-row seat to the man's glorious ass as it was bent behind home plate throughout the first half of the inning. The way that man winked at me each time he went up to take his position on the field made me swoon almost clear out of my seat.

Jamie was a completely changed man from the last time he was on this field. Gone was his typically stoic demeanor. He ran out onto that field with a spring in his step and an extra bounce to that booty I loved to squeeze. Instead of treating the game like it was all business, he was ready to have fun. And he learned all that by playing with the Sillys.

And me.

After a quick three outs, it was the bottom of the first. The coach must have been ecstatic to have him back as he slipped Jamie back into his coveted second place in the batting lineup. His usual walk-up song blasted over the ballpark speakers. I couldn't help but do a happy little dance from my seat. This was the fucking greatest.

With his first at-bat, I held my breath. He walked out onto that field with purpose to the roar of the home crowd. They were so happy to have him back. He was amazing. He was incredible.

He was mine.

Jamie lifted his bat, pointing it at me with a tip of the brim of his batting helmet before he stepped into the batter box. Baseball games were going to have a hell of a new meaning if I always got this special treatment when Jamie was in the starting lineup. After all the years I fantasized about the man maybe it was just my heart telling me that he was *the one* for me.

The crack of the ball against the bat jarred me from my tumble of happy thoughts. Around me, the stadium cheered as Jamie made a beeline for first base. But there was no need. I slowly rose from my seat, squinting to see the ball against the fading light of day. That ball was long gone. Clear over the fence in right field and into the first few rows of the second level, which only made the crowd cheer louder.

I screamed at the top of my lungs. What a hell of a return to his home field. My heart was in my throat as I watched him run the bases with the biggest grin on his face, playing it up for the crowd. As his cleats hit home plate, I rushed back to the safety net.

Jamie made a beeline for me but kept his respectable distance. I could tell the security guys were sending their warning stares at me. With all eyes on Jamie, we had to keep it at least PG-rated. Not that I wanted to. Nor did my mouth. When he was at the top step of the dugout, I slipped him a quick promise for later that was for his ears only.

"I hope for a repeat *home run* tonight, Slugger."

The look he shot me told my vagina that it was on like *Donkey Kong*.

"I can think of no other way to celebrate with my *good luck charm*." He gave me a wink as he ducked down into the dugout. There was another round of cheers and high-fives from his teammates as I floated back to my seat. Part of me didn't care if they won or lost, Jamie had his triumphant return and that was all that mattered.

It was a wonder to see him in his natural element. The Sillys had a much more lighthearted take on baseball. I only got to see little peeks of his true talent in person in between the dance breaks and other on-field nonsense.

This game was simultaneously exhilarating and going at a snail's pace. Especially with the filthy promises for later that lingered between us every time he went back to the dugout. With each free moment, he stole a glance, shot me a wink, or lifted his mask to enchant me with his knee-buckling grin. Or there was the token sultry comment when his teammates weren't within earshot. Which was a bit difficult given that most of the coaching staff hovered in the corner of the dugout near my seat.

It was finally the top of the ninth inning, and they were up by three runs. If all went well, they could hold on for half an inning to win the game. Jamie managed a home run on his first at-bat then a base hit to first. The other had been a pop fly, but at least he hit the damn ball.

The relationship between Jamie and all the pitchers had to be symbiotic. Jamie and the pitcher had to study their hitting opponents, but Jamie was the one who made the pitch calls. He had to know who would swing on the first pitch no matter if it was in the strike zone. And who had a weakness against left or right-handed pitchers? He had to know it all.

As he ran out on the field for, hopefully, the last time for the game, I gave him one last bit of encouragement. I caught his eye as he lingered behind everyone else outside of the dugout.

"Keep up the great pitch calls!" I yelled at him with a smile as I hopped from foot to foot. At the top step, he leaned in as close as he could manage between the netting and padded wall.

"Keep screaming my name. It will be good practice for *later*."

The smooth husky tone that slipped that doozy of a line had me gripping onto the safety net for support. My legs were one breath away from giving out completely. He gave me a wicked grin before he raced after his teammates. How could he drop something as epic as that and just…*walk away*? I was fairly certain I needed one of those security guards to grab a fire extinguisher for my thighs.

"Please God, if you can give me three pitches and three caught pop-fly balls, I'll do anything you want."

The chances were slim as I muttered out the words to the tangerine sky, but hey a girl could dream. Even if the game ended quickly, I still had to wait for Jamie to change out of his uniform and shower before I could jump his bones for the next twelve hours straight. Okay, maybe eight hours. The man did have to sleep at least a little bit before the next game tomorrow.

I didn't have to bother with sitting down. The opposing team's second batter was already up to the plate with two strikes. The crowd was on their feet, cheering on the pitcher to make this a quick top of the ninth. And since I had a very sexy reason to want this game to be over, I added my encouragement.

Like Jamie, the closer pitcher was on fire. He struck out the second batter and was well on his way to finishing off the third. The team was like a well-oiled machine with Jamie back in his usual position. The ease with which they fell back into their normal game flow was obvious to everyone.

With one voice, the stadium roared as the game was called with the last strike. You would have thought it was the team winning the World Series. It was bonkers. The announcers gave up on saying anything after the game. It was pointless over the deafening noise of the crowd.

My babe was back and kicking ass.

And I was here to see it.

The horde of baseball players celebrated on the field with special attention on Jamie. He certainly deserved it. From the first inning, he was back in his usual form, with a home run to boot. He certainly deserved to have the player of the game interview tonight.

I stood at the edge of the netted wall, anxiously awaiting Jamie to give him a congratulatory kiss. That was only the beginning as there was a hell of a lot more I had in store for him for the night. There was too much celebrating to do.

Once he managed to get away from the mass of his celebrating teammates, he swaggered up to me with a dusty, sweaty face and a big-ass grin. I didn't care how filthy he was. He was still utterly kissable. My grin mirrored his as he stepped up to me on the opposite side of the wall. Despite the cumbersome netting, he still managed to pull me in tightly against him.

"I told you that you looked so incredible in my jersey," Jamie mumbled against my lips as the safety net bit into my skin. "But it will look a hell of a lot better on my *floor* tonight. Be ready to round the bases, because I can't wait to *nail* you at home plate." Jamie swallowed my amused snort with a searing kiss.

Epilogue

FOR LIFE

KYGO & ZAK ABEL, FEATURING NILE RODGERS

"Cadence, report to the bullpen fifteen minutes before start time." I stopped in my tracks. That was an odd request coming from Topper. I always had spots in the ballpark during games. Watching the game from the bullpen was not one of them.

"What? Why?"

"Something with management. I don't ask questions." He shrugged nonchalantly as he shuffled out of his office and into the locker room. What in the actual fuck? My stomach suddenly dropped. Oh no, maybe this really was it. Unlike last time when I stressed over the possibility of being fired, but instead, it was Jamie's surprise. But that was well over a year ago at this point.

Glancing down at my watch, it was already close to the time Topper said I needed to be out there. With a heavy sigh, I turned on my heel and headed to the access tunnel leading to the bullpen by the LED scoreboard. Maybe it was something embarrassing? Or could it be something good again?

As I stepped out into the bullpen, there was a buzz about the crowd. Nervously I fingered the necklace I'd received as a gift from Jamie during his first night back in the majors. He had a matching keychain made and told me that it was baseball that brought us together. It was only fitting for both of us to have a piece of it.

Everyone I told the story to wilted at the gesture. Except for Tiffiny. I was pretty sure she dry-heaved. Deep down I knew she was happy for me. She made me promise to make her the maid of honor at our wedding. Hah! A wedding. Yeah right. Maybe one day. Jamie and I never really had a serious conversation about it.

Sure, it came up in little comments here and there. Jamie and I had been living together ever since the off-season after we met. And damn, that was one hell of a doozy of an off-season. Even though the baseball season for Philadelphia ended in the first week of the postseason, we still celebrated the end of baseball season.

We didn't leave the bedroom for at least a week straight. All of our groceries and meals had to be delivered. Damn, that was fun.

My thoughts were brought to a halt as the loudspeakers sparked to life. There was a peculiar music choice that suddenly filtered over the PA system. It wasn't any of the songs I had in the rotation for a dance number, and there wasn't a routine planned before the game tonight.

With a few more notes in, it hit me.

It was mine and Jamie's song.

The song we danced to at the bar when he finally showed promise in his dancing skills. Where we almost kissed. Where everyone could tell we were in love.

Except us.

But Jamie had a home game tonight, and he was starting. While he was happy to be back home with the Phillies, he knew he was on borrowed time, even with him playing like his old self. They reduced his number of games in hopes of giving some of the younger guys in the farming system their shot at the majors. Just the other week he brought up the possibility of retiring when his contract was up. I told him I'd support him with whatever path he chose, without question.

Maybe all of this was nothing. Or maybe it was the boys teasing me again. Ever since the guys on the Sillys caught Jamie and me, they hadn't let me live it down. Which was fine. I just worked their asses in practice and made them do more complicated and elaborate routines to get back at them.

Ender suddenly popped into view via the gated entrance to the field from the bullpen. Aside from his broad grin, he also came sporting a single red rose. I was rather taken aback by his romantic gesture.

"Ender, what–"

"Cadence, this is for you." His smile softened but was still warm as he extended the rose out to me.

"For me? Don't you mean, Tiff—"

"That's what I said, isn't it?" Biting my lower lip, I reached out and delicately clasped the rose with my fingertips. The scent of the flower hit my nostrils, mixing with the sweet summer air as I breathed it all in. "Besides," Ender's continued. "There's a few more of its friends you need to collect."

Raising a curious brow, I leaned to look to the side of him. Sure enough, there was Benson, a bit further in the outfield, waiting for me. In his hand was another rose.

Cautiously, I stepped out onto the field. My brain didn't even register that there were thousands of witnesses to this peculiar display. The entire team was lined up, one by one, each one with a rose in hand.

Well, damn, maybe it was my work anniversary? At the back of my mind I was thinking that this was going to make a hell of a video for social media. The female fans were going to go nuts. Heck, I was going nuts. This was overly adorable, even for my motley crew. I vaguely wondered who the heck had the creativity to organize it all. Considering the fact they helped Jamie with his epic surprise for me, nothing should surprise me at this point.

One by one the team offered their rose to me as I made my way towards home plate. Some gave a smile with their flower; some gave me a smartass comment that made me crack up in laughter. It was definitely a Sillys thing to do. The boys lived up to the team's name. They proved that daily.

I made my way through the entire roster before arriving at the catcher. He was at home plate with the last rose and down on one knee. I couldn't help but laugh as my arms were laden with roses.

"Let me guess, Schmidt. Ending this nonsense dance number?" I laughed as I took the last stem and added it to the rest of them.

"Nope, just a question."

My heart stopped.

I slowly lifted my gaze to his eyes as he pushed up his catcher's mask.

Except it wasn't Schmidt.

It was *Jamie*.

With one of his trademark grins and…

An engagement ring in a baseball.

This elaborate shindig all made sense now.

"But…but…the game?"

"That wasn't the question I had in mind." He chuckled as he leaned towards me a bit more. "Coach said I…needed a *night off*."

"I'll say…" I breathed out. Jamie reached out and took my hand in his. His calloused thumb caressed across my knuckles, calming me in seconds.

"Cadence," Jamie's voice softened as he gazed up at me. "I brought you to this field because this is the very field where I first laid eyes on you. I couldn't think of asking you this anywhere else." *Oh my god, be still my heart.* Regaining composure, Jamie continued.

"This is also the same field where I *fell in love with you*." A single tear broke free and danced down my cheek. "Day after day, of you torturing me to learn dance moves I couldn't dream of doing," A single huff of watery laughter broke from my lips. "I realized that you were the bright lights on my night game. The laces to my leather. The glove to my ball."

My lower lip quivered. I wasn't sure if it was from the imminent tears or from holding back my laughter at all his terribly corny baseball puns. Despite wanting to throttle him when we first met, he was truly meant for me. Terrible puns and all. He was my *everything*.

"I'm…an incomplete roster without you. And I know I couldn't survive another day without making you mine, forever. Cadence Andrews…*will you marry me?*"

I dropped to my knees, sending a swirl of red dirt into the night breeze. Setting aside the awkward pile of roses, I turned back to Jamie. Locking eyes with him, I carefully removed the catcher's mask and tossed it aside.

In one fluid movement, I launched myself at him. Tangling my arms around his neck, I slanted my mouth across his.

Jamie answered me by wrapping his strong arms across my lower back. His lips were heated against mine. If we weren't careful, things might get rather questionable in front of a few thousand people. We had to keep it child-friendly. With a gasp of air, I finally pulled away.

"You hit another home run, Slugger," I mumbled with a grin against his mouth. "The answer's yes."

The roar of the crowd was deafening as Jamie scooped his hands under my ass, helping me stand up with him. I let out a squeal of surprise that he quickly muffled with a barrage of kisses as we swayed together to the music atop home plate. Fuck the World Series. This was for sure a game neither of us would forget for the rest of our lives.

Stay tuned for
Tiffiny and Ender's
love story in

Working the Mound

Book 2

A
Philly Sillys
Romance

ACKNOWLEDGEMENTS

I want to give a hearty THANK YOU to my beta and ARC readers who went above and beyond to make this book happen. Without readers like you, I wouldn't be here! I am so thankful for all of your constructive feedback and kind words. Chatting with you in my reader group, via DMs, and through comments makes my whole day. The styled photos and snapshots of my book have been such a blessed gift.

To my beloved Phillies, thank you for being my escape in 2024 (and hopefully for years to come). Something clicked and it had me hooked on you. Your vibes are contagious. Rewatches of your games got me through the off-season until this book was released. By the way, can you PLEASE continue the base-hit shimmy for like...ever?

To my readers who have been here since the beginning, thank you, from the bottom of my heart, for giving me all the love and support over the years. You all will hold a forever place in my heart.

My love to indie bookstores who have given little ol' indie author me, a chance on their shelf.

About the Author

When K. Iwancio isn't attending a Phillies game or screaming at the Eagles on television, she's busy dreaming up her next book or creating…something. Born and raised in Northeast Philadelphia, her main food groups are soft pretzels, Dunkin', and wooder ice. Some of the fondest memories of her beloved late father are in front of the television yelling "Come on!" (in true Philly accent) at the umpires and referees. You can coax her from her writing cave with promises to visit indie bookstores and grab lattes. But if you want to win her over, ask her the number of the trash compactor on the Death Star where Luke, Han, Leia, and Chewbacca are trapped.

K. Iwancio

author

www.kiwancio.com